CONCERTO
BOOK I
Simon

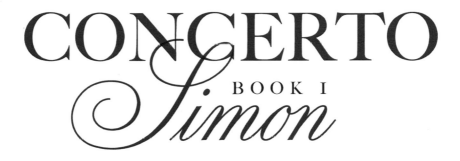

CONCERTO
BOOK I
Simon

One Boy's Struggle to Survive the Holocaust

FRED RAYMOND GOLDMAN

Charleston, SC
www.PalmettoPublishing.com

Concerto: Book 1 Simon

First Edition

Hardcover ISBN: 979-8-8229-1130-7
Paperback ISBN: 979-8-8229-1131-4
eBook ISBN: 979-8-8229-1132-1

To my grandchildren. May they never be in harm's way.

Contents

Part One

ONE

Morning of Saturday, September 2, 1939, Krakow, Poland

Simon was one of the first to notice the disturbance among the starlings roosting in the sycamore trees bordering the east and west sides of the square. He heard their pitched chorus and the flapping of their wings seconds before hundreds of them flocked to the sky, creating two formations before joining into one large configuration. They moved swiftly, twisting, turning, changing shapes, and creating an astonishing spectacle to those watching below.

As the progression of movements among the birds increased, Lena, and the other young girls with whom she was playing, ran to the benches where those caring for them were sitting. "What is it?" Lena whispered, pressing closely against Simon, her older brother. Simon put an arm around Lena's shoulder.

"Don't be scared," he said. "I saw this in a movie. Watch, it will be spectacular. You'll have something special to tell the others at lunch."

She pulled closer to him when the birds formed a spiral-like circle that temporarily blocked out the sun, causing a brief darkening over the square. Two worshippers wearing prayer shawls come out of the front doors of Beth David Congregation, a square shaped, flat roofed building on the west side of the square. Its congregants were comprised of Jews who followed the rules and practices of Halakhah, the strict observances of Jewish laws. They looked up into the partially blackened sky, stared at each other, and shrugged before returning inside their house of worship.

"This is unusual," an observer sitting near Simon said. "Starlings take flight at dusk."

An elderly woman, occupying the same bench, shook her head. "It's a bad omen. Something terrible is going to happen," she said.

Her bench partner waved his hand dismissively. "Nonsense," he said. "Something has frightened them, probably a predator, most likely a peregrine falcon."

"I've heard birds can sense sounds and movements from ten miles away," another woman said. Her lower lip and chin trembled. "Do you think there may be an earthquake coming?"

"Don't listen to her," Simon said, attempting to reassure Lena. She was holding on to his arm tightly as she watched the dazzling configurations above. "Something must have scared them, like the man said. Soon they'll move on to find other trees to roost in. You'll remember this for years and hope to see one again." The starlings executed the shapes of a duck, a feather, and a giant bird before flying off into the distance and disappearing.

With energy befitting a four-year-old, Lena skipped off to rejoin her friends soon after the starlings' show ended. "I wasn't scared," Simon heard her boast.

Simon sat quietly, listening to more chatter while watching over Lena. They were on the square opposite the bakery their parents owned and operated. It was his responsibility to care for Lena every Saturday morning from nine until noon, when his parents would turn the bakery over to their staff and call him and Lena in for lunch as a family in their quarters upstairs. After lunch, Lena would play under the care of their older sister, Katrina. Simon would be free to prepare for the Poland Independence Day Concert on November 11. His school, the Krakow School of Music, presented this concert annually.

Simon was the youngest student ever selected to represent the violin department at this event. He'd be performing the solo violin portions of the first movement of Tchaikovsky's Violin Concerto in D Minor, which required great skill in executing both its fast-running scales and its delicate main theme. None of his immediate family on his father's side had any musical talent. Simon wondered where his came from. His mother never spoke of her family. This puzzled him. When he asked her about them, she answered only that they were old and lived far away.

This year's concert was particularly important to Simon. The rector of the school had announced officials from the Alliance of Accredited Music Schools and Academies of Poland had accepted an invitation. This organization held a biennial competition and awarded prizes to experienced violinists and pianists seventeen or older. With the appearance of this delegation confirmed, Simon felt confident the coveted competition prize would be his in 1942, when he'd be eligible to apply. Winning this competition would earn Simon the recognition and money to attract the most distinguished teachers, and this would lead to his objectives of becoming a great composer and concert performer. Although his family earned a good living from the bakery, he knew it would cost them dearly to provide him with the continued education and training he'd need to attain his goals. He practiced the Tchaikovsky concerto every spare minute to reach perfection. Performing well and drawing the attention of the alliance attendees were foremost in Simon's thoughts.

Simon took his eyes off Lena long enough to see his fellow students, Bartek and Aleksander, walking briskly together on the walkway along the east side of the square. He waved to catch their attention. Bartek looked over at Simon and turned his head away. Aleksander gave him a weak nod. Simon rubbed his right hand, remembering the soreness he felt when Bartek congratulated him by shaking his hand too long and too tightly. At the time, Simon wondered if he were trying to break his fingers to replace him in the concert. Alexander's smile was overly broad in his concession. *They're still angry Professor Kaminsky chose me over them.* Simon thought. He understood their being upset and their envy. He would have felt the same if Professor Kaminski hadn't selected him. Disappointed by their dismissal, Simon turned his attention back to conversations among people sitting nearby on the square.

"I'm warning you. We're in for trouble, serious trouble," a woman said, pointing a shaking finger at a man, who seemed unconcerned. "The Jews must know something," she said assuredly. "The synagogue is unusually crowded this morning."

"They have reason to be alarmed," the gentleman sitting next to her said, scowling. "They have their own predators to fear. They're packing into their synagogues to ask for God's pity on them and their children. They've heard on the radio what's happened in Warsaw and in our other cities yesterday. They're afraid of more bombings and attacks and that Hitler will do to them what he's done to the Jews in Germany."

"God have mercy," another woman said. "We're all in for trouble. Germany wants our land. They'll take what they can get from us." She crossed herself. "We should pray for all Poles."

Simon's parents didn't talk about the Germans and what might be coming. They thought this would distract him from his studies. "Let him have his youth" he'd heard them say to his aunts and uncles. He now realized his parents were sheltering him from things going on in the world he should be prepared for. *I'm not a child anymore. I'm fourteen. They should trust me,* he thought. Oftentimes, however, when his parents didn't want him to hear something, they'd speak in his grandfather's native German. Simon learned to pick up the language to the extent he could understand what they were saying and eventually, could speak in it.

Simon looked at his watch. It was eleven forty-five. Soon he and the others on the square would hear the melodious sounds of the cantor chanting the closing prayer and the joyous voices of the congregants singing along. The rabbi, the cantor, and their families would be arriving at the entranceway to greet their fellow worshippers. Simon's parents would be handing over their aprons to their workers to manage the shop while they prepared to call him and Lena to lunch.

Simon felt a rumbling under his feet. He glanced around looking for what might have caused this. Lena and her friends were standing rigid, looking up the street. Simon's eyes followed theirs. He saw a parade of motorcycles followed by Nazi German-marked trucks moving toward the synagogue. The roar of their motors muffled the chanting and singing coming from the shul. Upon reaching Beth David Congregation, the motorcycles and trucks stopped. Simon felt a fluttering in his stomach.

German soldiers with rifles and pistols jumped from their vehicles and surrounded the synagogue. Elders on the square left their benches and scuttled away. Shopkeepers along the square and their customers came outside to see what had caused the commotion. Women clasped their hands over their mouths. Mothers with babies and children held on to them tightly. Soldiers grabbed the rabbi, cantor, and their congregants as they left the synagogue. They pointed rifles at them and pushed them up the street where the soldiers had moved their trucks. Other soldiers pulled the congregants into the trucks.

Simon's heart raced as he watched the scene unfold. He clutched his arms across his chest, trying to think what to do. Then he saw Lena run up and kick an offending soldier who was struggling with Rabbi Rosenschtein. The soldier grabbed his leg, and the rabbi was set free, but another soldier grabbed the rabbi and led him to one of the trucks. Simon ran toward Lena, maneuvering through the crowd of worshippers and soldiers. Instinct had taken over. He was moving by pure adrenaline.

Simon reached Lena and clutched her hand. She was crying. He knew he had to get her to the safety of their parents quickly. The throng of soldiers and worshippers struggling with one another made it difficult to get through. The intruders herded Simon and Lena away from the square along with everyone else. A woman in front of them fell. Two soldiers hoisted her up. She screamed and struggled to get free. Simon used the diversion to stoop and grasp Lena's shoulders so that his eyes met hers.

"Run as fast as you can toward the bakery," he said. She stood frozen. Her eyes darted back and forth. "Run," he shouted again and gave her a shove. He watched her little heels kicking up and down as she scampered away. Before he could see if Lena had reached safety, a German soldier gripped him by the back of the neck and propelled him toward the trucks. The screams of mothers and children crying out in search of each other pierced Simon's ears. He stumbled trying to keep his balance.

Simon heard glass shattering. The soldier dragging him stopped long enough for Simon to turn and see colored shards of glass falling from the second story of the synagogue. He looked up and saw two soldiers laughing. They had smashed the stained-glass Star of David. The soldier jerked Simon's head back and lugged him to one of the waiting trucks, where another soldier wrestled him inside.

Simon sat trembling in the shadows of the truck. He pressed his hands tightly between his knees and struggled to control his breathing. He prayed Lena had made it safely to their parents. With the reality of his predicament setting in, Simon wondered where the assailants were taking them. Had his parents seen what had happened? Would his father be able to rescue him? This was crazy, a mistake. He needed to tell the invaders he wasn't Jewish, that, in fact, he was part German and his family was waiting for him. Simon looked at his watch. It was twelve fifteen. He felt a pat on his knee. He looked over. Rabbi Rosenschtein was sitting next to him. He interpreted the rabbi's touch as a gesture of re-assurance, but he felt none. The only assurance he wanted was to soon be sitting safely at home with his family. Although he was fourteen and felt ashamed to cry, he broke down. He couldn't stop the tears from rolling down his cheeks.

Two

Later that same afternoon, Simon raced through the streets, looking behind himself at every turn. He prayed no one was following him. He heard gunshots in the background. Beads of sweat formed on his forehead and above his lips. He felt his heart racing, as if it would explode. *The bakery, I need to make it* to *the bakery*. These words circled through his brain.

He looked for someone who would help him if the enemy was following him, someone who would take him in if he didn't reach the bakery in time, but there were few people on the streets. Most residents, he thought, must have retreated to the safety of their homes after hearing about the incident on the square, waiting to learn what would happen next. He ran in terror, watching those on the sidewalk move away as he approached them. Couldn't they see he needed them? Why wouldn't they help him? Simon fell as he neared the bakery. He pulled himself up. Blood seeped from the right sleeve of his shirt, but he felt no pain. His only thought was getting home to safety.

When Simon reached the bakery, it was dark inside, and the door was locked. He pounded on the entrance. Finally, his mother arrived to let him in. His grandmother, Katrina, and Lena followed behind her. Once inside, Simon fell to the floor gasping for breath. His mother dropped to her knees and sat beside him. Simon clung to her, shaking uncontrollably.

"Get some water and a cloth," his mother said to Katrina. His grandmother stood by with her arm around Lena, who was hugging her leg.

His mother wiped Simon's forehead and waited for him to calm down. She spoke to him softly, repeating, "You're safe now. Just stay still."

Slowly Simon's breathing normalized. His mouth felt parched, and he gulped down a glass of water. His mother and Katrina helped him remove his shirt to examine his wound. His mother washed away the dry blood.

"The cut is superficial. It will heal without leaving a scar," she said to the others. "It won't affect your violin playing," she continued, offering comfort to Simon.

When calm, Simon told his mother how the German soldiers took their captives to the Jewish section and forced them out of the trucks.

"They instructed the prisoners to gather only those belongings that would fit into one suitcase per person and to leave everything else behind. The soldiers gave them three choices," he said. "They could either leave Krakow as soon as possible, find other living arrangements in Krakow, or be shot if they didn't cooperate." Simon stopped to inhale a deep breath. "Soon, they warned, more German soldiers would arrive and other Jews would be gathered and given the same options."

His mother swept a hand across her forehead. "How did you escape?" she said.

"Rabbi Rosenschtein persuaded the Germans to let me go. 'He's not one of us,' he told them," Simon said. "One of the soldiers pointed his gun at me and told me to run. I could hear him laughing to the others, 'Look at the little rat bolt.' While escaping, I heard shots fired into the air. I didn't look back. I ran as fast as I could."

Simon's grandmother bit her lip and covered Lena's ears as he described this horror. His mother and Katrina looked at each other, their faces turning white.

Simon looked around. "Where's Papa?" he said, becoming aware of his father's absence.

His mother reached a hand to her chest. "After your abduction he hurried to the police station for help. He hasn't returned yet," she said.

Simon stayed with his mother downstairs to rest while the others returned to the living quarters. When his father arrived, he looked disheveled and relieved to find Simon safe at home. His father shook his head and said, "The police didn't know how to help me. They couldn't respond to the Germans' sudden attack. They didn't have adequate manpower nor munitions." Catching his breath, he went on. "The Polish army in Krakow offered no help either. The unexpected appearance of the Germans found them in chaos." He looked into Simon's eyes. "Feeling helpless, I came home to think through other strategies to rescue you, Simon."

Later, upstairs, Simon's grandmother heated the food she'd prepared earlier for lunch. She gave him the first plate. "We couldn't eat, worrying about your disappearance," she said. "Now that you're back, we should nourish our bodies and thank God you're safe."

Simon remained uncharacteristically silent during dinner. He felt his family watching over him, but no one questioned him further about his experience, not even the usually inquisitive Lena, who kept peeking up from her plate to look at him.

Simon perked up when he heard his father speak to Lena.

"Lena," he said, "you must try your grandmother's soup. She works hard to prepare us nice lunches."

"But, Papa, I don't like peas in my soup."

"But they're good for you."

Lena sat up straight and placed her hands on her hips. "When I'm a grown-up and have children, I'll never make them eat peas," she said vehemently.

Mr. Baron put down his spoon and said, "Katrina, go get a piece of paper and a pencil."

"But why, Papa?" Katrina said.

Calmly he said, "Just do as I say."

All eyes turned toward him. His mother started to say something. She stopped when her husband put a finger to his lips.

Katrina left the table and returned with the pencil and paper.

Her father started writing on the paper, speaking the words as he wrote. "On Saturday, September second, 1939, at four forty-five p.m. Lena said, 'I will never make my children eat peas.'" He held the paper up for everyone to see and said, "There, I'll have this framed and hang it in your room. One day, when you have children, you may want to remember what you said." Everyone laughed but Lena. She folded her arms and pouted.

After the meal, Simon retreated to his room and prepared for bed. The events of the day reeled through his mind. He wondered what would have happened to him if the enemy hadn't released him. He thought about those he'd left behind. Some were classmates and their families from his previous years in public school. Images from being on the truck reappeared: the frightened little girl dressed in her Sabbath clothes grabbing on to her mother, crying; her brother staring into space, his elbows pressed tightly to his sides; a father squeezing his daughter around the waist while quietly repeating everything would be all right; an older man rocking back and forth in prayer, asking God to give him strength.

Later, Simon's father knocked on his bedroom door.

"May I come in?"

"Yes, Papa."

His father sat on the edge of the bed. He patted the mattress, inviting Simon to sit next to him. "You were quiet at dinner. How are you feeling?"

"I'm alright."

His father looked him straight in the eyes. "Are you sure?"

Simon looked down, fiddled with his fingers, and blurted out, "I was scared, Papa, scared and ashamed. Lena was so brave. She went right over to defend the rabbi by kicking that soldier. I didn't fight hard enough to get away. I was weak. I shouldn't have let them get me on that truck."

"You were very brave, son, and we're all grateful for your quick thinking in getting Lena to safety. After that, you had no choice. Everything happened so quickly you had no time to think."

Simon looked down. He wanted to believe his father, that he had no choice. He felt his father tap his knee.

"Tell me what happened when they took you away, son."

"They were animals, Papa. Solomon, my friend from public school, stood up to a soldier who was yelling at his mother. The soldier hit him in the forehead with the butt of his rifle and knocked him to the ground. He had blood on his face. His mother looked scared. She tried to help Solomon up, but the soldier pushed her away. When Solomon tried to get up, the soldier held him down with his foot."

Simon lowered his head. His voice quieted. "I watched, feeling helpless. Solomon had the courage to challenge the German soldier while I just stood there trembling. I was so relieved when the rabbi convinced the soldiers I wasn't Jewish and to let me go. I felt guilty leaving the others behind." Simon looked back up at his father. "Am I weak, Papa? I feel bad inside. I just want to crawl under my blanket and hide."

"Son, you're confusing courage with good judgement. Where would you be right now if you'd acted like Solomon? You'd be lying in the street with a smashed head. The invaders could have injured you permanently. Suppose they broke your arm or smashed your fingers? Don't you remember what happened to your classmate in the band when you were in public school, the one you once tried to help on the playground? A week later a Christian student beat him so badly he couldn't play his cello for months."

Simon remembered the incident. Some of his former class-mates were Jewish. A few were fellow musicians in the school band. He felt uneasy about the cruel treatment they'd received from their Christian teachers and students. Once, on the playground, he'd stepped in on behalf of a Jewish student, Nachum. A Christian student had snatched Nachum's yarmulke from his head and tossed it around. He caught the yarmulke and gave it back to Nachum. The snatcher called him a Jew lover. He said to the bully, "Your head is too pointed to wear it." The offender's face turned red. He stomped away when the other students laughed.

"Yes, I remember, Papa. You're right, but Jewish boys are considered men at my age. That's what I've heard them say. I should be a man, too, but I didn't act like or feel like a man today."

His father placed a hand on Simon's shoulder. "You are a man, son, in many ways. Your mother and I know how you treat Katrina when you take her to the movies, how you stare down people who take notice of her limp, how you take her early to get her a seat where she'll feel comfortable not having to trip over others. Your concerns for her are the actions of a mensch, as Rabbi Rosenschtein would say."

"A mensch?" Simon stumbled over the word.

"Yes. That's Yiddish for 'man.' Remember that's what Rabbi Rosenschtein called you when he came to thank you for coming to the aid of the son of one of his congregants?" His father tapped his forefinger on his forehead. "What was his name… Nachum, that's it, the son of Dr. and Mrs. Fridman. He's called you that many times when he's heard you playing your violin from across the square and come to the bakery to compliment you. He's made it a point to inquire about you when he sees me opening the store. He knows how respectful you are, how kind and considerate you are. 'He's going to grow up to be a fine man, a real mensch,' he's said to me often."

Simon remembered that visit from the rabbi, also. He felt awkward when his parents called him down to the bakery and the rabbi praised him. He had sensed a special interest in him from this strange-looking man dressed in black from head to toe whose widespread pink lips showed through his thick black-and-white peppered beard. He remembered the rabbi had come across the square often to compliment him. The rabbi never purchased anything. The bakery didn't adhere to kosher requirements and wasn't patronized by Orthodox Jews.

"Today you've learned the world is not always kind, son," his father said with a grim twist to his mouth. "Our family is blessed. Soon, however, we'll be in for terrible times, and we'll all be afraid and need courage. The radio tells us to prepare for the worst. This invasion will not affect just the Jews. It will affect all of us, even those of us with German blood." His father patted Simon's shoulder. "I need your promise you'll be prudent and not do anything to bring harm to yourself or your family. A little fear and guilt will be a good thing. Promise me."

"I promise, Papa."

Simon's father stood. "Your mother and I had a talk. We think you should stay home from school Monday and rest. I'll walk you to school for the next few days. German soldiers will be on the streets. We'd feel better if I were with you. I can explain to them, if we're stopped, that our family is of German heritage. Hopefully I'll be able to dissuade the invaders from bothering us, unlike the ethnic Poles, who are also in for trouble with the invaders."

"But…" Simon stood and started to object.

"No buts, Simon. It's decided."

Simon's father pulled him into an embrace and said, "Sleep well, my son." He turned off the light and left the room, leaving the door open a crack.

Although Simon knew his father's words were meant to comfort and reassure him he'd acted appropriately, he couldn't get past his doubts about his own reactions to what had happened, how he'd huddled in fear among the others when the soldiers removed them from their trucks and pointed rifles at them. He felt ashamed he'd whimpered and had been unsuccessful at holding back his tears. He still saw the fear on the faces of the captives and heard the laughter of the soldiers as they tormented the congregants of Beth David Congregation.

Simon realized his father's warnings about what lie ahead was a sign he was no longer treating Simon like a child, no longer sheltering him from the cruelties of the world. Despite his desire for his parents to treat him like an adult, Simon now saw this had its consequences. It left him feeling scared. Although his father and his two brothers were of German heritage, his mother and grandmother were Polish born. Would his father's and his uncles' heritage protect the others?

THREE

The following morning Simon woke up to find his room full of sunlight rather than the usual dim light of early morning. The stillness of the house confused him. His feet slipped quietly to the floor. He put on his slippers and walked cautiously down the steps to the kitchen, where he found his mother.

Relieved he wasn't alone, he said, "Where is everyone?"

"They've all gone to church. It's Sunday, remember? You were sleeping so peacefully after a restless night we thought it best to let you stay in this morning." His mother caressed his cheek and asked how he was feeling.

"I'm OK," he said, not convincingly, even to himself. "I'm hungry."

"I thought you'd be." She laid out freshly warmed pastries and bread on the table. "Would you like some scrambled eggs and sausage?"

"Sure." He pulled up a chair.

Simon watched his mother fuss over his breakfast. He thought how lucky he was to be home safe, unlike the others. He stood to help when his mother brought the plate to him.

"You're getting so tall, Simon, and I think you've gained a little weight. We need to get you new clothes. What do you say we go shopping this week? Your father and I think you should have a new suit for the concert."

"OK," Simon said, working on his eggs.

"Let's aim for Thursday after school, all right?"

Simon took a last swallow of milk and said, "Fine."

"When you're finished, bring me a pair of your trousers. I'll see if your grandmother can lengthen them for you."

When he had consumed his last bite of eggs, Simon got up and fetched a pair of his pants for his mother. Then he returned to his room, where he planned to spend the rest of the afternoon. The stresses of yesterday weighed heavily on him. He felt by putting his emotions to music, he might get better control of his feelings.

He went to his bureau and pulled out his violin case from the bottom drawer. He remembered when he was four years old his parents brought the chest to his room from the basement. They'd discovered the violin stored there. Initially, when his mother showed him how to plunk the strings, Simon was amused by the sound it made, but he quickly lost interest and went about playing with his toys.

When he was six, his mother took him to a concert. He was awestruck by the experience: the grandeur of the concert hall; the full volume of the instruments playing together; and the vigorous applause of the audience. He wanted to be a part of that one day.

Now, through his mother's stimulus in those earlier years and the encouragement of his instructors, Simon was a full-time student of Professor Kaminski, a well-respected teacher at the Krakow School of Music. The professor told Simon and his parents he not only had the dexterity, patience, and attention span, but, also, more importantly, the temperament needed to become a solo violinist. She told them, also, he had the special gift of being able to interpret his visual and emotional experiences into music. "You are blessed, also," she said to Simon, "with having an auditory memory, allowing you to replay your compositions without writing them down."

He now was using the violin his mother had shown him years ago, the adult-sized one she had stored away for safekeeping in a secret room behind the closet of his bedroom. He later learned the family living there at the time had used this room to hide their treasured possessions during what his father called the Great War. More recently, Simon used it to hide when playing hide-and-seek with Lena.

Alone in his room, standing straight, his head forward and his chin resting on his violin, Simon slid the bow across the strings. With swift movements, he created sounds representing the beauty and wonderment of the starlings' maneuvers in the sky. Soon his body quivered to the dissonant, erratic, screeching sounds he caused to emanate from the instrument by creating excess pressure on the strings. These sounds represented the arrival of the Germans and their resulting menace. The exercise of translating the experiences of yesterday onto his violin helped Simon process what happened to him the day before. If there was time during his next session with the professor, he'd play this for her. He didn't need to transcribe it on music sheets. He'd remember it.

Simon stayed home from his classes Monday, as his parents had insisted. He spent the rest of the day practicing his piece for the Poland Independence Day Concert.

On Tuesday, Professor Kaminski expected him to arrive at 9:00 a.m. sharp well prepared. He wouldn't disappoint her. She was a stickler for self-discipline. Simon rarely let her down.

Simon's father walked him to school. Simon was secretly relieved. He didn't like the idea of being alone on the street. His mother had called Professor Kaminski the day before to explain Simon's absence and how it might affect his schoolwork. Professor Kaminski greeted Mr. Baron and Simon. Without any pleasantries, she asked Simon how much time he had spent over the past three days preparing for the concert. With a gleam in his eyes, Simon said he'd practiced hard, and he was ready to begin today's lesson.

"Those damn Nazis," she said unexpectedly. "You aren't Jewish. They won't be after you. Don't worry. Besides, they love cultured people. You being a violinist is in your favor. Now let's get to work."

Four

O n Wednesday Simon couldn't wait to get to school. He felt he'd perfected his piece for the concert and wanted to play it for Professor Kaminski. Two blocks from the entrance, Simon asked his father to let him go the rest of the way alone. He didn't want other students to think he needed a parent to accompany him to school.

Mr. Baron looked around. The street looked safe. There were no signs of German soldiers. Shop owners were outside rolling out awnings and opening their doors. Reluctantly he agreed.

Simon walked away and turned around to make sure his father had gone. When he saw his father still watching him, he waved and waited for his father to leave.

One block from school, Simon saw two German soldiers walking toward him. He looked downward, hoping to avoid their attention. When they drew closer, one shouted, "Halt." Simon stopped, clutched his violin case tightly to his chest, and continued to avoid making eye contact with these men

"Where are you going, boy?" the taller one said in German.

Still holding on tightly to his violin case, Simon responded, "To school."

"I recognize this boy," the taller one said to the stouter one. "He was at the synagogue Saturday. We transported him from the square with the others. He's the one the rabbi said wasn't Jewish and who we let go."

"What's your name?" the soldier spit out.

"Simon, Simon Baron," he managed, stammering.

"Who are your parents?

"David and Karolina Baron."

Simon responded to their demand for his address and birth date.

"Are you Jewish?"

"No, sir. I'm Catholic."

"You speak German well. How is that?"

"My grandfather came from Germany. My father and uncles are half German."

The soldier wrote all this down on a pad he pulled from his jacket pocket. He replaced the pad and told Simon to go.

Simon headed toward school, but he stopped when he heard the taller one utter, "Let's go to the Department of Civil Records. Something is not right here."

Simon was curious. He decided to ignore his father's warning. He had to know what these soldiers were after. Mustering his courage, he followed the two soldiers, making sure they didn't see him. He watched them go into the Department of Civil Records. He stood under an open window and heard the soldier ask for his birth certificate. He hid behind a column when they came out, and he saw the taller one poke a finger at a line on the paper while the other looked closely. Then he scurried off to school, wondering what it was the soldiers were looking at that interested them so.

FIVE

After following the two Germans to the Department of Civil Records, Simon walked back to school thinking of excuses to give for being late. He worried Professor Kaminski might call his parents to ask why he had failed to show for his lesson. As he approached the entrance, Simon saw parents arriving and others leaving with their children. They all had worried expressions on their faces and walked with a heavy stride. He wanted to stop them and ask what was happening, but in their hurriedness, they rushed by him. He began to feel a quivering sensation in his body. Inside, the lobby bustled with students and professors moving in both directions. Their chatter bounced off the walls. The sounds of panicked gibberish rang in his ears.

Simon worked his way to Professor Kaminsky's classroom. His mind raced for answers to the clamor in the hallway. When he arrived, there was a note tacked on the classroom door. It stated the professor was in a meeting with the rector and that he should stay in the room and wait for her. He entered the room and sat hunched over on his chair, his violin case on the floor between his feet. *I should have let my father walk me all the way to school, and I shouldn't have followed those soldiers. If I had listened to my father, I'd be under his protection right now.*

When Professor Kaminski arrived, she lowered her head and tugged at the cross around her neck. She appeared both nervous and unhappy.

She cleared her throat and said, "We'll be closing early today. It's been reported a caravan of German soldiers has been seen on the outskirts of the city and is heading in. Krakow will soon be under siege. We're calling all parents to pick up their children. In the meantime, we're gathering students in the auditorium."

Simon said nothing. He wanted to flee or hide. *The Germans. I can't face them again.*

"Do you understand what I'm saying?" Professor Kaminski said.

Simon nodded. He couldn't speak. His mouth went dry. His mind retreated to last Saturday, when the invaders pulled him into the back of one of their trucks. He hoped his father would come soon to take him home.

Professor Kaminski led Simon through the bustling hallway to the auditorium, where the faculty had gathered a group of chattering students, most of whom he recognized as daily local pupils.

"The dormitory students have been escorted back to their rooms," the student sitting next to Simon said. "I don't know what all this worry is about. We're all Polish citizens. Our army will protect us."

Simon didn't tell him about his father's experience of finding the army unprepared for the German invasion. However, knowing this himself raised his anxiety.

Simon didn't have to wait long for his father. He jumped up when they called his name. Professor Kaminski walked him to the lobby. As he and his father were leaving, Simon heard her call out, "Remember, Simon, keep practicing your piece."

Simon and his father began their walk home in silence. Mr. Baron walked fast. Simon's violin case bounced across his thighs as he struggled to keep pace.

The scene had changed in the time since his father had walked him to school. Merchants had closed their stores and drawn the shades. Families living on floors above the stores peeked out from behind closed curtains.

Simon broke the silence. "How long do you think school will be closed, Papa?"

"It's hard to say. Until they think it's safe for the students to return."

"How will the invasion affect us, Papa?"

"I won't lie to you, Simon. The Germans will take over our city, and they'll have much support. Our army is ill prepared. Let's hope the British and French will help us. Right now, I can't answer how our lives will change, but they will. I'm praying that our German blood will make things easier for us."

Simon stopped asking questions. He had an empty feeling in the pit of his stomach and a sense something bad was going to happen. There was something his father wasn't telling him. He feared what he might find out when he got home.

They arrived at the bakery, where a CLOSED sign was on the door. His father let them in, and they went directly upstairs to a waiting family. Relieved to see Simon, they gathered around him. His mother poured him a glass of milk while he put his coat and violin case in his room.

Once settled, Mr. Baron asked the family to assemble around the kitchen table.

"First," he said, "I want to reassure you we're safe. There's plenty of food in the house, and, in an emergency, the bakery has enough flour and supplies to last us for a few days. The bakery will stay closed until your mother and I determine what the situation is. No one is to go downstairs. Is that understood?" he said with emphasis. They nodded. "Simon, until we hear school has reopened, you are to spend your time here practicing for the concert, like Professor Kaminski said."

Simon didn't argue. The concert was two months away. *By then things will have blown over, and we'll be safe*, he thought wishfully.

"All curtains are to remain closed, and we must play the radio quietly. Does anyone have any questions?" his father said.

When no one replied, he asked Katrina to get the family Bible.

When she returned, Katrina handed the Bible to her father. He turned to Psalm 3, David's Prayer for Deliverance. "Now let's pray for the Lord's strength and protection." The family closed their eyes and bowed their heads. Simon peeked up to see his grandmother's eyes open. She was rubbing her hands. He quickly closed his eyes when she looked back at him. His father began reading the prayer calling upon the Lord to shield them from their enemies and all despair and to bring restoration to their lives. When he finished, they crossed themselves, then Mr. Baron gave the Bible to Katrina to return to its place.

Afterward, Simon's mother and grandmother prepared lunch while Mr. Baron telephoned his brothers to make sure they were safe. Though Jakub lived only two buildings away, at a time like this, it could seem like miles. Fryderyk had taken similar precautions as his brothers. Simon heard his father tell his grandmother her other sons and their families were safe.

When lunch was over, his father followed Simon to his room and closed the door. He pulled up the only chair and sat. He told Simon to sit on the bed. The agitated tone in his father's voice caused Simon to move quickly. He waited for his father to speak.

"Your mother and I received a call from Mrs. Nowak, the clerk at the Department of Vital Records. She said two Germans were there this morning to retrieve a copy of your birth certificate. She said she watched them walk away and saw a boy who looked like you follow behind them. It was you, wasn't it, Simon?" His father's voice was stern

Simon stared into his lap. "Yes, sir." He'd hoped his parents wouldn't find out. When he'd arrived at school late to find Professor Kaminski wasn't ready for him, he'd thought his side tracking had gone undetected.

Simon felt ashamed. He had taken a risky action in following the soldiers. In doing so he had hoped to learn why they were so interested in him. It hadn't resulted in the outcome he had hoped. He still didn't know what his birth certificate contained that interested them. All his action had accomplished was to anger his father.

"Didn't we talk about your being more careful, about the danger of your being on the street alone and taking chances? You disobeyed me, Simon. You violated my trust. It's my fault. I shouldn't have let you walk the last two blocks alone. You may have placed us in danger, not just you, all of us."

Simon flushed. He sat quietly, unable to respond. His father had never spoken to him this harshly. He looked at him, tears welling up. He bit his lip, refusing to cry. He had no excuses, none that his father would accept, anyway. *Hadn't Papa ever disobeyed his father, standing ready to accept the consequences?* Simon thought, but he remained quiet.

"We'll talk more after dinner. Practice your Tchaikovsky," his father said curtly.

By midafternoon, outside their kitchen windows, the unmistakable rattling sounds of tanks and trucks, the roar of motorcycles, and the stomping of soldiers' footsteps echoed through the street below. The clattering seemed to go on forever. Lena and her parents peeked out from one window to see. Katrina, Grandmother, and Simon peered from the other.

Six

That night, after dinner, Simon got up to leave with his grandmother and sisters. His parents asked him to stay.

"We have a story to tell you," his mother said.

"But I must practice. I want to work on a composition I've been tossing about in my head." Simon was still reeling from the sting of his father's talk earlier. He wanted to avoid any more discussion and scolding. Right now, he wanted to be alone, play his violin, and think about the past three days. He'd play something simple, something he'd make up as he went along to help express his feelings.

"We know, but this is an important story you need to hear," his mother said. She stood at the sink with a dish towel in her hand, twisting and untwisting it. Her voice sounded strained. Simon sensed her unease.

His father sat with his hands clasped on top of the table and his body bent forward. The flickering candle in the dimly lit room cast a shadow across his father's face, giving him a solemn appearance. Simon returned to the table wondering what could be worrying them about him and not the others. His mother joined him and his father.

His mother looked at his father before speaking. They looked serious, he thought. His knee started bouncing. Finally, she spoke.

"Years ago, before you were born, when Katrina was three years old, a young couple came to Krakow from a small village northwest of here. The young man came to study violin at the conservatory, like you." Simon's ears perked up. His mother paused. She seemed to relax and smile at his reaction. "His goal," she continued, "also like you, was to become a concert violinist. They didn't have much money, just the small stipend from the conservatory, so they lived with us. They were young and in love. It was a joy having them stay here."

His mother's voice became warmer, sweeter. He himself relaxed as his mother told him how the young man entertained them with his violin playing and how during the day, while he was in school, the young woman took care of Katrina while they worked in the bakery. His mother's eyelids rose. "She was wonderful with Katrina. She assisted her with her leg exercises to help her walk better."

"Our family," his mother went on, "your father's parents and brothers, welcomed this couple with open arms. Their youthfulness and enthusiasm were contagious. It made us all feel proud to have a violinist among us. After a while the young woman became pregnant. It was a blessed time. After Katrina, my doctor told me and your father we likely couldn't have more children. The thought of having another baby in the house thrilled us."

His mother waited, as if allowing this information to sink in. Her voice lowered to a whisper, and her eyes filled with tears. "As the birth of the child grew near, the young woman became ill. At first it didn't appear serious, but soon it developed into a mild fever and cough. We wanted her to see a doctor, but she kept putting us off, promising she'd see a doctor after the child was born."

Simon's mother stopped speaking. His father moved his chair nearer to her and bent his head close to hers. He didn't say anything. He just took her hand in his. His mother pulled herself together. Her voice was sad when she continued.

"Soon the cough became worse, and she grew weaker. The week before the baby was to be born, we called the doctor. He insisted she go to the hospital. The doctor there said she had tuberculosis, and he should deliver the baby right away. The young woman passed away two days after the child was born—a fine, healthy son."

Simon wanted to interrupt the story sooner but couldn't make himself do it. He wanted to ask his mother if this couple was a part of the family she never spoke about, that part of the family from whom he got his talent. Something wasn't adding up. He had a feeling in the pit of his stomach, an impending feeling this story had something to do with him. *Does this have something to do with my birth certificate? Am I the child in this story?*

Now he couldn't stop himself. "Why are you telling me this?" he said, his voice rising.

The room turned as quiet as the night was dark. His parents looked at each other.

His mother reached across the table to touch him. Simon flinched away. Something told him he didn't want to hear what she had to say. His mother pulled back and said, "We're telling you this because the young couple were your biological parents. The young man was your father; the young woman, your mother."

Simon's posture stiffened. He felt cold. His eyelids closed tightly. He was unable to speak, unable to bring forth any thoughts or feelings. He crossed his arms against his chest, hugging himself as he rocked back and forth in his chair.

"Control your breathing," he heard the voice of Professor Kaminski saying. "Feel what you are playing. Go with the music; let it take you where it wants to go."

Simon kept repeating these words to himself, taking deep breaths as he tried to pull himself together. His parents were telling him they weren't his parents. He didn't understand. They'd taken care of him all his life. How could they be anything but his parents? He had many questions. Simon opened his eyes. His parents were watching him, as if waiting for him to say something. Finally, Simon found his voice.

"Are you still my parents?"

"You have two sets of parents, the young couple in the story and us," his mother said. "There is no doubt if your mother had lived, your life would have been different. Your father was my nephew, my sister's son, the sister I never spoke about. He and your mother would have raised you. We would have been your aunt and uncle, and we would have been an important part of your life. Either way we'd have loved you with all our hearts. We feel as if we are your parents, and you are our son."

Simon wondered about his real father. Where was he? He wasn't ready to ask. Right now, he was more interested in his sisters. His father wasn't yet real to him. They were.

Simon swallowed hard. Hesitantly he asked, "Do Lena and Katrina know I'm not really their brother?" Behind his question was a feeling of anguish. He loved his sisters. It was heartbreaking for him to think their learning what he'd been told might diminish their feelings toward him. He tried his best to hold himself together, to not cry.

Mrs. Baron looked painfully at Simon. "They have no reason to think otherwise," she said. "Katrina was only three when you came along. She's never thought of you as anything else. The same goes for Lena. She was born ten years after you, an unexpected blessing the doctor called it, a miracle. To them, and to us, you are their brother." In his mother's eyes, in her voice, Simon saw her love for him and the sadness she must have felt in seeing him hurt.

"Are you going to tell them?" Simon asked.

"Would you like us to?

"Yes."

"Do you want to be there?"

"No," he said, feeling he'd be unable to bear seeing the expressions on their faces, the twisting of their heads toward him and their mother in disbelief when their parents told them, especially Katrina's. He didn't feel he could bear the silence that might follow, nor their running to him with assurances of their love. Would they look upon him differently? Lena, he imagined, would be confused and ask questions. He knew he would cry, and he wasn't ready to handle such emotions. He needed time alone before they came to him.

Simon asked his mother, "What about Grandmother and my aunts and uncles?"

"They know the circumstances of your being a member of our family, and they've always treated you as our son. They love you dearly. Surely you must know that."

Simon struggled to ask his most important question, one directed at both his parents.

"Do you love me?" he said, his eyes glistening. He knew they did. He needed to hear them say it.

"Oh, Simon, of course we do," his mother cried out.

"As much as Katrina and Lena?"

Simon watched his father nod, wipe away a tear, and then turn sideways, momentarily hiding his face.

The question silenced them for a moment.

"Tell me about my real parents. What did they look like? Do you have a picture of them?" Simon asked, feeling guilty using the word "real."

"Yes, I do." His mother got up and went to the living room.

While he and his father sat alone, Simon said, "What shall I call you, Papa?"

"Son, I'm both your uncle and your father, but mostly your father. I will always be honored to be your father. I want you to think of me that way." Simon got up, walked over to his father, and hugged him around the shoulders. Their cheeks touched, and Simon felt his father's tears.

His mother returned with a photograph of a young man and woman standing side by side, wearing dress clothing. The young man was holding a violin. He and the young woman were both looking directly into the camera. They had posed for the photograph in front of the entrance of the Krakow School of Music.

"I took it before one of your father's recitals," his mother said. "See"—she pointed to the picture. The young man is holding the violin you're now playing, the one we found in the bureau drawer the day we brought it up from the basement. Look, you have your mother's features, brown wavy hair and brown eyes, and your father's talent. You're a perfect combination of them."

"May I have this?" Simon asked.

"Of course," his mother said, handing him the photograph.

He needed to hold on to the photograph, to study it in private. He stared at the young man and woman. They were a handsome couple, but it was hard for him to imagine these people as his parents, to see them in any way but as strangers he might pass on the street or see at a concert. The only things that connected him to them were the violin the man held and the image of his school behind them. He wondered if the man had purposely left the violin for him. He wondered, also, if any of the current professors at school had taught there when his father was a student. Did any of them know of the connection between him and this man?

"I think I'd like to go to my room now," Simon said.

His father shifted in his chair. "There's more, Simon. Please let your mother finish. It's important you know this."

What more could there be? Simon thought. He'd heard enough, but the look on his father's face told him to not question him. His mother was rubbing her wrists. She looked nervous, as if she were searching for the right words.

She began talking. "Your father was heartbroken by your mother's death. He stopped going to school and lost his desire to play the violin. As time passed, he began to heal, but he began to look upon Krakow as an unhappy place. The death of your mother shattered his dreams of a family. He was so talented, his professors encouraged him to move away. They wanted him to share his aptitude with the world and encouraged him to move to America to make a fresh start. He made us promise to love you and take care of you. That was all so easy to do. We loved you even before you were born. You became a gift from God to us, the child we were told we couldn't have after Katrina."

It started to sink in. His father was alive and out there somewhere. He was at a loss for words. How could his father still be alive and not have contacted him all these years? Pretending he'd misheard part of the story, Simon said, "My father is alive?"

His mother's lips squeezed together tightly. She nodded he was.

"Where is he now?" Simon asked, attempting to glean more information.

"He's in America, somewhere in New York, we believe," his mother said.

Simon was quiet. He was thinking, *Why haven't I heard from this man?* He wasn't sure he knew how to ask. He wasn't sure he wanted to know the answer, but he needed to.

"Hasn't he ever contacted you? Is he ashamed of me?"

"No!" his mother said. "You must never think that. He adored you. He was ashamed of himself, ashamed he fell apart with grief, that he left you motherless. He left you with us because he knew we could make a loving home for you, give you what he couldn't, raise you to be like him, to be a great—"

Simon interrupted angrily. "Like him? Raised to be a man who abandons his son? I don't want to be like him. I hate him! I hate you all!"

His father moved toward him. Simon held his hand up to hold him back.

"Please, Simon," his father said. His voice was shaking. "There is one final piece to this story. Then you'll know why I've been so firm with you since Saturday, why I've felt the need to protect you." Simon watched his father look at his mother and reach for her hand as the words came slowly. "Your mother was Jewish. That is what the Germans discovered on your birth certificate. In the eyes of the Germans, that makes you Jewish, as well."

Those words were like a shot to Simon's brain.

"But I'm Catholic," he sputtered. "I'm not Jewish. I don't know anything about being Jewish."

"That makes no difference to these damn Nazis. To them you are Jewish because your mother was Jewish" his father said.

Simon had never heard his father curse. It scared him, not only because of its forcefulness but because he had witnessed the danger firsthand when the Germans took him and the Jewish congregants from the square. These memories frightened him to the core.

Simon got up from the table, pushing his chair backward to the floor. He ran to his room and sat on his bed for a moment, shaking. Then he stood, tore the covers off the bed, and dragged his mattress onto the floor. He pulled out the drawers from his bureau and tossed the contents randomly. He reached for his violin, a symbol of the man who abandoned him. He was about to smash it against the wall when his father grabbed it from him and passed it off to his mother. His father wrapped his arms around him tightly so Simon couldn't move. Simon struggled, but he soon fell limp in his father's grip and began to cry, his body convulsing.

"We'll move him to Katrina's room for the night while you and Katrina put his room back together," his father said. His father took Simon to Katrina's bedroom and helped him undress. He stayed with him until he thought Simon was asleep. Words came from his father's lips, words Simon couldn't make out, but they sounded like a prayer.

Simon pretended to fall asleep and waited for his father to leave. He tossed and turned, his thoughts in turmoil. Everything about his life—or rather, what thought he knew about his life—was now a lie.

SEVEN

The next morning Simon woke up in Katrina's room to the sounds of movement around the house. Sleep had let him forget the shocking revelations of last night, but now they rushed back. He didn't feel prepared to face the new day, his family, or his own feelings. Everything was the same; nothing was the same.

Maybe last night was a dream. It never happened. It will go away. But he knew it wouldn't. He wanted to hide, to disappear. He rolled into a fetal position and pulled the blanket tightly around himself, hiding from the world. His chest hurt, and his stomach ached. He wrapped his hand across his shoulder blades, squeezed his elbows tight against his ribs, and closed his eyes, hoping to fall asleep, trying to make the uneasiness go away. He couldn't stop thinking about the scene in the kitchen last night and the story his parents had told him.

Simon needed to talk with someone, someone outside of his family who would understand his feelings and what he was going through. He thought of Rabbi Rosenschtein. He remembered how the rabbi had placed his hand on his knee in the German truck. He recalled the rabbi's words to the Germans. "Let him go. He's not one of us." Now Simon had found out this wasn't true. Did the rabbi know something about his past? He had to find a way to get to him.

A loud knock on the door broke Simon's thoughts. His mother and Katrina barged in.

"Simon, get up quickly. There's a German truck outside, and three soldiers are banging on the bakery door. You must get up," his mother said. Her breath was bursting in and out. She sounded terrified.

Simon unraveled himself and sat up. He felt panicked. He'd just been thinking about his capture by the Germans on the square and his release when they thought he wasn't Jewish. *Now they know I am. They've come for me.* He began shaking all over.

"Hurry," his mother said. "You must get back to your bedroom and hide. Katrina, make the bed."

Simon did as his mother said. He tiptoed to his room. He could hear his father's voice and the voices of the Germans coming from the bakery below. His mother followed him into his room. Someone had straightened it to look like it he hadn't used it. His mother opened the closet door and pushed the clothes hanging there aside. He released the lever that opened the back wall to the secret room. Once in, he closed the wall behind him and stood as straight as he could in the narrow space. He heard his mother rearranging the clothes back in place.

"Where is your son?" Simon heard a soldier ask. The voices were now coming from the kitchen.

His father's voice answered, "We don't know. He wasn't here when we got up this morning. He's probably out walking along the river. He sometimes does that before school." His father's voice was steady.

"You're lying. No one is out walking this morning. We'll search the house. If we find he is here..." His voice tapered off.

"Go search the house," the same voice ordered the others.

Simon remained very still, afraid to breath. He pressed his elbows to his sides to make his body as small as possible. He heard footsteps stomp from room to room, first downstairs, then rising to the second level. When he heard them enter his room, he put his fist in his mouth and held his body rigid to stop from making any sounds. His heart raced when he heard them open his closet door and toss clothing aside. "Look under the bed" he heard one say." "No one's here," said another. When he heard them leave, he relaxed enough only to breath air in and out slowly.

"What do you want with my son?" Simon heard his father say.

"We need to talk with him. We are recording the location of all Jews."

"My son isn't Jewish. He's Catholic."

"We have a birth certificate to the contrary. He was born to a Jewess."

"There must be some mistake. Ask Father Dempski. Our son was baptized and received first communion at Saint Mary's Church. We go there as a family every week." His father's voice sounded firm, assured.

"We have searched the house. There's no boy here," another voice said.

"We'll be back," the one who had spoken to his father said.

When Simon heard his father let the Germans out and lock the bakery door, he slid down the wall of the secret room and fell into a stooped position. He wrapped his arms around his knees.

"What am I going to do?" he whispered. All he could think of was the danger he'd placed his family in.

EIGHT

"Your mother and I received a call from Rector Holmes. He wants us to come to school with you Monday," Simon's father said to him Friday at dinner.

"Why does he want you to come?

"He wouldn't give me a straight answer, Simon. He just asked us to be there and said he'd explain. Don't worry. It's probably nothing."

Simon didn't sleep well over the weekend. He picked at his food during meals. His stomach was in turmoil. He tried to gain control over his worries by concentrating on the Tchaikovsky concerto, but he had trouble focusing. By the time Monday morning came, his anxiety had reached a high point. There was little conversation at the breakfast table.

Simon's stomach churned on the way to his school. At the entrance he tripped on a step. His father caught him before he fell. The rector and Professor Kaminski were waiting for them inside. Simon sensed the news wouldn't be good when he saw the look on the professor's face and the way she wrung her handkerchief. The rector led them to his office and asked them to sit. He was a tall, broad-chested man. He stood, towering over them.

Simon could feel the tension in the air. He was impatient to know why this meeting had been called. He shifted in his chair and looked over at his parents. His father gave him an easy nod. His mother offered the hint of a smile. The three looked at each other for a moment, then they turned their attention toward the rector.

The rector walked to his desk and stood behind his chair. He clasped his hands behind his back. With a solemn expression, he said, "I'm afraid I've got bad news."

Simon felt a sinking sensation in his heart. The rector's comment had warranted his worry. He pulled himself to the edge of his chair and held on tightly to both its arms, ready to pounce. He looked at his parents. His father glanced at him and held out an arm with his fingers spread, directing him to stay calm.

The rector paused and looked back and forth between Simon and his parents. He walked around to the front of his desk and sat against its edge. "An officer from the German Army came to see me Thursday afternoon. He told me about Simon's birth certificate. Is it true what he told me? Simon's mother was Jewish? You are his adoptive parents?"

Mr. Baron stood, and in a stern voice, said, "He's our son. We've raised him from birth as a Catholic. He's an outstanding Polish citizen."

"I'm sure that's true, Mr. Baron," the rector said. "We here have no reason to disagree with you. Simon is one of our finest students. We have the highest expectations for him. Please, sit down. Let's not have a scene. I understand how you feel."

"No, you don't," Mr. Baron said. He shook his fist. "The violin is Simon's life, his passion. He's put everything he's got into his studies. I won't let you or the Germans do anything to stand in his way. What is it you want to tell us? Why have you invited us here?"

"Please sit down, Mr. Baron," the rector said. "I'm getting to that, but you need to control yourself."

Simon glanced at his mother. There were tears forming in her eyes. He wanted to go to her, but he sat rigidly waiting to see where this was heading. He looked over to Professor Kaminski, who was staring at him, wiping her eyes with her handkerchief. He hung his head, unable to look back at her.

Mr. Baron breathed heavily, hiked the knees of his trousers, and slowly sat, looking at his wife and Simon.

Simon braced himself for what was coming.

The rector cleared his throat, stood, and walked back and forth before them with his hands behind his back. His voice seemed apologetic when he stopped and said, "The Nazis are insisting we expel our Jewish students. The ones who came here told me they are forcing all other conservatories and universities throughout Poland to do the same. If we don't conform, they'll close the school."

Simon's chest tightened. He slowly shook his head in disbelief. A slight noise rose from his throat. He fought an impulse to leap from his chair and swipe his arm across the rector's desk, letting the items scatter across the floor. To control himself, he squeezed his hands more tightly onto the arms of his chair. He looked at Professor Kaminski again for support. There was a look of helplessness on her face, a look of sympathy for what he must be feeling. He had grown to respect and love her dearly. The thought of losing her as his teacher devastated him.

His father raised his voice. "So what are you saying? You're expelling Simon?"

"It's most unfortunate, but the Germans have tied our hands. I'm afraid the answer is yes."

"When will this expulsion take place?"

The rector looked down and lowered his voice. "Immediately, I'm afraid."

Simon's face reddened. "Does this mean I can't represent the school at the Independence Day Concert?"

The rector stroked his forearm. "I'm sorry, son, I have no choice." The rector turned to Simon's parents. In a gentle tone, he said, "I want to repeat, Mr. and Mrs. Baron, we have the highest regard for Simon. It distresses us to have to take this action."

No one responded. The meeting ended with everyone looking dejected and unable to find the right words to say.

Professor Kaminski and Simon walked quietly to his classrooms to collect his belongings. Other students passed Simon and nodded. Simon's eyes averted theirs. When Simon finished, Professor Kaminski walked him to his parents. On the way she stopped, faced him, and placed her hands on his shoulders. "You're a fine violinist, Simon," she said. "You must never forget that. This war will be over one day, and you will resume your studies, here, I hope. In the meantime, hold your head high, and keep practicing and composing. I'll want to hear your compositions when we meet again." They hugged each other. Simon bit his lip to hold back his tears.

Simon and his parents walked out the front door of the school with their shoulders slumped and their heads down. His father attempted to put his arm around Simon's shoulder. Simon brushed it away and walked home ahead of his parents.

Once home, Simon retreated to his room and slammed the door. He threw his backpack on the floor and fell into his bed, stomach first. He hid his face in his pillow and cried.

NINE

Three nights after his expulsion from the Krakow School of Music, Simon stood at the front door of the two-story wooden house on Isaak Street where Rabbi Rosenschtein and his family now lived. He cleared his throat, took a deep breath, and rapped heavily, hoping someone would answer before he lost his nerve. He looked back toward his waiting father and fought the urge to flee back to the parked car.

Simon hoped meeting with the rabbi would answer his questions and get rid of the fears that had plagued him since he'd learned he was adopted, and his mother was Jewish.

Simon knocked again, this time harder.

A woman he barely recognized as the rabbi's wife appeared with a young girl around his age. The rabbi's wife wore a long black dress and shawl. Even in the dark, her skin and lips looked pale. Her hair looked unwashed.

"You're Simon," the rabbi's wife said, "from across the square, the young man from the bakery."

Simon was surprised she knew him.

His eyes widened. "Yes, ma'am," he answered.

Mrs. Rosenschtein invited Simon in and asked if he was alone. He told her his father was waiting for him in the car. She suggested his father drive to the back of the house, where it would be safer. She'd meet him there to let him in. Simon did as she urged and came back to the house, where the rabbi's wife and the young girl were waiting for him.

"My husband is upstairs leading a group in evening prayer. You can wait for him in the parlor. This is our daughter, Rachel.

She'll wait with you and keep you company while I go let your father in and offer him something warm to drink, won't you, dear," she said.

Rachel nodded and pulled her sweater tightly across her body. Simon shyly bowed his head and waved at her.

Mrs. Rosenschtein turned to Simon. "Please make yourself comfortable. The rabbi shouldn't be too long." She then walked down the hallway past the stairs, leaving Simon alone with Rachel.

The parlor, right off the entranceway, was cold and dim. A fireplace at the far end of the room was unlit. A small table lamp provided minimum light. Simon kept his coat on. Rachel lit an overhead light.

"Please sit, Simon," she said stone-faced.

He chose a cushioned armchair that looked comfortable. Rachel sat opposite in a straight-backed chair. Her posture was rigid. She folded her hands and placed them on her lap.

Other than his sister, Katrina, Simon had never been alone in a room with a girl. His chin dipped down. He felt uncomfortable looking directly at Rachel.

"My father says you play the violin," she said.

Simon looked up. Rachel's face was round and surrounded by brown hair pressed close to her head, as if she'd been wearing a hat all day. Her eyes were dark and sad looking. Wide eyebrows arched over them. Like her mother, her skin was pale and her lips were thin and colorless. Her nose had a bump in the center, perceptible only when she turned sideways. There was a small dark mole next to her left ear.

Simon's eyes widened. "He's mentioned me?"

Learning he was a source of conversation in Rabbi Rosenschtein's household gave credence to Simon's feeling that, in some way, there was a deeper connection between the two.

"How did you find us?" Rachel said.

"My father helped track you down after the Germans forced you from your home."

"Why are you here?"

"I need to ask your father some questions. Simon wanted to avoid being more specific.

"What kind of questions?"

"Personal ones, ones I'd rather talk about with the rabbi."

She lowered her chin. "I'm sorry. I didn't mean to be nosey,"

"That's OK," he said, picking at the buttons on his coat. It had taken three days for his father to locate the rabbi at his new location. The tension of having to wait made him edgy. He realized he'd come unannounced and this might not have been a good time, but he had important questions he needed answered. He was becoming impatient.

"How much longer do you think the service might be?" he asked Rachel, trying not to sound rude.

"Not much," she said.

Simon found her response unsatisfying. He looked around the room at all the photographs on the mantel and on the tables.

"Whose home is this?" he asked.

"This is my uncle's home. My mother's sister and her husband took us in when the Germans forced us from our house. My uncle's a photographer. He took most of these pictures of our mishpachah." Rachel looked down at her fingernails. "Soon they may be all we have left to remind us of our happy times together." Her voice sounded sad.

"Mishpachah?" Simon said, struggling with the pronunciation.

"Our entire family, relatives by blood or marriage. Other photographers took some of the pictures long ago. They go back several generations. Those no longer with us are so in spirit."

Rachel shifted in her chair. "When the Germans told us to pack only one suitcase each and leave our homes, the first thing

Mama told us to do was to remove our photographs from their frames. We divided them up and placed them in the bottom of our suitcases underneath our clothes."

"Mama rolled up our silver candlesticks and a wine cup for our Sabbath prayers in a coat. Father took whatever ritual items could fit into his suitcase. The soldiers warned us not to take any jewelry, but Mama hid some in her clothes. While here, she sewed them in the hems and false pockets of her coat and dresses.

"Oh." Rachel's hand flew to her mouth. She pulled herself forward and looked toward the entrance to the parlor. "I shouldn't have told you that."

Simon turned to see where she was looking. "No one's there, Rachel, and I won't tell anyone, I promise." He hoped she could hear the earnestness in his voice. "Please, tell me what else happened after your father persuaded the Germans to let me go."

Rachel looked off to the side, staring into space as she continued. Her voice was hollow.

"They did horrible things. The soldiers snatched babies and children from their mothers' arms, placed them in trucks, and drove them away. They shot the parents when they ran after them. For sport, soldiers told older men to run away, and then they shot them in their backs. They forced other men and women to dance in front of them and shot at the ground around them to make them dance faster."

Simon shivered. *The whole time I was running home, I heard shots firing. I thought they were aiming at me.*

"Wait until you see my father. What they did to him, and the other men, will shock you," Rachel said.

Simon listened intently as Rachel told him about her aunt and uncle taking her family in, about how upset her mother was by Rachel's brothers talking about joining the Polish Army, about how the Germans destroying the synagogue left her father with no income from the congregation and how her family was now dependent on her aunt and uncle. As she spoke, Rachel sank lower in her chair, her back curving. Her eyes focused on the floor, not on him. Simon wondered if she remembered he was sitting in the room. Rachel became alert. "I think I'll go to the kitchen and see if I can help my mother and aunt. I'm sorry if I frightened you, Simon. My father should be down soon." She got up from her chair and walked away with her shoulders slouched and her head bowed, without saying goodbye.

Simon was glad to be alone. Listening to how the lives of the rabbi and his family had changed so quickly only worried him further and made him feel more fretful for himself and his family. He wished the rabbi would finish his prayer service. He had to figure out a way to persuade the Germans he wasn't Jewish and spare himself and his family the horrible things he'd just heard from Rachel. He felt guilty thinking this way, but not being able to resume his life as a student or participate in the Poland Independence Day Concert was chiefly on his mind.

TEN

The clattering of footsteps down the stairs and men speaking rapidly to each other in what sounded like Hebrew broke Simon's reverie. He heard the rabbi saying, "Shalom," the thud of the front door closing, and the click of a lock.

The rabbi entered the parlor. He reached to turn off the light and saw Simon.

"Simon, what are you doing here?"

The rabbi's appearance stunned Simon. His beard and side-locks looked jagged, as if they'd been shorn by a knife. Simon couldn't speak. All he could do was stare. *This must be what Rachel warned me about*, he thought.

The rabbi responded to Simon's stunned face. "Yes, I know. I look different, but I'm alive and so are you. That's the important thing." He forced a smile, and after a brief pause, he said, "How did you find me? Does your father know you're here?

"He brought me here."

"Your father?"

"Yes. I pressured him to find you."

"But why, Simon?"

"I came to talk with you about my mother."

The rabbi's face showed concern. "Is there something wrong, my boy?"

"No, Rabbi. I mean my real mother, my birth mother."

"I see." His voice sounded cautious.

"I've learned she was Jewish. Is it true that makes me Jewish too?"

"Come, let's sit down, Simon. Would you like some water?"

Simon nodded.

"I'll get it. I'll be right back."

The rabbi returned with a glass of water. He sat and watched Simon start to gulp it down.

"Go easy with that water, Simon. Drink normally. Don't gulp."

When Simon finished, the rabbi said, "I saw your father in the kitchen. It seems you've been waiting for me quite a while. I wish I had known you were here. I would have turned our prayer session over to another participant. At any rate, my wife is taking good care of him, so we have time to talk comfortably. Now let's start from the beginning. What's brought you here?"

Simon held on to the empty glass and said, "The Germans visited our house with a copy of my birth certificate saying my mother was Jewish. My parents told me the truth about my birth. The soldiers told them if I hid or ran away, they'd punish my family and me."

The rabbi's posture stiffened. He pulled his chair closer to Simon's.

"I'm to blame, Rabbi. I don't know what to do. I feel like they've brought shame on myself and my family."

The rabbi shook his head. "I see, Simon. Now I understand. You and your parents must be under great stress."

"Yes, Rabbi. As if that weren't enough, my school has expelled me for being Jewish, and I can't participate in the Independence Day Concert. This meant more to me than anything in the world. Maybe God is punishing me for the sin of pride."

"I'm sorry, Simon. That must have hurt very much. It's no sin to be proud of your accomplishments. If it gives you any comfort, it's doubtful the Germans will allow such a celebration. There are rumors all Polish schools will be closed soon, Jewish students or not."

Simon raised an eyebrow. He felt a sense of selfish satisfaction hearing this.

"What's the most troubling to you now? How can I help you?" the rabbi asked.

"What I said before—is it true I'm Jewish?"

The rabbi sighed and paused before answering. "This is a complicated question, but right now, in its simplest terms, Hitler feels anyone with an ounce of Jewish blood in him is Jewish. So even if you consider yourself to be Catholic, the Germans will not agree with you, and they will treat you like a Jew."

Simon felt disappointed by the rabbi's response. He had hoped to hear otherwise. The rabbi's words confirmed what in his heart he knew from what his father had told him previously. They crushed any expectations he had of protecting himself and his family by freeing himself from the grips of the German Army.

"Simon," the rabbi said, "you must not blame yourself for things you have no control over. For your sake and the sake of your family, you must be brave, act smartly to protect yourself, and have faith that God will be with you."

"Rabbi, will people think differently of me when they learn I'm adopted?"

"I would hope not, Simon. Think about it. Your grandmother, aunts, and uncles, don't they treat you as a true member of the family? Haven't they loved you and taken pride in your accomplishments? Now that you know you're adopted, you must realize this. The community respects your parents, as well as you. They see you are good and kindhearted and of good character."

Simon knew the rabbi was trying to say all the right words. He'd never felt anything but a real member of his family.

Hesitantly Simon said, "I have another question to ask you, Rabbi." He looked down gathering his courage. "Am I wrong to think that over the years you've paid special attention to me?"

The rabbi bit his lip and slowly nodded.

"Is it because of my mother?"

"Yes, Simon, it is."

"Did you know her?"

"Yes, I did. Your mother came to see me while she was in the process of converting to Catholicism with Father Dempski. She was conflicted. Since she had lived so long as a Jew, the idea of conversion, of giving up her faith, was troubling for her. Her guilt over disappointing her father haunted her, and the prospect of giving up the God she had prayed to all her life felt like a betrayal. You can understand that Simon, can't you? You're going through the same thing now. She began to have second thoughts, but she felt it important a husband and wife share the same religion to provide a stable environment in which to raise a child."

"Soon, when she became pregnant with you, she continued her instructions with Father Dempski, but she never completed her conversion. After she became ill, she came to me and asked that if anything happened to her, I keep her in touch with you through my prayers. She asked me to look after you and let her know how your life was going. In a sense, I think she felt I could be her portal between earth and heaven so she could watch you grow. More so, I wondered if she saw it as a way to resolve the split between her and her family—if they somehow knew a rabbi was looking after you." The rabbi rubbed his shorn beard. "I agreed, and ever since her death, you've been a mitzvah, a blessing, to me, a tie between you and her. I have spoken with her about you in my prayers. It's given me a special bond with you."

Simon now understood the feeling he had about there being a special relationship between him and the rabbi. This knowledge filled him with emotion. He couldn't find the right words to say. Until this past week, he had never known any mother other than the one who'd raised him. Except for his feeling about the rabbi's extraordinary attention, Simon had never thought someone else was watching over him. To feel he had a guardian angel, his birth mother, looking after him, gave him a sense of comfort and grace. As his Catholic religion taught him, someday his family would meet in heaven. Maybe, through the rabbi, he and his mother had met already. *I have two guardian angels, my mother in heaven and the rabbi here on earth.*

"Thank you for what you've told me, Rabbi," Simon said. He could barely get these words out. "I know it's late, Rabbi, but I have one last question for you." He took a deep breath and said, "Is it wrong to hate my father—I mean, my biological father?"

"Hate" is a strong word, Simon. Are you sure you're not just angry or disappointed? He did give you life. Nothing is more precious. What would Father Dempski say about harboring hate? Think of the commandment about honoring your mother and father."

"But he abandoned me, never even tried to contact me. I don't know him. Besides, you broke the ninth commandment."

The rabbi's eyebrows raised. "When was that, Simon?"

"You broke the ninth commandment when you lied to the Germans, saying I was not one of you. That was giving false witness against your neighbor."

"That was a righteous lie, Simon. It's allowed to tell such a lie if it's to protect someone from danger or harm. I tried to protect you from the Nazis. Unfortunately, from what you've told me, the Germans have caught on to that lie."

"I'm sorry, Rabbi. I hope this doesn't get you in trouble. I didn't mean to…"

The rabbi waved his hand. "That's OK, Simon. Let's get back to your birth father. He is a human being with faults like all of us. He was once a happy boy like you who grew up and fell in love and who suffered a great loss as a young man. Perhaps he didn't handle his grief well. I can tell you he loved your mother deeply and that he wanted to raise and love you and watch you grow. I learned this from your mother when she told me she was pregnant with you."

Simon looked into the rabbi's eyes upon hearing these words.

"I'm not sure it's correct to say he deserted you," the rabbi said. "Maybe it was himself and God he deserted. We don't know what he's been thinking all these years. It could be he thinks of you every day but doesn't want to rip you away from the life you've come to know."

"You have a choice to make, Simon. You can be bitter about what you've learned about yourself and your background, blame your birth father, and rebel, or you can accept what has occurred and be grateful you have parents who have raised you with love in a good home and thank God you've been blessed this way."

The rabbi looked at his watch and said, "It's late, Simon. Your father has been very patient, but he must be tired. It's time for you to join him and mull over what we've talked about. I know I haven't answered all your question in the way you wished, but I hope I've helped you feel your mother's love and that I've given you something to think about with your anger toward your birth father so you can find peace with him. You put your coat on while I go tell your father to bring the car around."

When the rabbi returned, he walked Simon to the front door. Before opening it, the rabbi put his hands on Simon's shoulders, closed his eyes, and blessed him in Hebrew. He then translated it into Polish.

Simon was glad the rabbi translated the prayer for him. It was the same blessing Father Dempski gave to his congregation at the end of services. He appreciated this similarity in the two religions. He thanked the rabbi for helping him with his worries and telling him the truth about his biological mother.

"If you need me, son, if you feel I can be of help to you, please seek me out. My heart will always be with you."

"Thank you, Rabbi." Simon turned and waved back as he ran to the car.

Simon thanked his father for being patient. He'd been with the rabbi a long time. The ride home was quiet. When his father asked how things went, Simon answered, "OK." When he asked if the rabbi had answered Simon's questions, Simon said, "Sort of." His father didn't push Simon for more information.

On the drive home, Simon thought about Rachel's story, how the German soldiers had forced the rabbi and his family from their home, now requiring them to live with relatives in darkness and fear. Although he didn't like what he'd heard from the rabbi about Hitler's definition of who was Jewish, he suspected that would be the rabbi's answer. Eventually he would have to come to grips with his Jewish heritage and be ready for what lay ahead for him and his family.

What Simon couldn't accept was his biological father's abandoning him. *If he'd taken me to America, I'd be safely away from the Germans. Even if he couldn't take me right away, why didn't he come back for me later? Not only would I be spared, but my adopted family also wouldn't be in danger because of me.* He wasn't ready to forgive the man who brought these problems into his life and the lives of those he loved. He vowed never to absolve him. If they were to meet, he wouldn't acknowledge him.

That night, as he was lying in bed, his imagination took him further. One day he'd become a famous violinist and write a great concerto. His biological father would be in the audience and recognize him and come backstage to see him. Simon would refuse to acknowledge him. When people asked him where he got his talent, not wanting to give his biological father any credit, he'd say, "From God."

Eleven

On October 12 Simon delivered a container of his grandmother's soup to his aunt Ada and walked the twenty-two steps back home. As a child, he had skipped, hopped, and run this short distance many times. The sound of his feet hitting the sidewalk provided the beat, and the sounds around him provided the melody to form ideas for new compositions. Such travel was fun. Now any wandering just a few steps from the bakery might result in a confrontation with German soldiers, bringing a tightening in his chest and a desire to flee.

Ten steps from his front door, Simon saw two German soldiers walking toward him. He lowered his eyes to avoid looking into theirs. He hoped to go unnoticed to evade their engaging him in any form of mockery for their morning entertainment. Simon wished he could walk through them, separating them like a sharp knife splitting a heavily crusted loaf of bread. His hands clenched as he stepped down from the curb to let them pass. He made a misstep but caught himself from falling. The Germans, momentarily distracted by his near stumble, looked at him, laughed, and moved on.

In the four weeks since he'd visited Rabbi Rosenstein, life had changed for Simon. Now the Germans patrolling his area of Krakow readily identified him as a Jew, and he faced many restrictions, adding to his bitterness toward the invaders. New decrees prohibited him from public parks. He no longer felt safe outside of the house. As result, he spent his time caring for Lena indoors. She missed not playing on the square with her friends and didn't understand why they had to stay inside. He and Katrina were no longer able to enjoy their weekly Saturday evenings together attending movie houses because public buildings were off-limits to Jews.

Simon grew more resentful of the limitations imposed. His life became less joyful, less stimulating, especially so now that he was no longer a student at the School of Music. He missed his sessions with Professor Kaminski and the other students. Most of all, he regretted the lost opportunity to participate in the Poland Independence Day Concert, which now he realized, as the rabbi had suggested, the Germans would never allow to occur.

The restrictions imposed against Jews reinforced Simon's feelings of being different from the rest of his family. In addition to his worry about his own safety, he felt responsible for having placed them in danger.

One evening at dinner, Simon's father brought up the subject of him helping in the bakery in the mornings to take his mind off things.

Simon cocked his head. "When will I have time to practice and compose?"

"Katrina and your grandmother will cover for you in the afternoons, after lunch. You'll have all the time you need. Think about it."

It would be nice to be around others, and it might make the days go faster. I wouldn't have to put up with Lena's whining about spending her time indoors. Katrina could take her to play on the square. Having the entire afternoon free to keep up my skills with the violin and to compose might give me the time I need.

He accepted his father's offer.

On his first day, his father took him into the bakery kitchen to introduce him to the staff. They welcomed him with smiles and handshakes. When his father left, their tone changed.

Peter, the pastry chef, said to him, "We *knead* hard worker back here, not a slacker."

Lucas, the bread maker, shoved a broom at him. "Just because you're the boss's son, don't think you can *loaf* on the job!"

"This is our livelihood," Berta, the cake decorator, chimed in. "We work hard to earn our *dough*. We expect you to carry your weight."

Simon didn't catch on to their puns. He took them as admonishments. His ears turned red. He squeezed his broom tightly.

They began laughing.

"We didn't mean to scare you, Simon. It's our way of welcoming you with a little bakery humor, corny as it may be," Lucas said. He handed him an apron and explained their puns to him. From then on, Simon became a part of their team.

Contrary to his expectations, Simon found himself enjoying working in the bakery. As he pulled out sacks of flour, swept the floor, wiped off countertops, and helped with other chores, he became an observer of the fluid motions of the baking staff as they floured the surface of the dough, folded it, and stretched it with the heels of their hands. He watched their balletic movements as they skirted around each other performing their individual duties to finish their creations. They were kind enough to respond to his desire to learn their baking skills, especially how to make the German pastries his father had asked them to master to keep peace with the invaders. Slowly, Simon began to learn the basics of bread- and pastry-making.

It was in this back kitchen, among these artisans of a different kind, that Simon was introduced to his first sexual innuendos. The space between the preparation table and ovens was narrow. One day a passing between Berta and Lucas resulted in Lucas saying, "Watch it, Berta. You're getting me excited."

She said, "A pig would get you aroused."

Peter added, "Wasn't that a pig I saw you with at the movies last week, Lucas?"

"No, that was your wife," Lucas said, and they all had a good laugh.

Sometimes, when things got a little too risqué, Berta would shush them. "Not in front of the boy."

Simon hadn't had much contact with girls at school. He'd focused on his music. If any girl flirted with him, he either didn't recognize it or he was too shy to respond. Lately, however, he'd been thinking about Rachel. There was a sadness about her that had raised his feelings of protectiveness. Sometimes at night, while in bed, he thought about her. He looked past her unkempt appearance and concentrated on her timid brown eyes and the wide arched eyebrows that guarded over them. She was tall, only an inch or two shorter than he, and slender, like him. He judged her to be around the same age as himself. She was expressive, which in some ways scared him but in other ways made him feel comfortable. He didn't feel under pressure to carry a conversation. He felt a sense of connection with her, that he'd be able to share his feelings and she'd understand.

One morning, while Simon was in the back of the bakery sweeping the floor, he heard screams and knew something was terribly wrong. He dropped his broom and ran to the front of the shop. He saw his father run out the door toward the square. Simon ran after him, pushing past his mother and others who were standing with their hands over their mouths, eyes bulging, as if in disbelief.

Before he reached his father, Simon saw Katrina lying on the square walkway. He watched his father kneel and cradle her in his arms. Simon's body froze. He didn't know whether to run toward his father to help or run for assistance. He stood with his arms over his head, unable to speak. He wanted to pretend it was someone else his father was holding, and Katrina was still in the house. He blinked to make sure it was her. He heard his father shout for someone to call an ambulance.

Simon looked around. No one was moving.

"You heard my father," he yelled to a man standing nearby. Behind the man he saw his mother slumped in the arms of his aunt Ada. A crowd was forming.

Turning back, Simon saw the small figure of Lena standing behind his father. Her face was frozen with the look of a scream that appeared unable to come out of her mouth.

For a moment Simon stood still in disbelief, running both hands through his hair. He felt light-headed. His thoughts scrambled to understand what had happened and why.

His father cried out to him. "Come get Lena. Take her to your mother."

Simon did as he was told and ran back to his father, who was still holding Katrina and telling her to hang on, help was coming. Simon could see she was dead. Her eyes were open and blank, staring up toward the sky. Her dress was bloodied. Her arms hung limp as her father lifted her and carried her into the bakery, where he lay her down. Simon watched his mother cry softly as she held Katrina. It seemed to him it wasn't long ago he was on the floor of the bakery being held by his mother after escaping the Germans.

The ambulance arrived, and the medics pronounced Katrina dead. The ambulance took her to the funeral home. His parents went with her. Simon wanted to go, but his father asked him to stay with Lena and his grandmother. Seeing the enormity of his parents' grief, he agreed, but he was grieving too. He felt heartbroken, alone, and filled with rage, none of which he knew how to express.

Simon locked the front door to the bakery, leaving the staff to clean up and close. As he pulled down the shade to the bakery's front door, he saw two German soldiers at the far end of the square shaking hands and patting each other on the back. Simon later learned two soldiers had approached Katrina while she was sitting on a bench watching Lena. One sat down and put his arm around her. She resisted and got up to walk away. The soldier noticed her limp.

"A defective," he shouted to the other soldier. "Who wants her anyway?" He shot her, and the two soldiers walked away laughing.

It was never supposed to be Katrina who was in danger. If the Germans were going to hurt anyone in the family, it was going to be me, I always thought. I'm the cause of this. Will my parents ever forgive me? Will I be able to forgive myself?

Simon joined his family upstairs, waiting for his parents to return. His aunts prepared something to eat, though no one expressed any hunger. It seemed to him a way for them to keep busy. Lena sat on their grandmother's lap, not responding to anyone's efforts to soothe her. Simon couldn't wait for nighttime when he could hide in the darkness of his room.

When his parents returned, his father told them Father Dempski had met them at the funeral home, recited prayers for Katrina, and offered consoling words. Simon wondered what words could ever comfort them from such a horrible loss. His parents told the family a vigil for Katrina would take place at the funeral home in two days. The funeral would take place at the church the following day. They'd bury Katrina in the graveyard behind the church, next to their grandfather.

Alone that night in his room, Simon couldn't bring himself to cry. He was too full of hate and anger. He wanted to lash out and kill the two soldiers who murdered Katina and all the Germans who had taken the joy out of the lives of his family, the Germans who had come without warning, causing secrets to be revealed and disrupting the sanctity of their lives.

Simon knew even more carnage was coming. He needed to ready himself for whatever it would be. So far, his family's having

German blood and the bit of good will his father had developed among the Germans had protected him. But that hadn't helped Katrina, and his day was coming closer. His father was hinting the fate of the Poles was in serious question. Unless those Poles with German heritages made loyalty pledges to the invaders, the enemy would disarrange their lives as well.

As he lay in the dark, Simon heard a knock on his door. His father entered. When his father sat on the bed by his side, Simon broke down.

"This is all my fault, Papa. If I had been on the square instead of Katrina, this never would have happened. I didn't protect her. If I hadn't disobeyed you, the Germans never would have known I was Jewish and brought harm to our family."

"No, Simon, it's not your fault. Katrina loved you. She knew you protected her, and she was grateful. Your mother and I are grateful. Not only have you been a loving son; you were also a dutiful brother."

"No, no. If I hadn't agreed to work in the bakery, this wouldn't have happened. Katrina would have been inside working at the counter."

His father rubbed his forehead and let out a sigh. "It was the decision of your mother and me to have her be on the square with Lena. What happened there was the fault of the Germans, not you."

Simon listened, but no words would help him feel what had happened to Katrina wasn't his fault. He couldn't escape the feeling he was an intruder in this family who could never be forgiven for the death of their natural child. He would carry this guilt forever, along with his anger toward the father who abandoned him, causing this to happen.

Before leaving his room, his father said to him, "I want you to promise your mother and me, no matter how old you are, no matter where you are living, no matter what happens, you will always feel a part of our family, that you are our son." His father took hold of his shoulders and made Simon look him in the eyes.

"Promise me," he demanded.

"I promise," Simon said, taken aback by the forcefulness of his father's action and request. *Why is he talking like this? What does he mean by 'no matter what happens'?*

"One last thing," his father said. "I spoke with Father Dempski. He's agreed to allow you to play the violin at the funeral mass. Katrina would have wanted it and so do your mother and me. We're leaving it up to you to pick two hymns to play. We know you'll choose something appropriate."

Simon couldn't find the words to respond. He nodded. When his father left, he lay down sideways on his bed and his arms crossed on his chest. He didn't have to think about it. He'd play her favorite hymns, "Amazing Grace" and "Nearer My God to Thee."

Later that night, when the house grew still, except for the sounds of his mother's sobbing and the soft words of comfort coming from his father, Simon couldn't sleep. He changed into his clothes, walked into the kitchen, and gazed out the window upon the spot where Katrina's body had fallen. He saw the stain of her blood on the pathway. Washing Katrina's blood away was the least he could do for his parents. It also was his penance, his need to express his guilt.

Quietly he went down to the bakery storeroom. He filled a bucket with water and grabbed a bar of soap and a scrub brush. Nimbly he unlocked the front door and looked to see if the square was unguarded. When he felt safe, he walked to the stain. On his hands and knees, he scrubbed. He didn't wear gloves. He wanted to feel the pain. With each scrubbing movement, he pushed down with all his strength to wash away the smirks on the faces of the two Germans he'd seen on the other side of the square yesterday when he closed the bakery. He scrubbed until he had scraped his fingers and the knees of his trousers were torn. He scrubbed until he had washed away the signs of that horrible moment, though it would never be gone from his memory. When finished, he stood and looked down on the spot where Katrina had fallen and said, "Goodbye, dear sister. I'll never forget you. May God take care of you until we're rejoined in heaven."

Simon didn't attend the vigil for Katrina the following day. He stayed home to care for Lena. He couldn't bear the thought of seeing Katrina lying there and the realization that he'd never see her again.

The funeral took place at the church the day after the vigil. The funeral home had placed Katrina's coffin in front of the church altar. Simon couldn't look at it. He didn't want to envision what was inside.

Mourners had only partially filled the pews. Ethnic Poles feared being in public places as much as Jews. Simon sat in the first seat in the front row with his family. The night before, he and his father had discussed whether Simon felt comfortable taking Communion, given his new knowledge about his background and his meeting with Rabbi Rosenschtein.

From his talk with the rabbi, Simon knew he could choose what religion he wanted to live by, despite how the Nazis felt. He decided for the sake of Katrina and his family to take Communion. Now was not the time to draw attention to himself and create further problems for his family. When it came time, he swallowed the bread and drank the wine, but he felt guilty. He was feeling no spiritual nourishment from the ritual, only anger at God for not looking over his sister. He moved to the side, where he was handed his violin.

Simon closed his eyes and began playing the simple, but powerful, "Amazing Grace." He'd taken care to soak his hands the night before and use an ointment Professor Kaminski had recommended to him in the past to help heal his fingers. He wanted to play his best for his dear sister. As he played, Simon was filled with a mixture of sorrow and love. He thought of the things he'd miss about Katrina, how, in private, they'd made fun of their parents when they did silly things or rolled their eyes at each other when their parents treated Lena liberally but were strict with them. While playing, he pictured Katrina sitting on the floor at family gatherings admiring him when he played the violin for them and her applauding loudly when he finished. He couldn't imagine what it would be like without her. Simon found it difficult to swallow. His breathing grew heavy, and his body tensed the more he thought about times like these and the realization he'd never see Katrina again.

Simon wished the day soon would be over so he could go home and be alone. He wished he could see the rabbi and talk with Rachel. They'd understand his anger, his torment, his fears for his future. He tried not to think about three days ago: the sounds of gunfire coming from the square; the image of his sister in his father's arms; the blood on her clothes and on the square; his parents' anguish. However, these thoughts kept pouring into his mind. How would he be able to watch the undertakers lower Katrina's coffin into the ground?

When the congregation completed Communion, Simon returned to his seat and waited for the service to end, at which point he'd follow the casket up the aisle to the front of the church playing the solemn, "Nearer My God to Thee." A hearse waited there to drive the casket to the graveyard at the back of the church.

At the burial he blocked out the words of the priest. All he heard was the crying of his mother. All he saw was the priest giving the signal to lower Katrina's coffin into the ground. He tightened his fists as hard as he could to stop from crying. Knowing he'd never see his sister again, and his family would never be whole because of him, broke his heart.

In the days following the funeral, Simon couldn't sleep. He stayed in bed tossing until he finally gave in and went to the kitchen with his pen and tablet and tried to compose. The notes that came didn't seem right. Within a brief time, many pieces of paper lay on the floor. He worried he'd never be able to compose again.

Twelve

After Katrina's funeral, Simon returned to work in the bakery. It was awkward feeling the staff were tiptoeing around him, but he wasn't in the mood for talking or expressing his feelings. He kept his thoughts to himself and spent his afternoons playing his violin and attempting to compose. However, his heart was too heavy, his grief too raw, his anger too gut-wrenching.

Dinnertimes were quiet. He and the others felt Katrina's absence. Conversation about the comings and goings at the store and local gossip seemed forced, with long spaces in between. Lena remained quiet. She hadn't spoken since that day on the square. Her family tried to prompt her, but she remained mute. His mother stopped working in the bakery to spend more time with Lena. Aunt Ada took over behind the counter.

One night Simon overheard his parents talking about their worry Lena hadn't come out of her stupor. They decided to take her to Dr. Szymanski, their family doctor. A week later his parents told him there would be a family meeting at their home. They explained the meeting had to do with Lena's condition. They would tell him what they'd discussed and had decided afterward. They asked him to entertain Henryk and watch Lena during the meeting. Simon was skeptical, despite their telling him the gathering was about Lena. With the increasing attacks on Jews, he worried the meeting might also have something to do with his being an imminent danger to them. He didn't like their excluding him.

During the meeting Simon played with Henryk while Lena sat by quietly clinging to her teddy bear. He tried to catch pieces of conversation, but Henryk demanded too much of his attention, his voice distracting from the voices coming from downstairs. There was one word that caught his attention, however, and worried him. The word was "sanitorium." He'd heard that word before. A professor from school had disappeared. The rumor was he was in a place for people with mental problems called a sanitorium. The professor never returned.

When everyone had left the meeting, Simon's parents sat with him at the kitchen table. Grandmother took over Lena's care.

"We're sorry if we've made you feel left out," his mother said, wringing her hands. "It's just we had to make so many decisions, and you don't have to make the same adjustments as the others."

"What kind of decisions? What kind of adjustments?" Simon said uneasily.

"Dr. Szymanski said Lena is suffering a severe trauma from watching Katrina, you know…" His mother's voice trailed off. She looked down at her lap. "She's blocked it from her mind," she continued, composing herself. "The doctor said her refusal to talk is a sign she doesn't want to deal with what she saw. He recommended we take her to see Dr. Riddlehaus, outside Lodz, who specializes in such cases. We've arranged to take her there Wednesday."

Simon could see from the look on his mother's face she wasn't convinced this was best for Lena. Her eyes looked sad, almost fearful, he thought. He was feeling the same way.

"How long will you be gone?" Simon asked. He felt things were moving too quickly. "What about the bakery?" *What about me? Who will protect me?* He felt his face get hot. His gaze bounced back and forth between his parents. He ordered himself to relax to stop the mounting frustration causing his thoughts to run wild.

"In order to do this," his father said, "we needed to find someone to help with the store and be here with you and your grandmother. Uncle Fryderyk is out of work now that the Germans have shut down the university. He and Aunt Ada can move in here and take care of everything until we're back."

"Are you sure this will work?" Simon said, seeking confirmation. "Suppose the Germans come around again?" His speech began fluttering. "Will Uncle Fryderyk know what to do, how to protect me?"

"We're leaving your uncle enough money to take care of you and keep you safe. So far, the Germans haven't put pressure on us to sign the German National List pledging our loyalty to Hitler and the Nazis. Our German heritage has kept us out of danger. Your uncles should be able to protect you."

As much as Simon loved his uncles, and as much as they shared a strong bond, they could never protect him as well as his father. Their being part German might serve them well, but would it be enough to protect him, a Jew? However, his parents weren't asking his permission. He understood their concerns for Lena, and they were depending on him to help with the plan. He was torn, but he felt he had no choice but to express his agreement. He pulled himself from his chair, walked over to them, and hugged them both.

With a heavy heart, he said, "You can depend on me."

Three days later, Uncle Fryderyk drove Simon's parents and Lena to the railroad station for their trip to Lodz.

On November 11, the evening of Poland Independence Day, the new moon left the sky darkened. Street lanterns provided the only light. The night was cold. Simon stood on the roof of his parents' house in layered clothing, his bare hands holding his violin, determined to play Tchaikovsky's Violin Concerto, the one he would have played at the school concert.

The notes rang sweetly through the square as he played. Windows opened to listen. He paid no attention. His mind and body centered on his playing. He had no fear of the Germans catching him. They were busy squelching outbursts of the singing of the Polish Anthem that rang through the streets and alleys of Krakow in protest and resistance to the German occupation. The words of the anthem, though dating back to 1797, rang true today.

"Poland is not yet lost
So long as we still live.
We will fight with swords to take back
That which our enemy has taken from us."

The Germans rounded up and murdered many Jews and ethnic Poles alike this night as punishment for their act of rebellion.

Two days later, the telephone rang while Simon, Grandmother, and his aunt and uncle were eating dinner. Grandmother went to the parlor to answer it. She called out, "Come. It's David and Karolina calling from Lodz." The others hurried to the parlor and gathered around Grandmother, who held the phone up to let everyone hear.

"Lena's doing much better," his mother said. Her voice sounded cheerful.

Simon's grandmother smiled at him. "Thank God," she said, turning to his aunt and uncle and making the sign of the cross.

"She was admitted to the hospital soon after we arrived." his mother said. "Dr. Riddlehaus wanted to observe her to determine how best to help her. He's allowed us to visit her every day. We're staying at a small boarding house next to the hospital grounds. Lena is beginning to talk. The doctor said we may be able to bring her home soon for treatment in Krakow."

Back at the table, the discussion was cheerful. Simon's grandmother talked about making a new colorful bedcover for Lena. Uncle Fryderyk said he'd have Berta make a special welcome-home cake for her. Simon was more cautious. He hadn't gotten past the trauma of Katrina's death. Although he hoped Lena would be better, he suspected it would take her a long time to become again the happy little girl he supervised on the square.

On November 23, 1939, Hans Frank, the head of the General Government that the Germans had established in Nazi-occupied Poland, ordered all Jews over the age of nine to wear armbands with a blue Star of David on a white background on the right sleeves of their clothing. Those who didn't comply faced the threat of soldiers shooting them. Simon approached his grandmother.

"Please, Grandmother, I want you to make my armbands."

"Me? Why me?" she said. "No! I won't do it. I can't." She turned her head from him. "The thought of it sickens me. I've lost one grandchild to these savages. I won't give them a second. Ask your uncle, Jakub. He's a tailor. He can sew."

Simon knelt by his grandmother's chair and looked up into her eyes.

"Please, Grandmother. I'd rather it come from you."

Her head shook. "No, no, no. I won't do it!"

He laid his head on her lap. He felt her fingers run through his hair. A tear fell on his hand, then another. He threw his arms around her waist, his head against her breasts. He bit his lip, trying not to cry. He wanted to be strong for her, to help her feel, like his father had said to him, that this would be over soon, and to give her courage and solace.

She placed her hands on his shoulders and pushed him back. She held his chin between her thumb and forefinger and sniffed away her tears. Then she let him go and pulled out a handkerchief. She waved him toward her bedroom and said, "Go get some blue-and-white cloth from my bottom drawer and my sewing kit."

Simon did as she asked, and he sat with her as she formed four blue triangles. She sewed them together to form two Stars of David, one each for an inner and outer garment. He wished he could wash away the pain on her face like he had washed Katrina's blood from the square. He tried to appear calm and brave while he watched her sew the stars to the pieces of white cloth, but inside he felt a sense of dread and fear for what was to come. He hoped his parents and Lena would return soon from Lodz.

Thirteen

U ncle Fryderyk lived up to his word of protecting Simon
from the Germans. The newly formed General Government in Nazi-occupied Poland, headed by Hans Frank, forced
Jewish males into physical labor around the city and its sur-
roundings areas. The new government formed a Council of Jews
to make sure they met a daily quota of laborers from a registry
of Jews. With so many Jewish men out of work, hungry, and
suffering, Uncle Fryderyk found people to substitute for Simon
in these labor groups by offering them small amounts of money.
Other times Uncle Fryderyk called on a friend from his former
position at the university who was a member of the Council
of Jews. Sometimes he gave this friend bread from the bakery
or money as a bribe to avoid the council placing Simon into a
labor group.

Uncle Fryderyk did his best to shield Simon from the atroci-
ties the Germans foisted upon the Jews. Simon, however, learned
from the baking staff what was going on in the city. Lucas told
him about the influx of ethnic Germans arriving to settle in Krakow, forcing Jews and Poles from their homes to make room for
them. He learned the Germans were forcing Poles, as well as Jews,
into labor and were knocking them down and beating them on
the streets, sometimes for no apparent reason, sometimes robbing
and stripping them of their possessions. He learned, also, soldiers
were stopping Orthodox Jews wearing their traditional clothing
and grabbing their fur hats and tossing them back and forth, further taunting the Jews to get their hats back. Hearing these things
made Simon more fearful of going out. Berta confided she, Peter,

and Lucas, although Poles, were grateful, so far, to be protected by his father's German ethnicity. That was what allowed them to remain working at the bakery. Their skill at learning the art of German-style baking had made his father's business a popular place for the invaders and ethnic Germans.

The staff warned Simon news about his Jewish background had spread quickly through the community. Some of his parents' neighbors, who'd long ago forgotten the circumstances of his birth, now recalled his Jewish parenthood. With the harmony between Jews and non-Jews now threatened, and with antisemitism on the rise, his coworkers advised him to be cautious.

With the influx of both the German Army and ethnic Germans, food became scarce. People were hungry, and long lines developed at places where food was available. German guards kept order.

One Tuesday morning, the kitchen staff heard a loud scuffle in the front of the bakery. Simon, fearing another incident like the one involving Katrina, peeked with the others through the round window in the door separating them from the sales area. His uncle was talking to a police officer who was holding a young boy by the collar. Simon recognized the boy from his days at public school. It was the bully Simon embarrassed on the playground when the boy took a Jewish student's yarmulke and tossed it around. He was hiding a loaf of bread under his coat when the guard caught him. The boy spotted Simon peering through the round window in the door.

"Yid," the boy yelled, pointing to Simon. "Yid," he repeated five times.

This drew the attention of the German soldier trying to keep control outside. He entered the bakery. "Where is this Jew?" he demanded to know.

"He's my nephew," Uncle Fryderyk said. "This boy is mistaken."

Doggedly the German said, "Where is the Jew? I want to see him."

Simon didn't want to get his uncle in trouble. He came out from behind the door holding on tightly to a broom to stop his hands from shaking.

"Show me your identification cards," the German said to Simon and his uncle.

Simon dropped his broom and pulled his card from his back pocket.

His card showed the bold *J* that identified him as a Jew. He handed it to the German. His hand shook so much he almost dropped it. He tried to appear unafraid, but he was trembling all over. He saw his young accuser smiling, as if to say this was his payback for that day on the playground. Simon glared at the boy. *I'll get you back for this.*

When the German saw the *J* on Simon's card, he stood stiff and with cold eyes, said adamantly to Uncle Fryderyk, "I'd better see him report for labor tomorrow and the next day and whenever I say."

Uncle Fryderyk pleaded. "But he's too young, and his hands are soft. You see all he does here is push a broom."

The German smirked and waved his hand dismissively. "We'll toughen him up. Either he's in line tomorrow, or you'll be sorry. I'll personally see your bakery is closed and taken over by another ethnic German family." The German officer walked away.

Uncle Fryderyk held up his hands in frustration. Simon's fear intensified. He looked around and saw the alarm in the eyes of the bakery staff and their worry for him. He didn't know what to do. He wanted to run upstairs to his room and hide.

His uncle came over to him. Simon saw the troubled look on his face. "Don't worry, Simon," he said. "I'll figure something out."

That evening at dinner, his aunt and uncle and grandmother discussed what to do. They had two choices, as they saw it, to either comply and make sure Simon appeared for labor the next morning or to hide him.

"He's too young for such hard work," Grandmother said.

"If we hide him, we're all in danger," Uncle Fryderyk said. "If they catch him, he'll be treated worse."

No one asked Simon's opinion. He wanted to run away and hide at the rabbi's house.

"We should call David and Karolina," Grandmother said.

An hour later they reached Simon's parents in Lodz. After Uncle Fryderyk explained what had happened at the bakery, Simon's father asked to speak to him.

Simon listened to what his father said, then handed the phone to his uncle.

"Yes, I will. I'm glad to hear it. Godspeed, David," his uncle said and hung up the phone. He turned to the others. "David said to do as the German insisted, to make sure Simon appears for labor. If he doesn't, one way or another, he'll be in more danger."

Simon watched his grandmother turn her back. Her head turned down. It looked like she was praying. He wished he had a prayer to protect himself.

Aunt Ada slid into a chair and held her swollen belly. "Did they say anything about Lena?" she said.

Simon felt ashamed he hadn't asked.

"David said there's been progress," Uncle Fryderyk responded. "They hope to bring her home soon."

Grandmother turned back around and crossed herself. "Thank God," she said.

That night Simon couldn't sleep, worrying what would be expected of him. Would he be able to do what the Germans asked? He repeated to himself his father's words on the telephone: "Be brave. You're strong. Remember your psalms. Do as they ask, and don't take any chances. Keep thinking you'll be home for dinner tomorrow night. Your uncle has done a fine job of protecting you. He'll see the council doesn't select you every day, and he'll find substitutes for you when you're called upon too often. He has money and connections. Your mother, Lena, and I will be home soon."

The next morning Simon got out of bed when he heard his uncle stirring in the parlor. It was dark outside. The morning he dreaded had come after what seemed like a never-ending night.

"Good morning, Simon," his uncle said when Simon entered the parlor. "It will be cold today. I'll give you a pair of my gloves. They're extra tough and should keep your hands warm and protected from hard work. You might want to take a pair of your own mittens to wear under them. Also, take a scarf, and wear an extra pair of socks."

Simon wondered if he'd be able to move under all those clothes.

He entered the kitchen, still in his pajamas.

Grandmother turned toward him from the stove. "Sit down. I'm making warm milk and scrambled eggs for you. Eat a muffin while you're waiting."

His grandmother smiled, but he could tell she was forcing it. He was sure she was having the same butterflies in her stomach he was having.

Simon downed the milk, but he was too nervous to eat more than a bite of the eggs.

His grandmother didn't force the issue. She took the eggs away and handed him a muffin wrapped in a cloth napkin.

"Hide it in your coat pocket," she said. "Try to sneak a few bites during the day to give you strength."

Uncle Fryderyk appeared. "You'd better hurry and get dressed," he said. "We've got to leave soon."

Simon left the muffin on the table and went to his room. He dressed and came back into the kitchen. He felt scared and tingly cold. He wished he could run back to his room and hide under the covers, but he put on a brave front.

"Here, you forgot your wool hat. You'll need to pull it over your ears," Aunt Ada said.

His grandmother tightened the collar of his coat and kissed him. She stuffed the muffin deep inside his coat pocket.

It was as if the clock had slowed and was suddenly making up for lost time. He wanted time to drag on. He wanted every extra second to postpone what the day had in store for him.

FOURTEEN

Simon's uncle walked him to River Street, where the council had gathered at least four hundred men and women, men on one side of the street, women on the other. For a large crowd, it was quiet and solemn. German guards marched back and forth holding their rifles in full view. Soon the guards forced the people into rows.

Simon thought he saw Rachel across the street. He stood on his toes to see better, but it was still too dark to be sure. It was bitter cold. The vapors of men's breath filled the air. Those in front and beside him stood hunched over. They stuffed their hands into their pockets. They bounced up and down on their knees to stay warm.

An old man two rows ahead of Simon collapsed.

"Quick, remove him. Replace him," one guard said to another.

Simon's body stiffened when he heard the man pleading as the soldiers dragged him away. His body jumped when he heard gunshots. He wanted to run, but his feet stayed glued to the ground. No one else moved. *How can they take this?* he thought.

"They killed him," the man next to him said. Simon couldn't believe how matter-of-fact the man sounded. He thought of his father's words. "Be brave. You are strong. By evening you'll be home for dinner." Simon's fists loosened as he brought his breathing under control. He told himself he would overcome any obstacles that faced him today.

Buses arrived. Guards hurried Simon and the others on to them. The ride was short and quiet. Simon held his head down and pulled his coat collar around his nose to mask the body odor of the others.

The buses took them to their destinations, the men to a synagogue turned to rubble. Across the street the women's buses parked in front of one of Krakow's luxurious hotels.

"The SS is using the hotel as one of its headquarters," the man next to Simon said. "General Frank has taken over the Castle. The women have it easy in this weather. They work indoors and stay warm."

"Ha!" another man snarled. "Easy if the soldiers leave them alone."

The remark raised Simon's concern for Rachel's safety, if it were she he'd seen earlier among the women. He prayed for God to keep her safe.

The men quieted when a soldier holding a thick, threatening wooden stick entered the bus, telling them to get off by seat rows. Once they were off, soldiers divided the laborers into small groups. Large dump trucks, wheelbarrows, shovels, and picks waited for each group. The soldiers formed assembly lines for each waiting truck, whereby one laborer placed rocks and debris into the wheelbarrows, another wheeled the barrows to the trucks, a third laborer emptied the debris into the truck, and the man who had brought the barrow to the truck returned to get more debris. Simon's task was to place the rubble into the wheelbarrow.

This cycle continued for hours. It was backbreaking work. Simon's arms, neck, and back were in pain, but he couldn't rest. He saw the consequence when others did. Guards pulled them out, shot them, and replaced them with others. Simon couldn't believe such cruelty, but he realized he had to put it out of his mind. With every gunshot Simon's body jolted, but with the threat of a soldier at every line willing to crack his truncheon on a slacker, he kept moving.

Simon was glad he was wearing his uncle's thick gloves. The rubble contained concrete, stone, and glass, all with sharp edges he could feel through the gloves. His uncle's advice helped Simon protect himself better than most of the other laborers. He saw other workers looking at his hands and his warmer overcoat. He wondered if he had as much to fear from them as he did from the guards.

The laborers were granted a twenty-minute break. Guards set up lines for each worker to receive a cup of water and a piece of bread. Simon took one sip of water and felt silt in his mouth. He wanted to spit it out but was afraid the supervisors would call him out for it. He remembered the muffin his grandmother had stuffed into his pocket and wondered whether he could get away with eating it. He found a large rock away from the lines and sat on it. He looked around to make sure no one was watching him. He pulled small crumbs of the muffin from his pocket and pretended to cough, covering his mouth to sneak in pieces of the muffin. The cold weather had hardened the muffin, so it didn't leave crumbs on his coat. Another boy around his age joined him. Simon gave him a piece of his muffin, fearing if he didn't, the boy would cause him trouble.

"What's your name?" Simon asked.

"Joseph. What's yours?"

"I'm Simon." He started to shake Joseph's hand, but he pulled back when Joseph jerked away.

"The Germans might see us. We'd better not talk anymore," Joseph said. He stood and walked off.

After the break the labor continued until the sun began to set. Then, soldiers directed the laborers back to the buses to return them to River Street.

Uncle Fryderyk met him when the buses arrived.

On the walk home, his uncle said, "What did they have you do?" His tone was sympathetic.

Simon was sore, exhausted, and glad to see Uncle Fryderyk, but all he wanted was to get home, eat, bathe, and sleep. He wasn't in the mood to talk.

When they arrived home, Simon's grandmother gave him a hearty dinner of soup, potatoes, and meat. After gobbling everything down, he told them a little about his day, mainly the routine of his labor. He told it like he was speaking about someone else, like he was disassociating himself from it. He described what his task was and how others carried away his rubble. He didn't want to upset his grandmother with the horrible shootings he'd witnessed and their effect on him.

After dinner, he took a shower and got in bed early. He thought about the senseless cruelty he had witnessed, and he feared he wouldn't be able to keep up such labor regularly. He thought about Joseph. Simon was glad there was someone his age on the work crew, someone he might be able to connect with and make a friend of.

That night he dreamed of bullets coming from all directions. He tossed and turned on the bed trying to dodge them.

"Please don't shoot, please, please. Please don't shoot," he cried out in his bed.

Simon woke up to his uncle gently shaking him. He covered his face, thinking Uncle Fryderyk was a soldier glaring down at him. "No, no, don't hurt me," Simon said, twisting side to side.

He heard his uncle say, "Get him some water." Then Simon knew where he was. He looked up and saw his aunt and his grandmother were also with him.

He grabbed his uncle and hugged him tightly, hiding his face against his uncle's chest.

"It's OK, Simon. It's OK," his uncle said. "Cry it out, scream, yell, do whatever you need to do. You're safe here. Get it out of your system."

When his aunt returned with a glass of water, Simon was calmer. He took a sip and lay back in his bed shivering. He drew his knees up toward his stomach and wrapped his arms around them. His grandmother handed him a handkerchief and went to get him an extra blanket.

His uncle sat with him until dawn. Aunt Ada went down to open the door to let the baking staff in.

When Simon's grandmother came to check on him, Simon heard Uncle Fryderyk say, "I'll make sure he won't have to go to River Street today if I have to bribe every person on the Jewish Council and every German in Krakow."

Simon worried this would cause trouble for his family. He'd suffered yesterday but repeating the words of his father had helped get him through. He spoke with his uncle and told him he felt he could tolerate more days. His uncle saw to it that the council selected Simon as seldomly as possible.

During the following weeks, Simon worked on crews shoveling snow and unloading coal and supplies for the German Army at the train station. Now that the Germans had seen him at work crews, it was safer for his uncle to bribe the council.

FIFTEEN

At the end of one of his days of forced labor, Simon found his father waiting for him instead of his uncle. He ran into his arms. His father pulled him close and squeezed him tightly.

"How's Mama? How's Lena?" Simon asked excitedly, pushing away all thoughts of the pain of today's labor. "I can't wait to see them."

His father didn't answer. They walked home slowly. Simon talked about how his father's encouraging words had helped get him through the worst days.

Finally, he looked at his father.

"What's wrong, Papa? You look sad."

"It hurts me to hear what you've been through," his father said.

"Papa, I'm so glad you're home. I can deal with anything now."

When they arrived home, Simon ran to his mother and said, "I've missed you so, Mother."

He looked around, his face beaming. "Where's Lena? Is she sleeping?"

"Sit down, Simon," his father said. "There's something we have to tell you."

Simon's heart sank. He sensed from the look on his parents' faces he was about to hear something awful. He looked back and forth at them. "Couldn't they help her at the hospital?" he said. He looked over to his grandmother. She was wiping her eyes with her handkerchief.

"Lena's dead," his father blurted out.

Simon wasn't sure he'd heard right. He felt dizzy and grabbed on to the arms of his chair. He looked at his parents sitting opposite him on the sofa, a picture of Jesus overhead. His mother was biting her lip. Tears were falling down her cheeks. His father sat with his head and back hunched forward. His forearms dangled against his thighs.

Simon began shaking in disbelief. "What?" he cried out.

Simon's father brought his hands to his face and covered his eyes. "Lena died in the hospital," he said.

Simon's body pulled forward. His voice rose. "You mean that damn sanitorium? Professor Pabinski went to a sanitorium and never came back." Simon began pounding his fists on his knees. "I knew you shouldn't have taken her there. I knew it. I knew it. I should have told you."

"Stop it. You're hurting yourself," his father said and got up and walked toward him.

Simon raised his hand to wave his father away. They sat quietly until Simon calmed himself and asked what had happened.

"The day before, the doctor told us Hitler had ordered all patients in sanitoriums be put to death," his father said. "The doctor was preparing for the release of his patients. We were going to bring Lena home the next day. The Germans came the night before without warning."

Simon didn't understand. *I'm the Jew in the family. I'm the one the Germans hate. Why am I surviving while the invaders murdered my beautiful, innocent sisters, who had no Jewish blood?*

His mother twisted her hands together. "It happened so fast, late at night," she said. "We'd packed to get ready to come home the next day. While we were preparing for bed, we heard noises coming from up the hill."

"We opened the windows in our room and saw German trucks with soldiers jumping out and running into the building," Simon's father said. "We ran up, but they pointed rifles at us and forced us back. Children and staff were screaming. Soldiers were dragging and carrying children out of the building. Some looked lifeless. We never saw Lena. We were too late. The doctor was crying when he came to us. He told us the raid had come sooner than expected. He begged for our forgiveness."

"We should have brought her home the day before, when the doctor warned us." His mother wailed, rocking back and forth in her chair, and banging a hand against her knee.

Simon imagined his parents fighting to get through the German block, his mother falling to the ground and his father trying to figure out what to do, in what direction to turn, feeling helpless when the trucks pulled away. He felt bad for them and ashamed of his outburst when they told him Lena was dead.

That night in his bed, Simon heard his mother's crying for the second time in less than two months over the loss of a child. This time he didn't hold back his own tears. He rolled on to his stomach and pushed his face into his pillow to muffle the guttural sobs coming from deep inside him. He banged his fists on his mattress and kicked his feet until exhaustion overcame him. He felt more alone than ever.

There was no vigil for Lena. There was no body to bury. Her funeral consisted of a memorial mass at the church. Simon didn't play the violin. His parents hadn't asked him to, and he hadn't offered. He was too angry with God for allowing this to happen. Uncle Jakub and Aunt Natalia read from the scriptures. Uncle Fryderyk and Aunt Ada each gave a brief eulogy. His parents didn't work in the bakery the following week. His aunt and uncle took their places.

Feeling he had brought too much sorrow and dishonor into his parents' lives, Simon felt they'd be better off without him. He thought about moving away. His leaving would save his family.

Where could he go, he wondered. He thought about going to live with Rabbi Rosenschtein. He'd talk with his father about it.

"Simon," his father said, "I know you're thinking this way for unselfish reasons, but you're all your mother and I have left. We could never let you go. It's out of the question."

"I'm afraid, Papa. I'm afraid for you and Mother, for all of you. My being here has caused only grief."

"But you're our son. Remember, I told you to never forget that, whatever the circumstances. Besides, you'd be no safer with the rabbi, perhaps less safe. You'd still have forced labor, and the Rosenschteins can't afford to take on anyone else. They have no money, I'm sure. It would be a serious imposition. The matter is closed. You'll remain here with us, where you belong."

Sixteen

Wearing his armband and carrying his identification card, Simon sneaked away to the rabbi's house. He sat in the section of the streetcar set aside in the back for Jews. He looked out the window. On the walls of buildings and on lampposts, he saw posters depicting Jewish people with oversized crooked noses, yellowed teeth, and other distorted features. The pictures showed Jews wearing torn, dirty clothing and had hateful captions. Simon grew uncomfortable looking at them. He got off three blocks from where he and his father had last visited and walked the rest of the way.

Simon reached the rabbi's house and knocked. The rabbi answered the door.

"Simon. What are you doing here? Are you alone?"

"Yes, I'm alone. May I come in?"

"Of course." The rabbi stepped aside.

The rabbi took Simon into the parlor and told him to take off his coat and toss it on a chair.

Rabbi Rosenschtein eyed Simon up and down. "You've gotten taller since I last saw you, and your face is more manly, but you still have the deep, dark brown eyes and curly hair of your mother. You'll be fifteen soon, won't you?"

"Yes, sir, in March." Simon boldly said, "Do you see any resemblance to my birth father?"

"Yes, I do. You have his slim stature and bearing. He was very handsome."

"Yes, I know. I have a picture of him with my mother."

"It's hard for me to believe you're turning fifteen," the rabbi said. "You're so wise and sensitive for your age, but the times have forced our children to grow up quickly, I'm afraid. Your clothes are clean, and you look well fed, so your family is taking good care of you."

"Yes, I'm working in the bakery. I've learned to bake bread and pastries."

"That's wonderful," the Rabbi said. "My wife is teaching Rachel to bake too. Perhaps you can give Rachel pointers. Where are my manners? Sit. Tell me why you're here."

Simon sat in the straight-backed chair Rachel had sat in the evening of his previous visit. He looked at the rabbi. His beard was still short but trimmed. He looked thinner, his cheeks less full, but his eyes were still bright and welcoming. His clothes appeared worn. Simon noticed stitching where it looked as though there had been a tear.

"It's good to see you, Simon. I've thought about you and wondered how you were."

"I've thought about you too, Rabbi," Simon said, feeling pleased the rabbi had him in his thoughts.

The rabbi's voice turned serious. "You took a chance in coming here."

Simon told him about the deaths of his sisters, the circumstances surrounding them, and their effect on him. "If I weren't Jewish, Katrina wouldn't have substituted for me on the square, the soldiers wouldn't have shot her, and Lena wouldn't have suffered the shock of seeing what happened. My being Jewish has hurt my family deeply. I feel responsible for bringing so much grief to them."

The rabbi listened quietly, intently, then said, "It's not just Jews this is happening to, Simon. The Germans are persecuting Poles who are Catholic or who don't have German blood in their background. I'm sure you've heard about that. And Romani people and scholars, even priests. The Germans have destroyed churches back in Germany and thrown priests in jails and concentration camps. You can't take the blame for all of that, can you?"

"But I'm the one causing harm to my family."

"My point is none of us alone can stand up against an army of despots. It will take the rest of the world to bring down this craziness. You're not to blame for anything that's happened. You're just a young man. You didn't do anything wrong. Would you have Rachel or my sons hold me to blame for their being born and for their current suffering?"

Simon hesitated, feeling what he was about to say might sound selfish. He looked down in shame. "I'm scared for myself too. The Germans have forced me into labor. They said if I don't cooperate, they'll close the bakery. I come home very tired. I'm afraid the heavy work will ruin my hands and arms for playing the violin. I see terrible things like the Nazis whipping and killing people. I have bad dreams."

Simon looked up at the rabbi. "I shouldn't complain. I have warmer clothes than most, and I'm stronger than the old men at labor. I come home to a warm meal. Am I wrong to feel so selfish when others are suffering more?"

"No, of course not. You're working to protect your family, and you have compassion for the other workers. These are good qualities. The fact that you're afraid is normal. It may keep you and others alive. You should be afraid. I'd worry if you weren't, but like you say, you are young and strong, and you have the will and a reason to live. Use those strengths to get through these times. This won't last forever. These are the same things I tell my children."

"I thought I once saw Rachel standing in line to be bused to a labor site. Is this true?"

"You may have, and my sons and nephews too. They try to bring in as much money as they can so we can buy food and coal for heat. As you know, they're paid little, but every bit helps. It's become the way of life for all of us."

"What about you, Rabbi? How are you staying safe?"

"So far the soldiers and the council have left me alone to tend to my congregants. They need me to pray for the sick and to sit shiva with them when family members die. My sons and nephews have protected me by working for me to help meet labor quotas. Even my wife and sister-in-law work in the same hotel as Rachel, in part to look after her, but also to bring in extra money. I worry, though, that my time may be short, and I'll be threatened to work or otherwise be punished. No one is safe."

Sheepishly Simon said, "I came to ask to come live with you, Rabbi, in order to protect my own parents and myself, but I can't after what you've told me."

Seconds passed before the rabbi responded. "I'm honored you sought me out. You know how I feel about you and my promise to your mother. Even if I were to say yes, stay here with us, you know we can't protect you any better than your family can or love you as much as they do. It would be wrong to take you away from them." The rabbi leaned forward. "One day, if the time were to come and that was the only solution, then and only then would I welcome you. Go home to be with your family. You are a solace to them, as much as you may feel you are a burden. I will pray for you every day, for your strength and safety."

Simon felt embarrassed he'd put the rabbi in this position. He thanked the rabbi for seeing him and said he'd better leave before his parents worried about his whereabouts.

At the door the rabbi blessed Simon and warned him not to come again without his father to protect him. "I'm afraid I can't walk you to the streetcar," he said apologetically. "To be honest, they pick on old religious men like me."

"That's OK, Rabbi. I had no trouble on the way." Simon hoped this would hold true on the way home.

On the streetcar ride back home, near his stop, three young men got on and walked toward Simon.

"Hey, Jew boy. That's a nice coat you're wearing. Who'd you steal it from?" one of them said.

Simon bunched the coat around himself. "It's mine," he said. Simon felt his heart beating faster.

"Is that so?" the boy said.

Simon looked to the other passengers and driver for help. They sat rigid in their seats, acting as if they weren't paying attention.

The leader of the three stepped forward and grabbed Simon by the arm. Simon yanked his arm away. The streetcar jerked, and the boy fell into the empty seat next to Simon. His face turned red.

"OK," the boy said. "You want to play rough?"

He grabbed Simon's arm and called his friends to pull Simon from his seat. Simon couldn't match their strength. They threw him to the floor and stripped off his coat. Simon felt a punch across his nose and tasted blood. Then he felt a fist to his stomach and a kick to his knee. From the floor of the streetcar, he saw a passenger looking straight ahead, ignoring what was happening. The boys grabbed his arms and pulled him to the door. At the next stop, they tossed him out. He landed on the sidewalk, scraping his face as he fell.

"Take that, Jew boy. Thanks for the coat," Simon heard as the streetcar pulled away.

His father's face registered shock and then concern when Simon stumbled into the bakery. Customers turned to Simon. Their faces expressed confusion. His father came around the counter.

"What happened, son? Tell me."

Simon told the story.

"What were you doing on the streetcar? Where were you going?" his father said.

"I went to visit the rabbi." He knew this would make his father angry. He'd warned Simon not to put himself and his family in danger by being on the streets.

His father shook his head. "What am I to do with you, Simon? This is what happens when you don't listen to me. I'd hoped you'd learned your lesson by now. Come, let's go upstairs and get you cleaned up and see if we need to get you to a doctor."

This is not my fault, Simon repeated to himself. *I should be allowed to go out in public. This is the fault of the Nazis.*

Simon's wounds healed, and he wore a less stylish coat, something of his grandfather's his grandmother hadn't thrown away. It was old, but it was woolen and kept him warm. It showed moth holes from being in the closet without protection. His grandmother said she was glad she hadn't disposed of it. She was grateful Simon had something of his grandfather to remember him by. His uncle Jakub altered it to fit Simon. Now he looked like the other Jewish men working labor crews. He no longer had to fear anyone wanting to steal his coat.

SEVENTEEN

Simon continued to meet labor quotas on days his father was unable to get him relieved through bribes. Joseph worked on some of the same work crews. Their eyes met with recognition, but they didn't acknowledge one another. It was dangerous to stop one's work.

During a lunch break, as the guards tended to a disturbance among a group of laborers, he and Joseph spoke. Simon learned Joseph's family had been members of the rabbi's synagogue. He knew Rachel and lived near her. Their conversation, by necessity, was brief, but it gave Simon an idea. He would write letters to Rachel and ask Joseph to deliver them. If she responded, and if Joseph were willing, he'd sneak her letters to Simon when they were on the same work crew. It was a dangerous idea, but he hoped Joseph would agree. He did, after careful thought.

On December 21, 1939, Simon slipped Joseph his first letter to Rachel. In the letter he proposed they begin a secret correspondence using Joseph as their go-between. A week later Joseph sneaked Rachel's response to Simon. She wrote that although her father had arranged a marriage for her with the son of a rabbi in Lodz, she didn't consider herself and Simon corresponding a betrayal of that arrangement. "Right now," she wrote, "we need to be friends with people our age. It may help us to share our thoughts, feelings, and experiences."

Simon felt disappointed. In writing to Rachel, he'd hoped to form an exclusive relationship with her in which they'd share private thoughts and feelings and develop a personal bond. To learn Rachel was committed to someone was a bitter disappointment.

He began to lose heart over the prospect of corresponding with Rachel, feeling it would it be wrong to do this if her father had pledged her to someone else. He discussed his concerns with Berta.

"If it were wrong, she wouldn't do it," Berta said. "Chances are, with the way things are going, the marriage will never take place. It sounds like she feels she needs a friend."

That was a scary thought for Simon, not just because of his concern for Rachel but because Berta's implication was more terrible times were coming.

With Berta's encouragement Simon continued the correspondence. Becoming confidants with Rachel uplifted his spirits. He resumed practicing his violin and composing. She wrote she hoped to hear him perform one day.

Both shared their joys and sorrows, as well as their fears.

He shared his losses and loneliness: "I miss my sisters, and I'm reluctant to become close with Titus, Uncle Fryderyk's, and Aunt Ada's new baby. I'm worried I'll be a jinx to him as I feel I was to Katrina and Lena. The arrival of the German Army and learning I'm part Jewish has dissolved my sense of self, family, community, and my connection to the world of classical music."

She wrote back encouraging him not to give up and describing her own family's difficulties in gathering among other Jews and practicing their longtime traditions: "My family secretly celebrated Hannukah by making one candle last eight days and by giving home crafted gifts to each other. Please keep this a secret, but I stole a set of sewing needles from a pocket of clothes left for laundry by a German soldier and gave it to my mother. Papa admonished me for taking such a dangerous risk."

Upon reading this, Simon also expressed his concern for her and begged her not to take such chances.

Simon treasured Rachel's letters. He read them in the privacy of his room, and he stored them in a box in the secret area behind his closet, along with his compositions and the picture of his birth parents.

Their exchange of letters continued through March 1940. She wrote about the difficulties of her work assignment at the hotel headquarters for German officers. It was hard for her to see her friends mistreated by the Nazis. Sometimes, thinking wishfully, she wanted to pound an offending soldier on the chest or kick his shins. So far, she'd been able to avoid any physical abuse, only verbal. Her job in the laundry kept her away from soldiers, and her supervisor was kind.

Such writings raised Simon's concerns for Rachel. His unease for himself and all Jews increased when Rachel wrote the Germans were transporting Jews out of Krakow to work on farms, build roads, and work in factories manufacturing supplies for the German Army. Her father had heard rumors the Germans were secretly sending Jews away to die. This news caused Simon to think about what their futures, and that of their families, would be. Would he realize his dream of becoming a concert violinist? Would Rachel's dreams and hopes for the future come true? The war had continued for over six months, and there didn't seem to be any news of it ending, only getting worse.

Simon kept Rachel abreast of the happenings in his household. Business at the bakery had fallen off due to decreased supplies and people having less to spend. His parents had to let Berta go. When he turned fifteen in March, his family did their best to make it a celebration as in past years, but with Uncle Fryderyk and his family having moved to Berlin for a job opportunity and with business slow, everyone seemed weary. Grandmother, particularly, missed Titus. He'd given her something to live for with Katrina and Lena gone. She still had Henryk, but she worried his parents, too, would follow Uncle Fryderyk and Aunt Ada.

On the evening of May 2, 1940, Simon wrote to Rachel describing his day at labor unloading coal and supplies for German soldiers.

> My work is lonely which makes the day go slower. I take my mind off the repetitiveness of what I'm doing by composing music in my head. Sometimes it works. Sometimes it doesn't.
>
> It's unlike the way I felt at music school with Professor Kaminski. She was a taskmaster, but I knew she had a positive goal for me, and my obedience would lead to satisfaction. Before I learned a piece perfectly, I'd keep one eye on my violin and the other on her to catch her reactions. When she was harsh, I knew it was in my best interest so one day I'd be able to play with my eyes closed, concentrating on nothing but the music.
>
> At labor I keep my eyes open, not out of love but fear. There is no satisfactory ending. My goal is to escape into my mind until the day is over, only to be snapped out of my thoughts by a soldier's gunshot or the threat of a work supervisor whipping me into obeyance.

Simon carried this letter to Rachel in his coat pocket, hoping to have Joseph pass it on, but Joseph seemed to have disappeared. Simon worried about him, not just because his letter writing with Rachel had come to a halt, but, also, because Joseph had become his friend, and he missed him. He hoped he was alive and well.

Weeks and months passed without his seeing Joseph or having any contact with Rachel. He missed her letters terribly. Sometimes he thought about her before falling asleep, hoping she and her family were safe and well. He pictured her brown eyes and the arched eyebrows above them and her straight nose with the slight, barely noticeable, bump. He wondered if she thought about him and, if so, what about him she found appealing.

Eighteen

During the summer of 1940, on days when substitutes relieved Simon from work crews, he worked full shifts at the bakery. One evening he brought pastries upstairs.

"I made these," he said boastfully.

"You're trying to fool us," his father said, after taking a bite. "Lucas made these, didn't he?"

His grandmother licked her fingers between tastes. "This is delicious," she said. "The cream is perfectly distributed."

Simon knew they were overstating his accomplishment, but he knew, also, his baking had reached a higher level of skill.

In November Grandmother took seriously ill. She was unable to get out of bed. Dr. Szymanski said it was her heart. He told the family she should be in the hospital, but she refused to go. She insisted on dying at home.

Simon spent time by Grandmother's bedside every night, no matter how tired he was. Sometimes he played his violin for her. Other times he read to her. They talked about her past. She told stories about herself and Simon's grandfather, how they met at a picnic, how she didn't like him at first, how he grew on her, and how she fell in love with him. Simon enjoyed hearing her stories. Her last few days were painful for him. She didn't have the strength to talk. He'd sit with her and hold her hand and tell her stories he'd never shared with his family. He told her about his letters to and from Rachel. She smiled and patted his hand. "Young love," she managed to whisper. "It's wonderful."

Grandmother died on December 11. There was no priest for a service. Father Dempski had disappeared, as had other Catholic clergy, and the Germans had boarded up churches. The family held a vigil at the funeral home and arranged for Grandmother's burial the next day, between Simon's grandfather and Katrina. Simon was brokenhearted, but his grandmother's words to him the week before she died softened his grief.

"I've had a good life, with sadness, like we all have. Think of me with joy. Remember, always, I love you. We will meet again in heaven," she said softly.

In the year following Simon's visit to Rabbi Rosenschtein, when he had asked to live with the rabbi and the rabbi had sent him home, Simon realized the wisdom of the rabbi's advice. He thought about what he would have missed. His Aunt Ada, Uncle Fryderyk, and Titus would have moved without his being there to say goodbye. He wouldn't have seen the love between his parents and their support of one another as they went through their mourning for Lena. More important, he wouldn't have experienced the degree of his family's love for him and his contribution to them. He would have felt an unmeasurable sadness not being with his grandmother when she was ill and lay dying.

Part Two

NINETEEN

On March 3, 1941, sixteen days before Simon's sixteenth birthday, the German authorities announced the establishment of the Krakow ghetto. The new General Government required the approximately fifteen thousand Jews remaining in the city, after voluntary and forced deportations, be moved into this segregated area enclosed by a wall and barbed wire. Simon's parents went to Rabbi Rosenschtein asking if Simon could live with him and his family. The rabbi agreed this was the time to welcome Simon into his family.

Simon gripped the suitcase sitting on his lap to stop it from falling to the floor as his father drove the 1932 Polski Fiat across the bumpy cobblestone streets of Krakow on their way to the rabbi's home.

In addition to the clothes his mother had helped him pack, Simon had included a framed photograph of his family taken five years ago on Easter Sunday. In the corner of the frame, he'd placed the picture of his biological mother. The night before he'd taken a scissor and cut off that part of the picture with his father on it and tossed it into his wastebasket. His feelings about leaving his family had brought back his anger toward "that man." Later he retrieved the picture and placed it in the box in the secret room.

While listening to the rhythm of his flopping mattress tied onto the top of the car, Simon wondered if he'd made a mistake by not bringing his violin. He'd feared it would get damaged, lost, stolen, or taken from him. He wanted it kept safe for if-or-when he returned. The decision had been hard. His violin was often his source of refuge against the sad occasions in his life. He knew life in the ghetto would be difficult and lonely, and he'd wish he had his violin for comfort. Aside from his other reasons, it was his only connection with his biological father.

Simon watched his parents in the front seat. His mother's head moved from side to side with the movements of the car. She was holding three boxes of pastries and a bag of bread on her lap. They were a parting gift from Lucas and Peter to help Simon ingratiate himself with the rabbi's family. She squeezed two jars of soup she'd made the night before between her ankles.

Simon was sorry Berta hadn't been at the bakery to say good-bye. She'd stayed connected with the family after she left. He supposed she had to work. Within a block he saw a woman in a red coat waving her arms, running toward the car. It was Berta. His father stopped.

"I was afraid I'd miss you," she said, clutching her chest. For a moment Simon's anxiety left him when he rolled down his window and Berta stuck her head and arms in to kiss his cheek.

Afterward, Simon and his parents continued their ride. From the back seat, Simon saw his mother wipe away tears with the hand-embroidered handkerchief made by his grandmother. He reached over and placed his arms around her neck and rubbed his forehead against the side of hers. She held on to his hands.

The car went over a bump, and Simon let go of his mother. In front he saw his father's hands spread apart on the steering wheel as they so often had been when he placed them on Simon's shoulders to express his affection. Simon's own hands formed a tighter grip on his suitcase. He visualized his father pulling him closer by the shoulders into an embrace.

The car ambled along at a snail's pace. Simon was sure his father purposely was driving slowly to postpone their separation. His own anxiety increased the closer they came to the rabbi's street.

When they arrived, two young men whom Simon believed to be the rabbi's sons, Moses, and Aaron, were stacking the family's belongings onto a large, wooden four-wheel cart they would later hitch to a horse.

One of the brothers was taller, thin-bodied, and had muscular arms, probably from heavy labor, Simon thought. He assumed him to be Moses, the older brother. He wore black pants and a black vest over a white sleeveless shirt with fringes hanging from beneath his vest. His hair was black, and he had a thick black beard and deep brown eyes, almost black. When Simon got out of the car, he noticed a sneer on his face as their eyes met.

The other one removed his gloves and came to greet Simon and his parents. He was shorter than his brother and slightly built. His brown eyes were friendlier, and the stubble of his beard was brown, the same color as his hair. He was dressed similarly as his brother.

"I'm Aaron. That's my brother, Moses," he said to Simon's parents, pointing to the cart. Simon appreciated Aaron's greeting him with a handshake in the same manly way he greeted his father. "Don't worry, Mr. and Mrs. Baron. We'll take good care of Simon." Simon also appreciated how polite Aaron was to his mother.

Aaron relieved Mrs. Baron of her packages and led them to the house. "We're about packed and ready to leave. My parents are waiting for you, and Rachel is waiting to see you," he said to Simon, his eyes twinkling.

An irritated voice called out. "Hey, Aaron, I need you over here." Simon saw Moses's sneer directed at him again.

Aaron shouted back to his brother, "Be right there. Give me a minute."

Simon couldn't help but wonder if Moses resented him for invading the rabbi's household and taking resources away from his family

The rabbi came down the hallway. "What's all the yelling? Zey shtil. Be quiet. The whole neighborhood can hear you."

The rabbi came to the Barons with a smile, waving off Aaron. "Go help your brother," he said.

He invited Simon and his parents to the kitchen. Before Aaron ran off, he handed the rabbi the boxes containing the pastries.

"What's this?" the rabbi said.

"Just something to tide you over on your move to—" Mrs. Baron's voice cut off. Simon wished he could take her hand and blink and find he was in a dream and back at their kitchen table having breakfast, like the scene in the movie he and Katrina had once seen.

"Thank you," the rabbi said. Simon's thoughts turned back to reality. He looked at the rabbi. He looked tired.

"There's some homemade soup and bread in the car, also," Simon said. "I'll go get it."

"Why don't you take two of these pastries to the boys," his mother suggested.

Simon, grateful to have the chance to do something Moses might appreciate, jumped at the opportunity. He took two of his favorite kind, thinking the boys might like them also.

Aaron accepted his with a generous first bite, but Moses told Aaron to put his on the seat of the cart. "I'll save it for later," he said, not looking at Simon and continuing to work.

"Don't wait too long. It's good," Aaron said. "I might take it away from you."

"Take it, if you want," Moses said indifferently.

Aaron licked the last bit of icing from the pastry off his fingers. "We're waiting for Mr. Kowalski to bring us the horse to attach to the wagon," he said to Simon.

Rachel appeared at the doorway. Simon's eyes brightened. He smiled and walked with a lighter step to her and stared into her eyes. She was no longer the sad, withdrawn girl he sat with in the parlor two years ago. She smiled back. Simon thought she looked pretty in a clean blouse and skirt under her open coat, but he perceived an uneasiness, a cross between a happiness to see him and a fear of the circumstances that had brought them together.

"I'm glad you're here. It's so good to see you. I've missed your letters," she said. Her eyes looked downward.

"I've missed yours too. A lot has happened since we last wrote to each other. I hope Joseph is OK."

"He is. You'll get to see him soon."

"I hope so." Simon searched for words. He couldn't hold back his feelings. "I'm nervous," he said. "I'm glad your family is letting me live with you. I would have felt alone otherwise. You're the only Jewish people I know. It's scary not knowing what to expect."

"We're all scared, Simon. We've seen so much cruelty since the Nazis arrived, we'd be foolish not to be scared. Papa says being scared may save our lives."

Simon remembered the rabbi saying these same words to him at their last meeting.

"Papa is putting on a brave front, not just for us but for the community. He says our family must set an example, to show our people are strong, and our faith will help get us through this. We're wearing our best clothes to the ghetto to show the Germans our dignity and that we won't be beaten down."

"What will happen to us there?" Simon said, trying not to appear frightened.

"I'm not sure. Papa said the Jewish Council told him we may have it a little better than the others. We'll have our own apartment, but it won't be like it has been living where we are."

"Rachel, quit your talking and bring me your suitcase," Moses shouted impatiently.

She smiled at Simon. "Will you help me with my suitcase?"

Simon nodded. Their hands touched when he reached to take the suitcase from her. He felt a surge of electricity run through his body. They walked the suitcase to the cart as if the year's disruption of their letter writing hadn't changed their relationship. He wanted to catch up, to tell her about his past year and hear about hers. *This isn't the right time. We'll find time another day.*

"Do you want to put your things in now?" she said.

"No, I'll walk my suitcase to the ghetto. I'll put my mattress in later." He didn't want to deal with Moses right then.

"Put them in the cart," Moses quipped. "I'll need you to have free hands to help Aaron balance the cart as we move. The roads are bouncy. I don't want our things falling all over the street."

Simon tried the car doors to take the soup and bread inside and to hand his suitcase to Moses.

"The car's locked. I'll have to get the keys," he said to Moses. He went into the house and came back out. The horse had arrived. Aaron was holding the reins waiting for Moses to help attach it to the cart.

"That horse looks pretty old, and that's a pretty heavy-looking load," Simon said to Rachel.

"The slower the horse goes, the better chance Moses has of getting all our belongings there in one piece," Rachel said.

Simon went to the car to get the soup and bread. Aaron saw him taking them inside and asked him to alert his parents they'd soon be ready to leave. Simon came back carrying a sealed box marked "Kitchen." Mr. and Mrs. Baron and the rabbi and his wife followed behind carrying boxes.

While Moses and Aaron placed the boxes in the cart, Simon and his father unloaded Simon's items and took them to the brothers. Aaron helped untie the mattress.

Once Aaron and Moses had loaded and secured the cart and Mr. Kowalski had hitched the horse to the wagon, they'd be on their way to the ghetto.

Simon stood facing his parents to say goodbye. No one seemed to know what to do. Simon felt he needed to take the first step or his heart would burst. He didn't know how much longer he could put on a brave front, how much longer he could look at his mother's physical deterioration and his father's discomfort. He reached out to his mother as if she were a glass figurine he might break if he squeezed too hard. When they came together, he held her tightly to squeeze out every emotion from himself before letting her go. He didn't want her to see his fears. She burst into tears and pulled him back to her. His father came and wrapped himself around them. No one said a word. No one seemed to want to let go.

Simon's father pulled away and patted his wife's back. "Come, dear, it's time for us to leave. The rabbi and his family are almost ready to depart." Simon's mother held on a little longer before she let her arms slide off Simon's shoulders. When they did, Simon's father patted him on the back and said, "I love you, son. Remember what I told you. No matter where you are, who you're with, no matter what happens, you'll always be our son. Be brave. You're strong. Think of the day we'll be reunited. Use your brain and your talents to get by."

His father paused, then added, "Don't mind Moses. Don't let him fool you. He's scared too. Pull your weight. He'll come around."

Simon's father put his hands on his shoulders and pulled him in for another hug. When he let go, he said, "I've given the rabbi money to help with your keep. That way you should feel you're on an even keel, carrying your own weight. This should benefit you all." Simon felt better about his earlier concerns that Moses's sneers represented his worry Simon's presence he might deplete the family's resources in the ghetto.

Mr. Baron helped his wife into the car. She wiped away her tears with her handkerchief. Watching her, Simon could barely hold back his tears, but he wanted to be brave for her sake. His father saw that his wife was comfortably seated and closed her door. Simon kissed his fingers and pressed them against her window. She pressed her fingers onto the glass to meet his.

As he watched his parents pull away, Simon remembered the day when he was seven years old and his grandparents drove to the bakery to show them their new car. His grandfather had given each of his sons a ride around the neighborhood. He'd honked freely to show off. Simon couldn't wait for his turn. He remembered rolling down the window and holding his hand out against the wind.

After his grandfather's death, the car passed on to his grandmother, and it became shared by the family. With his grandmother and uncles gone, Simon's father was now in charge of it. The family had used the car for many happy occasions. Now it had taken Simon on the unhappiest drive of his life.

TWENTY

Simon and Aaron followed alongside the horse-drawn wagon. Moses had piled it high above the side slats. Although Simon and Aaron had taken care to pack it tightly with ropes, the jostling of the cart along the cobblestone streets resulted in the belongings coming loose and leaning to one side. Aaron called for Moses to stop so they could secure the contents. Moses looked back to see what their complaint was, but he didn't stop to heed Aaron's warning. Simon was sure Moses was doing this as a way of taking out whatever dislike he had of him.

Aaron stopped, looking like he was out of breath. He was bending over. His hands were on his knees. It was then Moses halted the wagon, got down, and pushed his brother and Simon aside. He pulled himself on top of the cart and started rearranging the contents. Aaron pulled himself together and joined Moses. After they felt the pile was steady, Moses told Aaron to sit on top of the pile for the rest of the journey to help stabilize it. Moses got down and stalked past Simon, ignoring him as he jumped back onto the front seat of the wagon.

Along the three-and-a-half-mile trek, they passed other Jews using diverse types of carriers to bring their belongings to the ghetto. Most were using small hand-pushed or hand-pulled carts or carrying only suitcases. The Germans had placed limits on the weight of the belongings they'd allowed Jews to bring. There were others like them, with larger, horse-drawn wagons, and others, especially children, carrying only a lamp or a chair or other single items.

The rabbi, his wife, and Rachel started off the same time as the boys, but they soon fell behind. Aaron, noticing this, called to Moses.

"Father has stopped to rest. Hold up for a while."

"He'll be OK," Moses said, unconcerned. "Rachel's with him and Mother. I'll come back for them later. If you want, you go back to him. I want to get this cart there before there's too long a line to pass through the gate. We have food that might spoil."

Simon couldn't believe Moses wouldn't even wait for his own family. None of this seemed real: the stream of refugees, the journey on foot, the ruthless young man on the cart controlling the situation.

They approached the double-arched entrance to the ghetto on Limanowskeigo Street.

"Moses and I helped build that wall," Aaron said to Simon. "The German Army forced us to work over Passover to build their cage. Their damn wall is over ten feet high and built of stone and barbed wire to keep us in. Many of the stones are monuments from the Jewish cemetery. Moses and I broke our backs dragging and lifting them. I hope one of the stones over the entrance comes loose and falls on the head of a German guard."

Simon understood the strong emotion in Aaron's voice. He'd experienced forced labor and its cruelties. More so, he couldn't imagine the sacrilege of removing the headstones of his own grandparents and sisters, or anyone, to build a wall to contain even the worst of one's enemies.

Aaron spit down from the cart onto the street. "One day, when this war is over, I'll make the Nazis build a wall of stone swastikas and cage them in the filthiest parts of Germany," he said.

"Be quiet. They'll hear you," Moses said, pointing to the German soldiers guarding the entrance.

At the gate they showed their documents. The soldiers directed them to their street. Once there, Moses dropped the boys off and went back to get his parents and Rachel. Simon and Aaron sat on the steps outside waiting. The rabbi had the only key to get in.

Simon looked at the peeling paint on the porch and front door and the loose nail on the step and wondered about the condition of their apartment inside. He watched people walking back and forth with their belongings, holding pieces of paper with the addresses of their assigned residences. They were tired and haggard looking, and they wore old clothing. Simon remembered what Rachel had said about her family wearing their better clothes to show their dignity, to show the invaders wouldn't beat them down. The people passing by looked as if the Nazis had crushed their spirits through this experience.

Twenty-One

It was late and they were tired when they came together. Their apartment was on the first floor of one of the many two-story buildings in this area of Krakow. There were two apartments on the first floor separated by a stairway.

They entered the apartment. The kitchen was in the front room. It was as wide as the apartment. It had a window, which faced the street. An open doorway beyond the kitchen led to a hallway, off which was a tiny room with a sink only. Beyond were two small bedrooms, one on each side of the hallway. Windows facing the side and back of the house were boarded. The only natural light came from the one window in the kitchen.

Aaron whistled. "This is one-quarter the size of Uncle's house. We'll be cramped."

"Count your blessings," the rabbi said. "Be grateful we have this to ourselves. Most of the apartments have two or three families living in them. The Jewish Council has given me special privileges to help them keep order. I need you all to set an example and cooperate."

Aaron nodded, but Moses shook his head. Simon saw Moses narrow his eyes in disgust.

Simon said nothing. He was a guest, but the apartment above the bakery was at least three to four times the size of this one, and he had his own bedroom. He could foresee the problems he'd have sharing one with Moses and Aaron, especially with Moses.

"Let's get as much in as we can before dark," Mrs. Rosenschtein said. "If you bring in the kitchen table and chairs and boxes marked 'Kitchen,' I'll try to have some of the soup and bread the Barons gave us ready for dinner."

"What about the horse and wagon?" Rachel asked.

"Mr. Kowalski gave me a bag of feed for the horse. I'll give him that and some water tonight and take them back tomorrow morning," Moses said.

The boys helped unload the wagon. It was getting dark. They decided to bring in everyone's suitcases, bed frames, and mattresses before dinner. Moses and Aaron agreed to put their bunk bed together the next day. They would sleep on their mattresses on the floor that night. They assembled their parents' bed, however. Rachel, too, decided to sleep on the floor that night, on her mattress. To give herself and her parents privacy, she chose to sleep in the narrow hallway area between the two bedrooms.

"What should we do with the parlor furniture we don't have room for?" Moses said.

"Pile what you can in the hallway beside the stairs," his mother said. "Tomorrow we'll see if there's any basement storage."

Exhausted and achy, they sat down for dinner. The rabbi asked them to hold hands for the blessing.

Rachel was sitting next to Simon. She took his hand.

"There's more for tomorrow, thanks to the Barons," Mrs. Rosenschtein said when the meal was over.

Simon felt pleased his parents had provided this food. It made him feel more welcome, until he saw the sneer on Moses's face.

Rachel patted Simon's hand and said, "Thank you."

Simon saw Mrs. Rosenschtein glance at her husband, catch his eye, and nod toward Rachel's hand where it lingered on Simon's.

Self-conscious, Simon said, "You're welcome" to Rachel, and he gently pulled his hand away. She let go and smiled. Simon hoped no one was offended by what they saw.

"Can we have some of the Barons' pastries?" Aaron asked.

"How about at breakfast?" his mother said. "I may even heat them for you."

"OK," Aaron said, sounding disappointed.

Exhausted, they went to bed early.

The next morning, while they were eating the remains of the soup and bread, there was a banging on their apartment door. A messenger handed the rabbi a note instructing him to appear at ten o'clock for a meeting at the office of the Jewish Council at the corner of Limanowski and Rynek-Podgorski streets.

The rabbi sipped one last taste of his soup and got up from the table to prepare.

"Don't forget the pastries," Aaron reminded his mother. "You promised some for breakfast."

The rabbi turned toward his wife. "Give me one of those boxes of pastries to take to the council meeting," he said.

"But…" started Aaron.

Simon looked up, puzzled, wondering why the rabbi wanted to take the pastries to the meeting.

"Don't 'but' me," the rabbi said. "I've got an idea. There'll still be two boxes left. There were two dozen in a box, plenty for us, plenty."

"How do you know?" Aaron said.

The rabbi patted his stomach. "I snuck one last night, and I counted."

Aaron frowned and crossed his arms.

Rachel let out a laugh.

"I'm glad to hear you laugh, my child," the rabbi said. "It may be your last one for a while."

His words caused everyone to stop eating.

Rachel's laugh evaporated. She turned serious. "You will tell us about the meeting when you come home?"

"Of course, my *haim sheli*." Simon could tell by the rabbi's tone this was a term of endearment. When the rabbi patted his daughter's cheek, Simon's heart twisted. The image brought his mother into the room for an instant, but then reality returned and she was gone.

After breakfast Moses left to return the horse and cart. Simon helped Aaron put the bunk bed together. Aaron put on the sheets and covers while Simon dressed his mattress on the floor.

The bunk bed was against the wall that separated the apartment from the common hallway to the other apartment on their level. Simon's mattress was by the door, which meant the brothers would have to step over or around him every time they entered or left the room while he was in bed.

Aaron stuffed some of his clothes into the drawers of a dresser he and his brother had brought, and he hung other clothing in the small closet in the room. He left space for Moses. Simon guessed his suitcase would have to serve as his dresser. He wondered if there might be a secret room behind the closet. He'd check when he was alone in the room.

The rabbi left for his meeting at the Jewish Council, and, after they got their room settled, Aaron and Simon went exploring to see if there was a basement where they could store the parlor furniture. They found the entrance to one behind the house and walked in through the unlocked door. Their hands brushed away cobwebs. They didn't find a light switch, but it was light enough for them to see it was an area half the size of the first floor of the building. Nothing was stored there except empty boxes. It provided plenty of space.

Aaron cursed. "It will a take a lot of cleaning before we can store anything here."

Simon shook his head in agreement. "Do you think we can get the furniture through the door?"

"We'll have to try to see. If not, we may have to chop it up and use it for heating later."

They walked in a little further. Simon hit his head on a low beam.

"Darn," he said, holding his hand to his head.

"Don't you ever swear?" Aaron said.

Simon shrugged. "Does it help?"

Forcefully, Aaron answered it did, with another profanity. Though he'd heard Lucas and Peter swear, Simon never did. His father would have scolded him if he'd heard him cursing.

Simon saw another door in the corner further back. It led to another room with a furnace and pipes for the building's plumbing. Cobwebs covered everything.

"We'll have to get a couple of brooms," Aaron said. "Let's clean up this sewer, get the furniture out of the hallway, and wait for Moses to get home to help move it back here."

"Why doesn't Moses like me?" Simon asked. He decided to see if Aaron trusted him enough to tell him.

Aaron hesitated before answering. "Let's get out of here."

When they were outside, they stopped to breathe in the fresh air.

"Promise me you won't tell him what I tell you," Aaron said.

Simon promised.

"You're a threat to him."

"A threat? How?" Simon asked, not able to understand how he could threaten the rabbi's oldest son, four years his senior and a blood relative.

"As the oldest, he feels responsible for our safety and for our survival, by bringing in income and providing food. We all do that, but as our senior, he feels the most responsible to look after us, to protect us. Rachel and I look up to him as the oldest."

"But how am I a threat?"

"He has feelings about your family giving us money and providing food. It takes away from what he sees as his role. He's also aware our father has special feelings toward you."

"That makes no sense." Simon wished he hadn't said that. He didn't want it to sound like he was arguing with Aaron.

Aaron kicked his heel into the dirt. "It does to him."

"Thanks for telling me the truth. I don't want to be a threat. I just want to fit in and pull my weight."

Aaron put his arm around Simon's shoulder. "Come on. Let's tell my mother what we found."

Mrs. Rosenschtein gave them a broom and rags to clean the space before storing the furniture.

"Let's take all the furniture outside to the front of the house before cleaning the basement," Aaron said. "Moses will be tired from walking back. Let's give him a break so he won't have to bring it out. He'll only need to help move it around back and store it."

Aaron and Simon had just finished cleaning the basement when Moses appeared out back.

Moses looked confused. "Where's the furniture?"

"It's out front. We brought it out to make it easier for you," Aaron said.

Moses glared. "It's not there."

They walked around front. He was right. It was gone.

"You stupid fool, leaving it out here," Moses said, directing his words at Aaron. "Someone has stolen it. What were you thinking?"

Aaron stared at the empty space where the furniture should have been. Then he spun away, hiding his face in his hands, slamming one heel against the hard ground.

Moses shook his head in disgust and walked away.

"Stupid putz." Aaron scolded himself.

Simon felt just as much at fault. Moses should have blamed him too. Why hadn't he? Simon went over to console Aaron, but Aaron turned away from him. Simon decided it best to leave him alone.

He went into the house. Rachel was in the kitchen unpacking some of the boxes they hadn't unpacked yesterday.

"Can I help?" he asked.

"Sure. You can hand me the things I've set out on the table. I'll put them away."

Simon was glad to have something to do to take his mind off what had just happened outside.

Rachel took a bowl from Simon and placed it in a cabinet. "It must be awful for you, being separated from your family," she said.

"It is. I keep thinking how lonely my parents must be." The image of his mother setting dinner plates on the table for her and his father and his not being home to share their meals came into Simon's mind as he watched Rachel. He felt so far apart from his parents, even though they were in the same city.

Rachel gave an understanding nod. "I'm glad you're here. I've missed your letters. They were comforting. They helped take my mind off our troubles."

"I've missed yours too," Simon said. "I looked for Joseph on every labor crew I was sent to, hoping to give him a letter for you or to see if he had one to give me."

"The German Army sent him to work on the ghetto wall with my brothers. You'll see him again once we and his family settle in."

"I hope so." Simon reached for another bowl and handed it to Rachel. "I've never had a real friend before. I concentrated so much on my violin studies, there was no time for friendships. Katrina was my friend. When she died and my school closed, I was lonely."

"That must have been an awful time for you." Rachel stopped what she was doing and pulled out a chair to sit down.

He sat down too. "It was. I miss the routine of my life, knowing every day had a purpose, and I was accomplishing something. Professor Kaminski had confidence in my talent and pushed me to bring out the best in me. Without her and Katrina, I've lost my inspiration. I want to get it back. I'd love to compose a tribute to her and Lena."

"Did you bring your violin with you?"

"No. I was afraid someone would take it from me. It belonged to my biological father. It's the only connection I have with him."

Rachel rubbed her hands together. "We'll have to find you a violin." Your music will bring joy to us during our time in this terrible place, under these tight conditions. Sharing a bathroom among the six of us without a toilet and shower, we'll all want to keep far apart," she said. Her body rocked back and forth with laughter.

Her warm and sudden burst of joy lit up her face and enchanted Simon.

Simon joined her laughter. "We'll all smell so bad, it won't matter. We can blame it on each other so no one of us is embarrassed," he said. He hadn't laughed so hard since before Katrina's death. It felt good.

"I'm glad you're here, Simon," Rachel said to him again. "It feels good to laugh like this."

He felt his face turn red. He'd never made a girl laugh before. It felt nice to hear her say that. Her compliment quieted him. He looked down to the floor to hide his embarrassment and the surge of emotion he felt toward her at that moment. To distract from her noticing his self-consciousness, he said, "I'm not sure about Moses. He doesn't seem to be happy with my being here."

"Don't worry about him. It's not you. His girlfriend and her family left Krakow just in time to avoid the ghetto. He misses her. He loves her very much and hoped to marry her. He's taking out his feelings on everyone. Since you're new, it's easier for him to take it out on you than on his own family."

Tell that to Aaron, Simon thought. He'd forgotten, for a little while, how Moses had humiliated Aaron outside. Aaron hadn't mentioned Moses's girlfriend. Simon thought he'd be more comfortable if what Rachel said was right, that Moses's bad mood had nothing to do with him.

"What about the boy your father arranged for you to marry?"

"My father received news he and his family are in the Lodz ghetto. None of us can plan a future right now. Our lives are on hold."

"Too bad," Simon said, but he couldn't ignore the quick hope that darted through him.

Twenty-Two

The rabbi arrived home late that afternoon. He brought vegetables and beans for Mrs. Rosenschtein to make more soup.

Aaron collapsed into his chair and frowned. "Soup again?" he said.

"Be still," the rabbi said. "Your mother works hard to feed us. Be grateful."

Respectfully, Aaron said, "Yes, sir."

"Tell us what you learned at the Jewish Council meeting, Father," Rachel said while she helped her mother place soup and bread on the table.

"First things first, prayers before eating," the rabbi said.

Rachel and her mother sat at the table. The rabbi took a piece of bread from the basket on the table and said, "Baruch ata Adonai, Eloheinu Melech ha'olam, h'-motzi lecham min ha'ar-etz."

Simon watched the rabbi pull off a piece of the bread and pass the rest around the table for everyone to take a piece and eat. It was strange for him to hear blessings in another language. It was the same blessing said at yesterday's meal. It must be important, he thought. He'd memorize it quickly.

"Now," Rachel said, "tell us what happened."

The rabbi took a sip of soup. "Rabbis Kranz and Lieb were at the meeting too. The council has given us each the responsibility for a section of the ghetto. The council wanted us to understand and explain to the residents of our sections that members of the council would remain the intermediary between us and the German authorities." The rabbi took a sip of water. "I'm sorry. It's been a long day. Let me catch my breath."

Rachel started to rise from her chair. "Are you all right, Father?" she asked.

The rabbi wiped his lips. They were barely visible through his beard. "Yes, yes. Sit still. I'm fine. I haven't gotten my bearings yet. I got lost on the way home. I walked more than I'm used to, I guess."

Aaron ignored Rachel's concern for their father. "How did they like the pastries?" he asked.

Simon was curious to know also.

"I'll get to that, son. Let me finish about the meeting." He took another sip of soup and went on. "The Germans will continue to determine what work crews they'll need and the quotas required. The council will remain responsible for fulfilling those quotas. The council will also coordinate the distribution of our food and our hygiene requirements."

Flippantly, Aaron asked, "Can they put a toilet and shower in our apartment?"

"They'll be installed tomorrow," the rabbi answered without delay.

Aaron's eyes widened. "Really?"

"Of course not, schlemiel," the rabbi said.

Everyone laughed but Aaron and Simon.

"What does that mean?" Simon whispered to Rachel.

"It means 'fool,'" she said.

Simon couldn't hold back his laughter, but he felt guilty after knowing the humiliation Aaron had suffered earlier.

His face red, Aaron said, "You still haven't told us why you took the pastries."

"I took the pastries to show them how useful Simon would be either working in a bakery or in food distribution, anything that would make it possible for us to have access to food."

There was silence.

"Father, is it fair for us to have greater access to food than others?" Rachel said.

"I know Simon will be fair to everyone in distributing food and will give equal portions in ration lines. Did you think I had a selfish motive for us? That would be a *shanda*, a shame. All I did was give them the pastries and tell them the young man living with us made them. I planted the seed. Let's see how it grows. Wouldn't you want me to try and get all of you jobs that didn't involve hard labor?"

"There's a drawback to your reasoning, Father," Moses said.

Simon looked up to see what Moses had to say that might disparage him.

"What's that?" the rabbi said.

"Simon didn't make those pastries. His parents did or at least their bakers."

Everyone turned to Simon.

"Is that true?" Rachel said.

"The staff made the pastries my mother gave you, but I've worked along-side the bakers for the past two years, and I've learned to make breads and pastries. I could easily have made them." He tried not to sound boastful so he didn't embarrass Moses, but at the same time, he wanted to convey confidence in himself.

Moses's face turned crimson. "Well then, let's see if Father's scheme works," he said.

Rachel gently threw her hands up. "The worse that can happen is we sacrificed a box of sweets."

"Tell us quickly what else was said at the meeting, *meyn tayer*, my dear," said Mrs. Rosenschtein. "We're all getting a little tired and need to get ready for bed."

"OK. I'll try to be quick. Also at the meeting were representatives of the Jewish police, the OD, and people from the

Social Welfare Office. The OD told us how they planned to keep order among us. There will be no German guards in the ghetto, but they will guard the outside gates. The welfare people told us about the hospital services.

The rabbi covered a yawn. "I'll finish tomorrow. Your mother is right. It's been a long day, an exhausting day. We all need rest. I think I'll take a shower first, though," the rabbi said. He winked at Aaron and rubbed Aaron's hair when he passed by him.

Simon wasn't used to seeing the rabbi interact with his family. He was surprised by the rabbi's sense of humor, given their circumstances. Since the deaths of his sisters and grandmother, humor had vanished from his house.

Twenty-Three

It wasn't long before the Jews in the ghetto were faced with continued exploitation. They received low, if any, pay for their labor, and they struggled against hunger, and trying to stay well amid diseases associated with poor plumbing and limited access to good hygiene. Keeping spirits up among the residents in his section was a difficult job for the rabbi.

Compared to other families, the Rosenschtein household did better. The rabbi's ploy of taking the Baron's pastries to the council meeting landed Simon a job with kindly Mr. Mandelbaum, who ran the ration distribution center in a small church turned over to the rabbi to use for people in his district. Supervisors brought laborers to the center for their meager lunch of a cup of soup and a piece of bread.

Simon helped Mr. Mandelbaum by uncrating the daily delivery of vegetables for the soup, storing bags of flour, and baking bread for the daily rationing among the laborers in the rabbi's district. While Mr. Mandelbaum pealed potatoes and prepared other vegetables for the soup, Simon baked bread. During lunch Mr. Mandelbaum ladled out a cup of soup to each scrawny worker. Simon handed them a piece of bread.

When their supervisors took the laborers back to work, Mr. Mandelbaum and Simon filled themselves with leftovers. Mr. Mandelbaum made more soup than was needed to feed the laborers. He came to work daily with jars to fill so he could take soup home. He never used all the vegetables in preparing the soup. Anything left over went home in his pockets, except for the one or two he'd give Simon. Later in the afternoon, two women came to help wash the soup cups and spoons. While Mr. Mandelbaum washed the large cooking pots and serving pieces, Simon cleaned the ovens and swept the floor.

Simon found time to stack the empty crates near the door to make room for the new crates that would arrive later that afternoon. If the supply distribution center didn't deliver the crates and flour the day before they were needed, Mr. Mandelbaum sent Simon the long three blocks to pick them up. Fortunately, this didn't happen often. The crates were heavy and awkward to lift and place into the wooden two-wheel cart Mr. Mandelbaum provided. Simon wore thick gloves to protect his hands. Regardless, the wood from the crates sometimes scratched his face and tore his clothes.

Despite his position and influence, the rabbi was unable to keep his sons from strenuous work. The council assigned Aaron to a garbage crew. He and others went house to house following a garbage truck and emptying garbage cans in their district. Moses worked on a crew sweeping sidewalks and streets. The brothers came home smelly and dirty.

Rachel and Mrs. Rosenschtein worked as seamstresses at the Gruber Textile Factory, owned by Paul Gruber, who provided humane and comfortable working conditions. His workers received a generous lunch every day, and he permitted them to take home left-over portions. With what Simon, Rachel, and Mrs. Rosenschtein brought home and what their supervisors provided them for lunch, they ate better than others in the ghetto. They knew they were more fortunate, and they shared their food with those in other apartments in their building, as did the rabbi, with the sick and hungry he visited.

The rabbi removed items from a small chapel in the church and, with a blind eye of a council member who stopped by periodically, he led a group of men in morning prayers. He visited the laborers during their lunch to offer spiritual comfort, and he visited the children in the building where his wife and Rachel had established a day care center before they found work in the textile factory.

In the afternoon the rabbi visited the hospital to see sick patients from his district. The Polish community had built the hospital to serve the five thousand gentiles who lived in this area of the city before it had become a ghetto. The hospital was not large enough to tend to the needs of fifteen thousand people. As a result, the rabbi spent a part of his day making visits to the apartments of those the hospital could not care for, many of whom were ill and dying from malnutrition and diseases spread through unsanitary conditions. Others, not so ill, seemed to give up the will to live.

One night Moses awoke Simon from a dream by kicking his feet when leaving the bedroom.

In the dream Simon was pounding on the door of his parents' bakery. Someone stuck his head out the upstairs kitchen window

"I'm Simon Baron. I'm looking for my parents."

"The Barons don't live here anymore," the stranger said.

Disheartened, Simon turned away.

"Wait. Come back. I have a letter for you."

The man disappeared and came back. He tossed a letter out the window.

Simon grabbed it as it fluttered downward.

He crossed over to the square and sat on a bench to read the letter in the moonlight.

Dear Simon,
You're strong. Be brave. Use your talents. Do what you must to survive. We'll meet again when the war is over. Remember, you will always be our son, no matter what, no matter where.
Love, your father

Disturbed by his dream, Simon left his mattress and went to the kitchen, where he found Rachel. She was sitting at the kitchen table wrapped in a blanket over her clothes. She had pulled her knees close to her body and rested her heels on the edge of her seat. Her teeth were chattering.

He looked at her admiringly. She never complained. She had pulled her blankets above her mouth and nose, and she was wearing a woolen cap to cover her ears and forehead. Only her eyes showed. They were watery and glistening from the wind ripping through the cracks around the loosely framed window. Her parents were in their room. He suspected her brothers were waiting in line, shivering, at the public outhouse.

Simon pulled up a chair to join Rachel. "I feel guilty working inside while your brothers are laboring outside in the cold," he said.

"Don't be. Father says he's seen you lifting and carrying heavy crates of vegetables."

"That doesn't compare with Moses and Aaron being outside in the cold all day, and at least I don't stink as much when I come home."

Underneath her blanket Rachel giggled. "I know I shouldn't make fun of him, but Aaron does reek of garbage when he gets home. Life is hard for him, but he's always been the good-natured one in the family, not like Moses, who takes life so seriously. Last night Aaron came into the apartment just in his underpants. He took his smelly clothes off on the front steps and left them there. You should have seen his expression when mother sent him right back out to bring them in so she could wash them."

Rachel's chuckle faded as she stared off into the distance. "I don't like the way Father's looking," Rachel said changing the subject. "Mother, too, but Father looks worse. He's under so much strain trying to tend to the needs of so many people who are sick and starving."

Simon shared her concerns. Things had worsened since they came to the ghetto. It felt like the Nazis were purposely attempting to weed out the strong from the weak, the young from the old, or get rid of them all.

Twenty-Four

"The High Holy Days will soon be here, Father," Rachel said. "What are we going to do?"

"We'll observe. That's what we'll do," the rabbi said.

With cynicism, Moses said, "We'll certainly have no trouble fasting."

"Have faith, my son. Be positive," the rabbi said.

Moses's nostrils flared. A vein in his neck twitched. "Like our faith in the Allies, that they'll come to our rescue," he spat out. "And what about the Americans? Should I have faith in them, that they won't continue their abandonment of us?"

The words "American" and "abandonment" aroused strong feelings in Simon. Since moving to the ghetto, he had fantasized the Americans would enter the war. His father would come to his rescue, ask for his forgiveness, and they'd reconcile. He never genuinely believed this would happen, but the idea never left him.

Later, when they were alone, Simon asked Rachel to explain the significance of the High Holy Days.

She explained this was the beginning of the new year according to the Jewish calendar.

"For you this is 1941. For us this is the year 5701, soon to be 5702."

Simon scratched his temple.

"It's confusing, I know," Rachel said. "The Hebrew calendar is based on the age of the world according to the Bible. The Gregorian calendar was started in 1582 by Pope Gregory XIII."

Simon was embarrassed he didn't know this. His ears turned red.

"Let's sit down. I'll explain it all to you," Rachel said. They each pulled out a chair and sat opposite one another at the kitchen table. She went on to explain. "Our year begins with Rosh Hashanah and Yom Kippur during the Jewish month of Tishrei. This year it begins the night of September 21."

Simon sat attentively with his hands loosely folded into fists atop the table. "Rosh Hashanah, Yom Kippur, what do they mean?"

Rachel placed her hands on top of the table, also, and leaned in toward Simon. "On Rosh Hashanah we believe God inscribes a person's fate in the Book of Life. He doesn't seal our fate until Yom Kippur, ten days later. We're to use the time between to atone for our wrongdoings and seek forgiveness from those we've offended during the previous year."

"What did Moses mean about fasting?" Simon asked.

"On Yom Kippur we fast all day. We refrain from eating and drinking for twenty-four hours."

"I have a lot to learn about being Jewish."

Rachel placed her hand over his. "Don't worry. I'll teach you." Her tone was warm, her smile inviting.

Simon felt those feelings for her stir again. They were becoming more frequent. He tried to push them aside. He was a guest in the rabbi's home. He wasn't sure how the rabbi and Mrs. Rosenschtein would feel about his having such emotions toward their daughter. The rabbi had promised her to another, and he remembered the look Mrs. Rosenschtein had given the rabbi when Rachel took Simon's hand their first night in the ghetto. Simon found himself thinking about Rachel increasingly. He wondered if she shared his feelings.

He shook these thoughts away and said, "It was strange to learn I'm Jewish when I've been a Christian all my life. You'll have to be patient with my ignorance."

"We will be. Father told us about your background. He felt it important we know so we'd understand why your parents asked that you come live with us. He told us about his promise to your biological mother and how he felt a special connection with you. That made us all want to make you feel welcome and safe, at least as safe as anyone can feel right now."

Does this mean Rachel is only being friendly toward me? Am I making more out of her attention than is there?

Simon tried to shake away his thoughts about Rachel. "Even Moses? He resents my being here."

"Moses is a good person. Give him time."

There was a pause between them.

Rachel's voice rose. "I have an idea," she said excitedly. "The meal on the eve of Yom Kippur is special. We may not be able to eat as well here as we did back home, but you know how to bake. We can surprise everyone with challot. Maybe Mr. Mandelbaum will let you use the church's oven."

"We'll need flour and yeast," Simon responded, thinking about recipes for different breads.

"And lots of butter," Rachel said.

The fact that Rachel could find enthusiasm about something amid so much suffering raised Simon's own spirits, if only for a while. That night he went to bed thinking of Rachel again. Under his blanket he folded his arms across his chest and stared up at the dark ceiling, envisioning her face. His body was tingling, and he was aware of the beating of his heart. Simon wanted nothing more than to please Rachel. He wondered if she was thinking of him. He thought about her idea of his making challot for the Yom Kippur Eve dinner. He didn't know if Mr. Mandelbaum would go along with the idea, but he'd ask him.

When the High Holy Days arrived, the Rosenschteins recited special prayers at dinner on Rosh Hashanah Eve. Simon thought about a God sitting in heaven inscribing his fate for the new year. *Will I still be alive? Will the Allies rescue me? Will I meet my American father? Will my parents and I reunite? Will my relationship with Rachel grow and endure?*

The week before Yom Kippur, Simon spoke with Mr. Mandelbaum.

"I have an idea, if you agree," he said.

"What's that?"

"I'm a good baker. I can make your family's Yom Kippur Eve meal special by baking challot if you help me get the ingredients."

"What will you need?" Mr. Mandelbaum said.

Simon was encouraged by Mr. Mandelbaum's readiness to consider his proposal. "Extra flour, yeast, eggs, and butter."

"I'll see what I can do," Mr. Mandelbaum said. Simon couldn't wait to tell Rachel about Mr. Mandelbaum's reply. His efforts were meant to please her. The Yom Kippur Eve meal had no real meaning to him at this point.

Mr. Mandelbaum brought him enough ingredients to make the challot. The day before Yom Kippur Eve, Simon prepared the dough, rolled it into braids, and made four large loaves. He brushed them with butter while they baked. They cooled a golden color. Mr. Mandelbaum and Simon each took two. Mr. Mandelbaum split the extra butter with Simon and gave him three potatoes to take home.

Mrs. Rosenschtein thanked Simon with a hug. "We shouldn't be greedy," she said. She cut one challah and a potato into three pieces. "Take these to the other apartments in the building," she told Simon and Rachel.

At Yom Kippur Eve dinner, Mrs. Rosenschtein placed a challah on the table with butter. The soup she made was thicker because of the extra potatoes. Everyone was surprised by the challah. Rachel explained Simon made it with the help of Mr. Mandelbaum.

Simon smiled and looked at Rachel. "It was Rachel's idea for me to make it. I wouldn't have known it was special for this meal if she hadn't told me."

Rachel was sitting next to him. She leaned so their shoulders touched. She smiled at him and then at those around the table.

"Mr. Mandelbaum gave me extra potatoes for the soup," Simon told them.

"God bless Mr. Mandelbaum," the rabbi said. "May we all be inscribed in the Book of Life for many happy, healthy, sweet years to come."

That night Simon pulled out the photograph of his biological mother. He spoke to her through his thoughts.

We celebrated the High Holy Days, Mother. I'm learning what it's like to be Jewish. The Rosenschteins have taught me a little, but Rachel's taught me the most. I hope God puts me down in the Book of Life to survive this year. I'll be praying to Him every day for this. I hope you are looking down on me and are proud.

He kissed the picture and put it back into the corner of the frame of the picture of his family.

TWENTY-FIVE

With the arrival of winter, Simon and the others felt the sting of cold in their ghetto apartment. Many nights they went to sleep in their clothes trying to keep warm.

"Keep your chattering teeth to yourself," one might hear one or another of the three boys chiding the others while rolling over and pulling a blanket over his ears.

When Moses proposed they break into Mr. Mandelbaum's kitchen to steal wood from the crates, Simon tried to dissuade him by giving reasons why this wouldn't work. Simon appealed to Moses's sense of morals and his being the son of a community leader. Not only would they be breaking the eighth commandment, but if they were caught, there would be more dire consequences than being cold, consequences that could lead to their death. He promised his father he'd be strong and do what it took to survive. He'd tolerate the cold if that's what it took to return home. Moses's idea horrified him.

"How would it look if we were caught?" he said.

Simon's words didn't deter Moses. "We're only after wood, not food. The Nazis have plenty of wood to make new crates. They can deliver the food in sacks. What difference would that make?" he said. "We wouldn't be hurting anyone." Moses kept it up. He pushed Simon. "My father's sick. Look how pale he is. And I can hardly sleep from the sound upstairs of Mr. Askin coughing all night. This is for the building, Simon, not only us. It would be a mitzvah. If you and Aaron hadn't been so stupid and left our furniture unattended, we'd have wood for heat."

That final statement shamed Simon into agreeing. The next day he regretted he'd given in to Moses's pressure. Mr. Mandelbaum had been kind to him, and the rabbi's family benefited from his kindness. Simon felt guilty at the possibility of disappointing him if anyone caught them.

At 2:00 a.m. Simon felt Aaron's hand on his shoulder to awaken him. The three boys had slept in dark clothes to be less visible for what they were about to do. They tiptoed shoeless from the apartment and put their shoes on quietly on the porch. They walked in the shadows to the back of the rabbi's building to the entrance of Mr. Mandelbaum's kitchen, where in the morning Simon and Mr. Mandelbaum would open the crates of food for the laborers' lunchtime meal.

Simon was scared. He knew if the police caught them, they would shoot them. He wanted to turn and run back home, but he felt intimidated by the brothers, especially Moses.

When they arrived at the kitchen door, Moses jimmied the lock open. "Where are the knives?" he asked Simon.

Simon pointed to a drawer. His hand was shaking. Moses pulled out three of the sharpest and handed one each to Aaron and Simon. They started cutting open crates and placing the wood into piles. Each boy had a sling to make it easy to carry the wood home in bundles. When they thought they had as much as they could bear, they slipped out of the kitchen and back into the cold, dark night.

They weren't a hundred feet from the building when a whistle blew behind them and someone shouted for them to stop. A man came running toward them holding a gun. It was a member of the Jewish police. Simon froze. His bundle of wood slipped from his shoulder to his elbow before he caught it and slipped it back. Aaron stopped a foot behind him.

"Run," Moses cried out. His voice echoed down the street.

Simon turned and saw the OD holding Moses by the collar. They were struggling. Moses's bundle of wood fell to the street, scattering. Simon watched Aaron drop his bundle and run to Moses. Aaron picked up a piece of wood and tried to help Moses by hitting the OD officer. Moses managed to get free of the OD's grasp. He reached down and grabbed a piece of wood. He hit the officer until the officer fell to the ground motionless.

Simon stood frozen, torn between whether to run as Moses said or to turn back and help the still-looking man laying at the feet of Moses and Aaron. *No one was supposed to get hurt.* Breathing heavily, Simon made a split-second decision to heed Moses. He dropped his bundle of wood and ran as fast as he could to their apartment. The other two followed close behind. Window lights went on as the three boys fled through the streets, leaving their wood strewn everywhere.

They snuck back into their apartment, leaving the lights off. Out of breath, they jumped into their beds and covered themselves. The three of them lay there, their lungs heaving. Simon's heart was beating fast. His body squirmed. He prayed the OD officer wasn't hurt badly. *Why? Why did I give in to Moses? This is a disaster. Please, God, don't let that man die.*

Simon heard Aaron whisper to Moses, "Are you sure? How can you be sure?"

"I saw his eyes. They were blank, just staring back at me," Moses whispered back.

Simon's heart sank. Had his worst fear come true?

The boys heard pounding on the apartment door. The voices of men called out, "Police. Open the door."

The brothers and Simon turned on their sides and pulled their blankets higher. Simon couldn't stop shaking. *They've found the man Moses beat. If he's dead, if the police are knocking on our door, they must suspect we're involved. They'll point their guns at our heads, drag us into the street, and shoot us as an example. I'll never see my parents again.*

"Keep quiet," Moses said. "Act like we're asleep."

Simon realized he still had his shoes on. He kicked them off so that if the ODs called them into the kitchen or burst into their bedroom, it wouldn't look as if he'd been outside.

The three listened as the rabbi opened the door.

"There's been a robbery," an unfamiliar voice said. "One of our ODs is dead. Witnesses heard three men shouting in the street. There was wood from crates left on the ground. The crates were from the kitchen in your building. We're searching for suspects. Where are your sons and the boy who lives with you?"

Simon pulled his blanket higher. The tone in the man's voice caused his heart to race.

"My sons and Simon? They're asleep in their room."

In a scathing tone, the voice said, "Bring them out."

Simon remembered the night three Germans appeared at his parents' home looking for him, how he hid in the secret room behind his closet and how scared he was while they scoured the house looking for him. He wished he had a place to hide now. There was no secret room in his bedroom here. He'd checked one night when the boys were out.

The rabbi entered their room and roused them from their beds. The three of them followed him into the kitchen, rubbing their eyes, stretching their arms, pretending to yawn from the rabbi waking them suddenly. The OD asked if any of them had been out within the past hour. Each said no. Simon tried to hide his trembling by crossing his arms across his chest and pretending he was shivering from the cold, not from his fear of their catching him in a lie. He blinked his eyelashes and swayed back and forth, hoping the officers would think he wasn't used to the light and was trying to stay awake.

One of the ODs said, "A policeman's been killed. A neighbor heard someone shouting, 'Run.' Neighbors said the voice sounded like that of a young man. They heard running in this direction."

Simon locked his knees and stood straight, trying not to look intimidated. He thought of the trick Professor Kaminski taught him and his classmates to avoid stage fright. Stand tall, pick a spot in the room, focus on it, and concentrate on the piece you're playing.

The rabbi looked at the three boys, worriedly, and turned back to the officers.

"They've been here all night. It couldn't have been them," he said.

"Why are they in their shoes?" one of the men said, pointing to the feet of Moses and Aaron.

Simon, seeing the boys fumbling for a response, focused on the armband of the questioning OD, and said, "They always wear their shoes to bed. They've been at work all day. They're tired. They fall asleep before they can get undressed." Professor Kaminski's advice helped him remain calm for the moment.

The officer looked at Simon's feet.

"Me?" Simon said. "My job is easier. I don't get as tired."

"I'm afraid you've come to the wrong house," the rabbi said. "You can see you've woken us all from our sleep, and we have to be up very early."

The officers wore suspicious faces. They left, saying their investigation wasn't over and to expect a return visit.

When the rabbi closed the door behind them, they could hear one of the ODs say, "Let's head to the Schreiber's apartment. A young man lives there." Simon pulled at his collar and shook his head at the prospect of the ODs harassing and frightening someone else for something he and the brothers had been responsible.

The rabbi's wife and Rachel were standing at the hallway entrance observing what was happening. The ODs' knocking had awakened them. The rabbi told them to go back to bed.

When his wife and Rachel left, the rabbi looked the three boys straight in the eyes and said, "Did you boys have anything to do with this?"

"No, sir," both Moses and Aaron said.

The rabbi stared longer and harder at Simon.

"No, sir. We've been in bed all night," Simon said, feeling he'd betrayed the man who had taken him in, provided him a home, and who could get into serious trouble if the truth were to come out. He was furious with Moses, but mostly with himself, for allowing himself to be put in this position.

"Go back to bed," the rabbi said. Simon and the other two obeyed. Simon could feel the rabbi's gaze searing into his back as he tried to decide whether he was telling the truth.

When they were back in bed, Aaron said to Moses, "Do you think Father believed us?"

"I don't know. I hope so. Be quiet before he hears us talking."

Simon couldn't get back to sleep. He hadn't touched the OD officer himself, but he'd been there and stood silently by while Moses beat him. Then he had lied about it. Those truths lay on him like weights he couldn't lift. The rabbi had once told him about righteous lies, white lies one told to help another from being harmed. Were the lies he told to save his life and the lives of Moses and Aaron righteous lies? But they had killed another Jew. It wasn't intentional. It was self-defense and accidental. Did causing the death of another person erase the idea his lies and those of Moses and Aaron could be considered righteous? He wished he could talk about it with the rabbi, but that would mean betraying Moses and Aaron, even though he suspected the rabbi knew they hadn't told the truth that night. Was the rabbi himself telling a righteous lie by ignoring the truth to save his sons and Simon?

Simon lay in bed waiting for another knock on the door that would lead to their arrest and probable death. His mind replayed what had happened that night. He wished he could go back and change things. He thought about what Mr. Mandelbaum would think in the morning when he came to work to find the lock on the door broken and vegetables lying on the countertop, uncrated. Would Mr. Mandelbaum accuse him of being involved in the break-in? Would he lose his job and the extra benefits that came with it? Worse, would Mr. Mandelbaum's suspicions cause the OD to return—if not tonight, tomorrow? What would become of the rabbi and his family and him then?

Simon made a bargain with God. If He would help him and the rabbi's family get away with what happened, he'd never again do anything that went against God's teachings. He vowed not to let himself come under the influence of another person, to stand his ground and do what he knew to be right. Exhausted, he fell asleep. The ODs didn't return that night.

The next morning Simon overheard a conversation between Rachel and Moses.

"I heard you leave and come back," she said.

"You must have been dreaming."

"Turn around," she said.

"Why?" Moses said.

"Just do it."

Simon couldn't see what was happening.

"What's that?" Simon heard Moses say.

"It's a splinter of wood. I saw it in your hair last night when you had your back to me."

There was silence.

"Don't worry, I won't tell. Don't ever do it again, and don't let Aaron and Simon either."

Simon thought of Katrina. He felt she would have reacted the same toward him as Rachel had toward Moses, such was the bond between them. The thought of Katrina touched a tender spot in his heart. While brushing his teeth, he looked in the mirror and spoke to her silently. *I miss you, Katrina. I hope you're still proud of me after what I did. Keep an eye out for me up there. I need you more than ever.*

Mr. Mandelbaum and a member of the Jewish Council were waiting for Simon when he arrived at work. Mr. Mandelbaum stood by silently while the council member told Simon the council was transferring him to another job. Simon felt, from the stern look on Mr. Mandelbaum's face, he suspected he'd participated in the break-in. The council member escorted Simon to the distribution center, the same one where Joseph worked, for his new assignment.

For weeks Simon lived in fear a police officer would return to accuse him and the brothers of the OD's death. He, Moses, and Aaron never spoke of the incident again, and Moses never asked him to participate in another crime. The sneers disappeared. Moses treated him with respect. Simon hadn't noticed it immediately. He felt the difference one night at dinner, not long after, when Moses gently patted his shoulder when he passed Simon's chair on the way to his own. When Moses sat down, his and Simon's eyes met. Each gave a quick, knowing nod to the other.

Twenty-Six

Simon was reassigned to the strenuous job of unloading cargo brought to the ghetto in trucks from the train station. Joseph had the same assignment.

Labor in the ghetto was hard but not as brutal as it was when the Nazis watched your every move and were prepared to strike you down for any reason. In the ghetto the Jewish Council assigned fellow Jews to watch over the labor. If you worked steadily and you didn't interfere with the work of others, your supervisor treated you fairly, except for the occasional one who felt the need to show his authority through cruelty. The kinder ones allowed their workers to sing while they worked, and Simon heard many songs sung in Polish and Yiddish.

When Simon learned Joseph played the piccolo, he told Joseph he played the violin but hadn't brought his instrument to the ghetto. One evening Joseph appeared at the Rosenschteins' doorway with his piccolo in one hand and his other hand hidden behind his back.

"For you," Joseph said. He brought his hidden hand forward. It held a violin.

Simon held his arms out as if to hug the world. He took hold of the violin and examined it. The craftsman who made the instrument had used solid maple wood on its back and sides and spruce on its top. He'd used ebony for the fingerboard and its parts. The instrument was hand-varnished and well cared for. It looked as well made as Simon's own violin, made by his grandfather. He peered through the f-hole see the maker. It was not a name he knew. "Where did you get it?" he said.

"Mrs. Goren in our building gave it to me," Joseph said. "Her husband died. I asked if I could have it for my friend who is the greatest violinist in the world."

"Where is the bow?" Simon asked.

"Mrs. Goren said I had to bring you to her to get the bow. Her husband was a fine violinist. She said she wanted to make sure she was passing down his violin and bow to someone worthy of them."

"Take me to her. I'll play for her."

Joseph took Simon to Mrs. Goren's apartment. The boys listened as she told them about her husband's music training at the Prague Conservatory and of the symphony orchestras he'd performed with. Simon promised to care for the violin and honor her husband's memory. He told her about his studies at the Krakow School of Music and his desire to compete in the Alliance competition before the war intervened. He wanted to assure her she had given the violin to someone worthy.

While Simon played for her, Mrs. Goren listened attentively, her hands clasped together, her eyes closed. He thought she was imagining her husband playing. He hoped his expressions of joy in receiving the instrument would make up for her sacrifice of giving something precious away.

The gift of the violin raised Simon's spirits. As he loaded and unloaded trucks and stored their contents in the warehouse, his head filled with sounds, images, and movements. His preoccupation with these detracted from his hunger to the point that when it was time to break for lunch rations, his supervisor had to remind him to stop. Simon feared he'd lose the momentum of the music that rambled through his head.

Simon and Joseph worked well together. Their manager noticed their teamwork and paired them often to unload trucks and store the contents in their designated areas in the warehouse.

Joseph was tall and lanky. His arms and legs were long compared to the rest of his body. It was easy for him to squat on the back of a truck and stretch his arms down to Simon's. The two were able to keep up a pace their manager noticed, and this gave them extra privileges.

Twenty-Seven

"You've changed since you got your violin," Rachel said to Simon one night as they sat in the kitchen while she was sewing.

"How do you mean?"

"You're happier."

"I've got my music back. It's like I've gotten my life back. One day I hope to compose great music and have it played around the world. What do you want to do with your life, Rachel?"

When Rachel didn't respond, he wondered if his burst of optimism that there might be a future for either of them beyond the ghetto had upset her.

Rachel put down her needle and gave a shallow sigh. "My future was determined before I was born. Don't get me wrong. My childhood and youth were happy and filled with religious observances and celebrations during which I dressed up as Jewish heroines in the Bible and pretended to be them." She put the coat she was mending on the chair next to her and her needle and thread on the table. "When Father started looking for a husband for me, I began writing down my dreams about the kind of husband I wanted and the children I wanted to have. I created a happy fantasy to help me get through the unknown of Papa matching me with a stranger. After the invasion started, I turned to writing poetry."

"Poetry? That's great. Did you bring any of your poems with you?"

"No. I thought they were silly. At home I was able to hide them from my brothers. I was afraid they'd make fun of them. I didn't want anyone to find them here."

Simon straightened. He felt disappointed. "That's too bad. I would like to have read them. I bet you're an incredibly good poet." He paused and cocked his head. Scrunching his eyebrows, he said, "Be honest with me, Rachel. Have you written anything since you've been here?"

Rachel crossed her arms. Her lips curled into a secret smile.

"You have, haven't you, you little stinker." He said it with affection, like he had with Lena when she did something naughty and he chased her around the house, pretending to try to catch her while she ran away from him screeching with both pretend fear and laughter. Simon leaned back and slapped his thighs. "Please, I'd like to read your poems."

Rachel leaned forward in her chair. "Promise me you won't laugh at them and you won't tell anyone about them."

Simon crossed his heart.

Rachel left the kitchen and returned holding papers. "You're sure now? You won't tell anyone, not even Joseph."

Simon promised again, and Rachel handed him her poems.

Simon sat on the edge of his chair and stretched his body over the table. He placed the poems down and spread his arms around them as if he were guarding them from prying eyes. His lips moved silently as he read the first poem.

"I Forced a Smile"
I forced a smile today to remember how it feels.
The muscles in my mouth grew tight.
It hurt because it wasn't real,
but I had to try, and
I'll try again and again so I don't regret,
that when there is a reason to smile for real,
I'll be happy I didn't forget.

When Simon finished, he read the poem again, moving his mouth to see how it felt to pretend to smile. He felt his cheek and jaw muscles tighten, as the poem described. He pictured Rachel going through this exercise as she wrote the poem.

Simon looked up. "Gee, Rachel, this is good. It's so clever. How did you ever think of this?" He wondered if it reflected a sadness in her he hadn't noticed, deeper feelings he'd missed.

Rachel blushed, then shrugged. "I don't know. It just came to me."

Simon kept his eyes on her for a moment, trying to decide if she was being modest. Then he began reading the second poem.

"Hopeless Cries"
I felt my heart today,
to see if it was beating.
It felt a little slow,
but it was there.

I blew my breath into my hand
to feel the flow of air across my palm,
and when I was sure it was real,
I blew it into the atmosphere.

I wiggled my toes and pulled my hair,
and begged for an itch to scratch,
To prove I was alive and strong enough,
to sew another stitch.

I walked with others in the street.
I looked for hope in their eyes.
They fixed their brows to the ground.
Their shoulders were bent from their cries.

The promises made in childhood,
now had turned to lies.
All hope seemed gone.
They were robots, waiting for their demise.

Simon ran his hand across his brow. "Wow, Rachel. This is heavy stuff. I don't know what to say. It's beautiful." *Where did this come from?* he wondered. He didn't have the words to tell her what he thought of the poem, how insightful it was. She had a gift for looking into people's souls. He realized she was a person of deep feelings, like him. He wanted to wrap his arms around her and tell her everything would be all right. He held on to the poems for a while, to feel this connection with Rachel, before giving them back to her.

"You shouldn't be shy about sharing your writings. You should be putting them into a book for all the world to read someday." He looked at her with pride, and with a burst of exhilaration, he said, "Someday you'll be a famous poet and I'll be a famous violinist, and people all over the world will read your poems and listen to my music. We'll be rich and live in an apartment in the sky in New York. We'll have lots of children to pamper and servants to take care of us. Our life here will be long forgotten."

Oops, he thought, realizing what he had said and how he must be sounding to her, but he couldn't stop himself. His excited utterances gave him the courage to blurt out, "You must know how I feel about you, Rachel. It must be obvious. Even Moses and Aaron have noticed the way we act toward one another. Sometimes Joseph teases me about it." He raised his eyebrows. His voice lowered. "They say you like me too." Simon looked into her eyes. He barely blinked. He decided he better stop talking before he sounded idiotic.

Rachel gave him a yearning look. She reached over and took his hand and squeezed it. "The war has interrupted our dreams. Let's wait to see what happens."

Simon could tell from her touch and the smile on her face she shared his feelings. From then on he knew their relationship had taken a turn. They were bound to one another, and this bond would help them get through the war together.

Twenty-Eight

Simon and Joseph were unloading crates when they heard someone running through the streets shouting. They looked up to see a frantic man rushing toward them, waving his arms.

"He's sick from hunger," Joseph said. "He's lost his mind."

"Let's go see," Simon said.

People stopped and gathered around the man. Simon and Joseph joined the crowd.

"The United States has declared war on Japan," the man said. He leaned forward, bracing his hands on his knees, trying to catch his breath.

"Give him room," someone said, waving the group back. People obeyed reluctantly.

When the man caught his breath, he told the gathering Japan had attacked Pearl Harbor, and the United States had declared war on that country.

"What about Germany?" a voice in the back said. "Did they declare war on Germany too?"

"No," the man answered.

Simon looked at Joseph. "My father lives in the United States." He said nothing else, but he wondered if the United States might soon enter the war and, if so, whether he and his father would meet as a result. Would his father be among the rescuers?

Three days later people ran through the streets of the ghetto announcing the United States had declared war on Germany. That night Simon had a dream.

American tanks were driving down the streets of the ghetto. The residents were in front of their houses shouting their praises to the American soldiers marching alongside and behind their tanks. A loudspeaker was calling Simon's name, telling him to come to the main gate. Simon ran as fast as he could. A soldier was standing at the main gate holding his cap. He was tall with blond hair. Simon stopped a few feet from the soldier and stared at him. There was a metal nameplate on the soldier's breast pocket. It read Sgt. Adrian Mazurek. He and the soldier ran to each other and embraced.

Twenty-Nine

On an early morning in June 1942, German military trucks entered the ghetto. Simon heard whistles blowing and German voices ordering everyone out onto the streets. SS guards entered every building to make sure residents obeyed. Some Jews hid, but German soldiers scoured every apartment, found them, forced them into the streets, and lined them up. They looked at each other scared as jackrabbits, not knowing what was going to happen. German Army officers began selecting people and pointing them to the trucks.

Simon watched as the soldiers pulled away older ghetto residents and children, those too old or too young to be of value to the Germans. The stronger ones the soldiers hadn't selected clung fiercely to those family members not yet yanked from the lines. Heart-wrenching cries rose from among those the occupiers had ripped away. Armed soldiers escorted them to the trucks. The bodies of the victims twisted back toward their relatives, their free arms stretched out, begging for those not taken to rescue them.

The rabbi stepped forward from the line too quickly for anyone to pull him back.

"What are you doing? Where are you taking these people? You can't separate families like this. Have you no hearts?" he said.

Two soldiers grabbed the rabbi's arms, holding him back. He started struggling.

"You have no right," he said. The rabbi's voice sounded thin and weak. Simon was frightened. With the Germans picking the frailest among them to export, Simon wished the rabbi hadn't called attention to himself.

A superior officer came to the rabbi. In a bone-chilling, disdainful voice that could only forecast trouble, he asked, "Who are you?" The officer looked down at him, his cold blue eyes expressing contempt. Simon closed his eyes and asked God to have the officer ignore the rabbi intervening and send him back to the line with only a warning.

"I'm Rabbi Rosenschtein. I'm in charge of this district."

The officer took out his gun. The soldiers holding the rabbi let go of him and stood aside, leaving the rabbi standing alone in front of the officer. Instinctively, Simon knew what was about to happen. He'd seen it all too often when he worked in labor crews. The German soldiers pulled out those who complained and shot them.

Everything passed before Simon in slow motion: the gun rising from the officer's holster toward the rabbi's head, the look of fear and foretelling on the rabbi's face as he turned toward his family, Simon's hand tightly grabbing on to Moses's coat and pulling him back to stop him from attacking the attacker, Moses's knees sinking against the pressure of opposite pulls, a shot ringing out, the bullet piercing the rabbi's head, and the screaming coming from all directions. The rabbi fell to the ground. Simon watched the red blood pooling on the asphalt. He felt he'd been trapped in a nightmare. He shook his head as if to wake himself. It was no dream.

"Take him away," the commanding officer ordered to the two soldiers who had been standing by.

Mechanically, they followed their orders. Each of them took hold of one of the rabbi's legs and dragged his body away as they would have a fallen tree.

"Anyone else want to say something?" the officer spit out as he walked back and forth among the lines of Jews standing in shock.

No one answered. The only sounds heard were sniffling, crying, moaning, and praying.

Simon clutched Moses's leaning body to prevent him from falling to the ground. He saw Rachel and Aaron on each side of their mother, holding her up by the waist. Tears were rolling down Rachel's cheeks. Mrs. Rosenschtein's face looked downward, her shoulders slumped, her knees buckled. Aaron's eyes were closed tightly. His mouth was open wide. His body was rasping for air.

They stood waiting as the soldiers selected more men, women, young boys, and girls to go on the trucks. A soldier stopped in front of Mrs. Rosenschtein.

"No!" Rachel said sharply, grabbing her mother's elbow and pulling her away.

The soldier smiled and grasped Rachel's chin. He rolled his tongue over his lips and leered at her. Simon wanted to go to her, protect her. He held back, ashamed of his own fear. He watched the soldier stare at her for a few seconds more and walk away.

When the soldiers had taken all those deemed unable to work, they gave orders for the trucks to be driven away. Those in the trucks cried out for their relatives left behind. Those left behind clung to each other weeping over the loss of their young children and older parents. Mothers and fathers, knowing their efforts would be futile, chased after the trucks only to collapse in profound sorrow as the vehicles outpaced them.

Moses, Rachel, Aaron, and their mother circled around each other, their heads together buried in grief. Moses lifted his head from the others. He put out his arm to Simon and beckoned him with his fingers. He drew him to them. Simon cried with them like he hadn't cried since he'd heard about Lena. The rabbi was his beloved guardian, his mentor, his moral compass. He loved him, and now he was gone. How were they to go on? For the first time, he wanted to murder a Nazi soldier, to take revenge for what they did to the rabbi.

Despite the prohibition on religious services, at least two dozen men, along with their wives, daughters, and sisters, arrived at the Rosenschtein apartment for Maariv, the evening prayer service, and the recitation of the Kaddish. Rachel explained to Simon this was a prayer said by those suffering recent and past loses. It was a prayer proclaiming the greatness of God. Men squeezed into the kitchen with the remainder settling in the hallway, shoulder to shoulder, and on the stairs. Women who came to lend support and comfort stood behind Mrs. Rosenschtein and Rachel in the hallway leading to the bedrooms.

Moses led the service. Aaron stood by his side. The brothers insisted Simon stand with them. Moses wore his father's tallit and yarmulke and held his father's prayer book. Simon observed the men were wearing clean shirts and pants. Their faces looked cleanly scrubbed, their hair and beards brushed. The women wore long black dresses. Simon was impressed with the outpouring of mourners. Despite what they had witnessed on the square earlier that day, they pulled themselves together to honor the rabbi's memory.

During the service Simon kept his head low, moving his lips, pretending to utter the Hebrew words said by the other mourners. When he saw their upper bodies rock back and forth as they prayed, he imitated their movements. He felt uncomfortable not knowing the words of the prayers. He hoped no one noticed his awkwardness.

Simon looked up toward Mrs. Rosenschtein and Rachel. Mrs. Rosenschtein clung to a handkerchief. Her eyes were red and sore looking. She wore a black sweater curled around her slim shoulders. Rachel was to her left, her arm around her mother's waist, their heads leaning into each other's. Simon remembered the feelings he had on the drive to the rabbi's, how he leaned from the back seat to place his head against his mother's while she cried into her handkerchief. He prayed he'd live to be reunited with his parents and hoped they were taking care of themselves.

After prayers Moses asked Simon to join the family in a line to greet people as they filed by to express their condolences. Mourners shook his hand and expressed their sympathy. They accepted him as part of the grieving family.

After everyone left, Mrs. Rosenschtein, exhausted, went to bed. Simon joined Moses, Aaron, and Rachel in the kitchen.

Rachel stared down at her clasped hands. "Poor Father. He didn't deserve to die that way."

"He died the way he lived, taking care of people," Moses said. He pounded the table, causing it to shake. "The Germans will not get away with this."

His anger made everyone jump.

Rachel's eyes went toward the bedroom. "Don't wake Mama," she whispered. "This day has been one of anguish. She needs to sleep."

Aaron stared down at the table. "At least he didn't suffer," he said. "We've seen so many suffer long, tormenting deaths."

Simon sat quietly. He felt out of place among the rabbi's children. They were saddened and hurting from the loss of the father they loved and respected. He wondered whom he'd have to share his grief with if one of his parents died. He watched and listened with envy to how they had each other to share their feelings. They had welcomed him into their family, even Moses, but it wasn't the same. He didn't share their history, their experiences with each other and with their father.

Soon their anger turned to remembrances.

"We could never fool him or make him angry, could we?" Rachel said.

Aaron smiled. "That's true. Remember when I snuck out during my bar mitzvah celebration and was late to dance the 'Hava Nagila.' He came looking for me. I was smoking outside the back of the synagogue with my friends. He sent everyone else back inside and told me I was a man now and should act like one. He told me to take my coat off and shake out the smell of cigarettes so Mama wouldn't be upset and to come back in. I'll never forget how scared and ashamed I was, but he never said another word about it."

"Really?" Rachel said. "I never knew about that."

"You were only eleven. Papa wouldn't have told you," Aaron said.

They each had comparable stories about how their father had rarely lost his temper with them, how he showed them off with pride at every religious and social occasion, and how he expressed his love for them freely.

Simon remembered when the ODs came to the apartment to question them about the robbery and the death of another police officer and how the rabbi stuck up for him and his sons. All the while, Simon felt the rabbi knew about their involvement but had protected them.

"You look deep in thought," Rachel said to Simon. "What are you thinking?"

"I'm envious of you," he said, looking around at them. "You have each other to share your grief with. My sisters are dead. If I lost one of my parents, I wouldn't have them to share my grief and stories with, like you do."

Rachel moved her chair closer to him and put her hand over his. She looked at her brothers. "We're your family now," she said. Her brothers nodded in agreement.

"Thank you," Simon said. "I loved your father too. When I found out I was Jewish, he was like a guardian angel to me. He was the only person I could talk with and ask questions I needed answers to. He was my lifeline. I know I can't feel the same loss you do, but I'm grateful for the way you've accepted me into your family."

The boys pulled closer to the table and reached over to Simon and Rachel. They all held hands in a moment of emotion and a display of unity that Simon felt he'd never forget.

Thirty

Each member of the family reacted differently to the rabbi's violent death. Moses seemed more irritable and defiant and spoke of retribution and joining the resistance. His eyes looked cold, his body tense. His fingers and arm muscles flexed as if he were ready to explode. Mrs. Rosenschtein became withdrawn, unable to concentrate on simple things like preparing meals, making her bed, and her appearance. Rachel's smile seemed false. The sadness in her eyes showed through. Aaron became quiet. He lacked pleasure in joking around. He developed stomach aches.

Simon was careful not to step on anyone's toes. He helped Rachel clean the apartment and prepare dinner. He listened to Moses's outbursts without judgment, realizing the pain Moses was feeling. He even said curse words to Aaron to make him laugh. He tried to control his own grief to hold the family together. He felt the same pain and anger, but, as an outsider, he felt it wrong to compete with their grief and tried to be helpful in whatever way he could.

One evening, after Moses and Aaron went to their room, Rachel expressed her concerns about Moses's anger and her fear he might do something rash. She asked Simon to look after him.

"He respects you after..." She didn't finish her sentence but reached out to put her hand on his arm. He knew she was referring to the night Simon lied to the OD and her father about their involvement in the death of another OD.

"I will," Simon answered. He didn't really think he could do much to control Moses, but he wanted to comfort Rachel.

When Simon returned to the bedroom, Moses and Aaron were in bed.

Aaron leaned up on his elbow, his hand behind his head.

"I see how you look at my sister," he said. "You like her, don't you? She likes you too."

Simon was glad the light was out so Aaron couldn't see him blush.

"It's late," Moses said sharply to Aaron. "Leave him alone. Go to sleep."

That night Simon lay on his back thinking about Rachel and how she had touched him. It hadn't been the first time. He smiled and turned over on his side. Aaron was right. He did like Rachel, more than Aaron realized. He had professed his feelings to her the night he read her poems. He respected her response, knowing from the touch of her hand, she felt the same.

Thirty-One

Simon was in the washroom in the apartment when he heard Rachel screaming. He, Moses, and Aaron ran to her.

Rachel was in her mother's bedroom leaning over Mrs. Rosenschtein, shaking her. "She's not moving. I can't wake her up," she said. She stepped aside to make room for Moses and leaned into Aaron. She covered her mouth with both hands. She was whimpering. Aaron put his arm around her. He and Rachel waited for Moses to speak.

Mrs. Rosenschtein's room was too small for all of them. Simon stood in the doorway, watching and waiting. All he could see was their backs.

Aaron turned to Simon and said, "Get Dr. Schoenfeld."

"Don't bother," Moses said. "She's gone. She must have died in her sleep. Get Rabbi Lieb. He'll know what to do. Don't tell the ODs. They'll just take her away. The rabbi will know the proper rituals. Hurry."

When Rachel turned, Simon could see her head lying on Aaron's shoulder. Her eyes were squeezed tight. Tears were falling down her cheeks. Her body was convulsing. It hurt him to see her in so much pain. She had lost her father recently, now this. He felt the grief of all three of the Rosenschtein children. He was grieving too. Mrs. Rosenschtein had become his mother away from home. He was grateful for her kindness and for treating him as if he were a family member. But he wasn't a blood relative. He was more like a cousin whom they needed to rely on to take care of matters to ease their burden. Right now, they needed the rabbi. This is where he had to direct his attention. He'd share their grief later, after he'd helped them take care of all necessary matters.

Simon ran as fast as he could to the next district and knocked on Rabbi Lieb's door. The rabbi answered, wearing his morning prayer shawl.

"Come quick, Rabbi. Mrs. Rosenschtein is dead. She must have died in her sleep."

"Give me a moment, son. I'll be right with you."

Simon stood waiting, lifting one leg, then the other trying to stay warm. He wished the rabbi would hurry. He envisioned the Rosenschtein children waiting in the kitchen, Rachel still in shock and crying, Aaron comforting her, and Moses trying to figure out how best to arrange for a proper burial. He wouldn't want their mother hauled away like their father.

When the rabbi returned, he and Simon walked briskly to the Rosenschteins' apartment.

Neighbors stood in the hallway and nodded to the rabbi when he walked in. The Rosenschtein children were waiting in the kitchen. Rachel was still in her nightgown and robe. She was clutching a blanket around her body. Her eyes were red and swollen. Aaron was sitting opposite her, his head down, his forearms on the table, his hands clasped. Moses was leaning against the sink, his back to it, his arms behind him, holding on to the ledge.

The rabbi went to each of them. "She was a wonderful woman, such a perfect wife to your father and a caring mother." Rachel burst out crying. The rabbi patted her back and said a silent prayer. When the rabbi walked over to Aaron, Aaron stood politely and thanked the rabbi for coming. Moses got right down to business. "She's in the bedroom," he said.

"Please take me to her," the rabbi said.

Moses did as the rabbi asked, then left him alone with his mother.

From the kitchen the four of them heard the rabbi quietly reciting prayers. When he came back to the kitchen, the rabbi said, "I suspect she died of a broken heart. She had a terrible shock when your father passed."

Moses narrowed his eyebrows and squinted. "You mean when he was murdered," he snarled.

The rabbi patted Moses's shoulder. "I'm obliged to notify the ODs."

Rachel, still crying, asked, "Where will they take her?"

"I suspect they'll take her to Plaszow and bury her with others from here who died at that camp," the rabbi said. Simon had heard rumors about the mass graves at Plaszow. *If she's buried there*, he thought, *her children won't have a tombstone to visit.* He thought of Katrina and his grandparents. Would he ever get a chance to visit their grave sites again?

Moses stood and placed his hands on his hips.

"Don't protest, Moses," the rabbi said. "She's gone now. She's at peace. That's probably where they buried your father. That's what she'd want. Protect yourselves."

Moses sat down. He covered his face.

Simon sat with Rachel and her brothers as they sat shiva for their mother that night. He saw how attentive Moses and Aaron were to their sister, how concerned they were for her fragility. At night Simon heard Moses tell Aaron how he would find a way to avenge the deaths of their parents. Moses had been coming home later nearly every evening after his father's death. Simon had wondered if he was involved in the ghetto's underground.

The Rosenschtein children and Simon sat shiva for only two nights. Then they went to their jobs. Moses urged Rachel to stay home, but she insisted on returning to work. She was the main provider of food.

Thirty-Two

In October 1942 additional deportations of Jews to the ghetto began. Each deportation resulted in a reduction of the area comprising the ghetto. As the area decreased, the ghetto became more crowded by the Nazis requiring Jewish residents from twenty-nine surrounding villages to move into its confines. This resulted in the Rosenschtein children and Simon being forced to share their apartment with two other families.

Conditions in the ghetto became more horrific. Food became scarcer. With no medical attention, people were dying of starvation and disease. Corpses lay on the streets, ignored. Body collectors and grave diggers became overworked and stressed from hunger and exhaustion. Simon passed beggars on the streets on his way to and from work and blessed the fact that he, Rachel, and her brothers were doing better than many others, thanks to Rachel continuing to work at the sewing factory and he and the boys keeping their work assignments. But the suffering of others wore on him, and he began to question how God could allow such things to happen.

In early December 1942, the Germans divided the ghetto into two parts. Ghetto A was for people able to work. Ghetto B was for everyone else. Rachel and her brothers lived living in ghetto A, now sharing an apartment with three other families. Soon the German invaders sent many of those remaining in the ghetto to the Belzec concentration camp.

THIRTY-THREE

On the morning of March 15, 1943, Simon was leaning against the wall outside the washroom of his apartment waiting for his turn to use the sink. He suddenly heard the shouts of German soldiers on the streets bellowing orders for everyone to quickly pack their personal belongings and gather outside. The shouts made him sick with foreboding. He turned to see Rachel run past. She was throwing a blanket over her shoulders.

She looked around and saw Simon. "Where are Moses and Aaron?"

"They're in line to use the outhouse," Simon answered.

Rachel looked scared and helpless. Her thin face was pale. Her worn hands fumbled at her hair. Simon felt as lost as she did. What new trouble had come to them?

Moses and Aaron came running in. "There're soldiers everywhere telling us to pack and come out to the streets," Moses said. "They have attack dogs with them."

"We didn't even get a chance to use the outhouse," Aaron said. "They chased us away and laughed at us. 'Let them mess their pants,' they said."

Soon the frenzy inside the apartment, resulting from occupants stepping over and around each other deciding what belongings to pack, drowned out the shouts of soldiers and barking dogs.

There was no time to hesitate. Simon grabbed his violin and bow and the pictures of his family and his birth mother. He put them in the flour bag his mother had given him to pack his bedding in. On top he threw in some clothes and all the papers

171

he'd collected, on which he'd written his compositions while in the ghetto.

Outside, families gathered in the streets. Parents with suitcases by their feet clung nervously to their children. Simon heard mothers comforting their crying babies, the quiet prayers of righteous men, and the murmurs and whispers of people speculating about what was happening. They'd heard rumors of the camps in the east and of the horrific conditions inside them. Simon wondered, in terror, if that would be his future.

When everyone had assembled outside, those SS officers with search dogs went into the apartments looking for hideouts. They announced they'd shoot anyone found concealing themselves. The Jews waited in the streets, guarded by other soldiers pointing rifles at them. One soldier dragged a nine-year-old girl out by her arm and threw her to the ground. Another soldier pushed the girl's mother to the street next to her.

One of the soldiers shouted to an officer, "They were hiding in a closet."

The officer ordered the two to get up. The girl's shoe had fallen off. She stumbled and gashed her knee.

The officer smirked. "Does anyone else want to try to escape?"

There was silence.

"Good," he said sharply. He ordered the two soldiers to take them away and shoot the mother and her daughter.

As the soldiers dragged them away separately, the mother begged, "No, please." She managed to stay on her feet. Simon watched her twist her body to see the guard dragging her daughter by her arm along the ground. The guard laughed as the girl's body scraped on the pavement.

Simon felt sick. He shut his eyes but couldn't shut out the cries of the girl screaming for her mother. He envisioned Katrina. He felt the fear she must have known in the instant before the soldier shot her on the square. He remembered the horror in Lena's eyes when he saw her behind their father as he held Katrina's limp body in his arms. Simon squeezed his eyes tight, trying to shake away these images. If only he could forget them.

The sounds of gunshots dragged him out of the past. He heard distant cries of other people begging the invaders to not slaughter them. The Germans pulled elderly people and anyone who looked sick or infirm from the lines and took them away in their trucks. Simon watched the enemy parading members of the Jewish Council and the Jewish Police past his cluster of ghetto residents. Their arms were raised in surrender as the soldiers escorted them toward the main gate.

Simon heard one soldier say to another, "These filthy Jews will be killed, so they won't be able to tell anyone how badly they were treated."

Hours later, other soldiers arrived to march the exhausted remaining Jews out of the ghetto gate into Plaszow Square, where more trucks waited to take them away.

Simon stood in line with Rachel and her brothers. Soon, soldiers packed them into a truck. It took them to the Krakow train station, where other vehicles were unloading prisoners. When Simon jumped down from his truck, he heard an SS officer tell the driver to return to the square and bring another load.

Moses uttered under his breath, "To them we're just a 'load.'"

"Quiet," Rachel whispered.

Simon, standing in front of Rachel, turned to see beads of sweat on her forehead. He turned back quickly when he heard a dog bark. His stomach felt as hard as a rock.

Soon, soldiers with truncheons led them to one of a lengthy line of cattle cars and told them to get in. Simon grabbed Rachel's suitcase and helped pull her up into the car. The soldiers had packed the car with people shoulder to shoulder, chest to chest. Mothers held their little children in their arms so they wouldn't suffocate. The boxcar lurched as it started to move, jostling the prisoners inside.

A woman cried out, "I've dropped my glasses. I've dropped my glasses. I can't see without them."

An unsympathetic voice responded, "Be quiet. There's nothing to see. It's pitch-black in here."

The occupants of the transport vehicle jostled against one another as it rattled over the rails. "Are you all right?" Simon quietly said to Rachel.

"I'm frightened," she said. "As terrible as life was in the ghetto, we knew what to expect. It's the fear of the unknown ahead that scares me."

Simon took her hand and squeezed it. "Remember our dreams. You're going to be a great poet one day and I, a concert violinist." He felt her squeeze his hand back. To stay calm, he repeated the words of his father: *You're strong. Be brave. Use your skills. Do what you need to survive. We will be together again. Do not give up hope.*

Rachel lowered her voice to a whisper. Still holding his hand, she said, "Your birthday is next week. You'll be eighteen. We've lived in the same house for two years. I've grown…" She didn't finish her sentence, but he knew she was trying to say how fond she was of him. It meant more than he could say, here in the dark with the unknown bearing down on them.

"I know," Simon said. "Me too."

They remained quiet in the car listening to the whimpering of women and children.

The train stopped. It was a short ride, and soon they heard the rattling of locks. The train car's door clanged open, letting in the cool March air and a flood of light.

Simon covered his eyes until he got used to the brightness. Voices shouted for them to get out. Soldiers pulled people down

and ordered them to assemble on the platform with their possessions. The soldiers used their sticks to prod their prisoners along.
People were stiff and had difficulty moving as quickly as ordered.
Simon looked around for Joseph. He hadn't seen him on the
square, but he hoped he'd been on another truck behind his and
placed in another cattle car.

There was pandemonium on the platform. Simon saw soldiers
beating people on their backs, buttocks, and heads. Dogs were
barking, whistles were blowing, and guards carrying rifles were
ordering the hundreds of people into groups. All Simon could
think about was to make sure he, Rachel, and her brothers weren't
separated. He waved his arms and called to them to stay together.

Up ahead was an arched metal gate with German words
across the top.

"What does it mean?" Rachel asked.

The sharp voice of a guard answered, "Work will set you free."

Simon laughed to himself at the irony. The Germans had
no intention of setting them free. He had watched people work
themselves for the Germans until they could no longer stand.
Then their overseers killed them. Death was their freedom.

Simon heard an orchestra playing as they neared the gate. He
recognized the music. It was a march by Mozart. The orchestra
at the music school had played it during a graduation procession.
He turned to Rachel. "How bad can this place be if they have
an orchestra to welcome us?" For an instant, despite everything
he had lived through, he thought he, Rachel, and her brothers
might be all right. Then he heard shrill whistles blowing. Up
ahead, guards dressed in black pointed women and children in
one direction and men in another.

"Leave your things here," a guard said. "They'll be taken care of."

Simon didn't want to leave his violin. His voice shaky, he told
the guard, "I'm a violinist. My violin is in my bag. I studied at

the Krakow School of Music. I'm good enough to play with that orchestra."

"Leave the bag here. We'll get it to you later," the guard insisted. "Move on, quickly."

Simon looked back at the sack marked "FLOUR." It was the only baggage like it among suitcases, bed sheets, and pillowcases tied together among whatever else the ghetto residents could find to quickly pack their possessions. He could only hope he'd get it back.

Simon realized he'd been separated from Rachel. Before he could speak up, Moses yelled out to the guard.

"You can't separate us. She's our sister."

"Move on," the guard said. "Everything will be all right. You'll meet later."

Simon saw Rachel's face as she turned her head back to look at him and her brothers. Her fear made him feel angry and helpless. His hands clenched into fists.

THIRTY-FOUR

The guards divided the men into groups. One took Simon, Moses, Aaron, and about hundred others to a large gallery where he told them to strip. A man in a prisoner's uniform shaved their heads and bodies.

Simon rubbed his hand over his bald head.

"Don't worry," the barber told him. "You have the hair of Hercules. It will grow back just as thick and strong."

Simon remembered the day he sat beside his grandmother and she rubbed her fingers through his thick wavy hair as she told him she didn't want to make him his Stars of David. He was glad she wasn't alive now to witness what was happening to him.

Next, guards took the prisoners to the showers and deloused and powdered them for lice. Simon stood naked alongside Moses and Aaron until someone brought them blue-and-white-striped, ill-fitting uniforms that looked like pajamas. Simon's pants were short and above his ankles. His jacket sleeves came to his thumb knuckles. On his jacket were two yellow and red triangles forming the Star of David. His jacket fit loosely. A guard handed him a cap that, without his hair, fell halfway down his forehead. The prisoners weren't provided socks to wear under the wooden clogs they were given in place of shoes. Simon looked at Moses and Aaron. Their clothes fit no better.

German guards then took the group to an area where men at desks wearing the same blue striped clothing asked them their full names, their dates of birth, what languages they spoke, and what skills they had. Guards weighed the prisoners, measured their height, and took mug shots of them. Finally, another prisoner tattooed them. Simon looked down to see six numbers embedded into his arm. *Am I just a number now?* One guard gathered all the information on each prisoner and placed it on a form. He pointed to a desk and told the detainees to present it to a uniformed guard standing nearby.

Simon, Moses, and Aaron stuck together in line. Another guard marched them to an area of brick and wooden barracks in the Birkenau Men's Camp of Auschwitz. Along the way Simon sniffed a peculiar odor permeating the air. He became less aware of the smell when he noticed other groups from their transport had arrived. His eyes searched to see if Joseph was among them. Simon recognized the other arrivals. They were primarily the younger, stronger men from the ghetto. It seemed to him there were half as many men here as had gotten off the railcars when they arrived at the camp. *Where are the other men? Where is Joseph?*

Simon worried about Rachel. Had women disappeared too? Would he, Moses, and Aaron see her again, as that one guard had promised?

An SS officer barked at Simon's group. Simon jerked to attention. The officer introduced two other men as special prisoners in charge of their daily activities. They reported to him. One of the two, a large, yellow-toothed man whose nose looked as if it had been broken more than once, gave them a stern look. He was their block elder, and it was his job to supervise their barracks to ensure all of them kept it clean, made their beds, and appeared for roll call on time. The other was a work supervisor, a capo, who would assign them jobs. He was of medium size, wore glasses, and blinked a lot.

Simon's stomach growled. Hours had passed since the Germans had rounded them up on the streets of the ghetto. *When are they going to feed us?* He felt Aaron's nudge, and he heard the SS officer say, "Does anyone play the violin?"

Simon's ears perked up. *They found my violin, and he wants to return it to me.* Simon raised his arm. "I do," he shouted.

"Come with me," the officer said.

Simon caught sight of his badge. His surname was Muller.

Simon walked behind SS Muller in silence. He felt awkward in his wooden clogs. Along the way he, again, became aware of the foul odor in the air. The officer led him to a different area near the barracks. There, they went into an office containing a desk and two chairs. A picture of Hitler hung on one wall, a mirror on another. The officer sat down behind the desk. He didn't invite Simon to sit. Simon looked around, hoping to see his violin and bow.

For a moment, the man didn't speak. Then he said, "Sit." Simon did as the officer instructed. "Tell me about your violin training," the officer began.

Simon told him he started private studies when he was five and later studied at the Krakow School of Music. He told the officer his goal was to be a concert soloist and a composer.

"The commander has asked me to find a violinist for the camp orchestra. I am not sure why. The orchestra plays mainly marches when the prisoners are sent out and return from their daily labor assignments. However, it is not my job to question him." The man's accent was thick, but he spoke formally and pronounced every word clearly, making it easy for Simon to follow his German. "What is your name?" Muller said.

"Simon. Simon Baron."

"Where are your parents now, Simon Baron?"

"They're in Krakow."

"How did they escape Auschwitz?"

"They're not Jewish, sir. My father is half German. They raised me since I was a baby. My biological mother died in childbirth. She was Jewish." Simon squirmed in his chair. He felt uncomfortable sharing information about his parents without knowing how the officer might use it.

"What about your real father?"

"He's a concert violinist in America." Simon hoped sharing this information would work to his advantage

The officer's eyes lit up. Simon saw the pleased look on his face. He decided not to reveal his true relationship with his father.

"What do your parents do in Krakow?"

"My parents own a bakery. I learned to make breads and pastries."

The officer picked up a pen and scribbled a note on a piece of paper from the pad on his desk. Simon took note of the pad. The bright white paper would be perfect for writing down compositions.

"I shall see to it the commander knows you are here and recommends the orchestra capo interviews you."

He put his pen down and scratched the underside of his chin.

"Perhaps you can assist me from time to time."

Simon tilted his body forward. "Oh! How so, sir?"

"I am in love with a young woman back in Germany. She is studying violin at the Leipzig Conservatory of Music. I would like to be able to impress her with a knowledge of the violin."

His eyes crinkled when he mentioned his woman friend. He sat straight in his chair with his hands folded on his lap. He looked loose and comfortable. Simon felt slightly more comfortable also.

Puzzled, Simon asked, "In what way?"

"We correspond regularly. I get a letter from her. I send one back. When she writes me what she is learning and playing, you can help me write back in a way that will make her appreciate my knowledge of music."

"Would I have time to meet with you if I were assigned to the orchestra? Would the commander approve?"

The officer leaned back in his chair and looked up to the ceiling. "We shall have to see."

The officer had spoken to him as if he were a good friend with whom he could share a confidence. As strange as it all was, Simon felt a spark of hope. Maybe the officer would sympathize with his feelings for Rachel, help him find her, if he made himself useful. Cautiously he said, "It would be helpful if I had my violin."

"Do not worry. We have many violins here. I shall find you one."

"I left mine on the platform of the train station along with the other luggage. Would you find that one for me? It would be easy. It's the only one that's in an old flour sack."

"I shall see."

Simon dared to push a little further. "I'd really appreciate it. There is also a picture of my family in the sack. Could you get that too?"

"I make no promises," the officer said. He rubbed a finger against his lower lip.

"I shall try to find your violin, but, if not, I shall find another."

"Thank you, sir. If you do find mine, please bring the pictures of my family too."

"You are a very brazen young man to ask this."

Simon froze. "I'm sorry, sir."

"Come, I shall walk you back and tell your work capo that the commander may want to have you transferred to the orchestra's barracks. With your background in baking, I shall see that you are assigned to the kitchen."

Simon's stomach rumbled loudly as he and the officer walked, the officer in front, Simon stumbling behind. He tried ignoring the growling. In the office, Simon had temporarily lost awareness of his hunger at the prospect of getting his violin and family pictures back. Now he couldn't stop thinking how badly he needed food. He became aware again, momentarily, of the strange odor in the air. He was about to ask the officer what it was when the officer said to him, "I shall see you get something to eat."

Thirty-Five

Back at the barracks, Simon found the men exchanging clothing to find more suitable sizes. Moses and Aaron came up to
him wanting to know what had happened between him and the
SS officer. Simon explained.

"So there's a chance we may be separated?" Moses said.

"It's up to the commander."

"What about his wanting to see you?" Aaron said

"He didn't say exactly. When he gets a letter, I think."

"Did you ask him if he would return the favor by helping you
find our sister?" Aaron said.

Simon swallowed. "Not yet. It wasn't the right time, but I
think he may be sympathetic once I prove I'm useful to him."

"How will you do that?" Aaron asked.

Simon lowered his head. "I don't know yet. I'll have to wait
until I see one of the letters he receives. I don't even know if I'll
see him much at all. I don't know how this stinking place works."

Moses ignored the frightened tone in Simon's voice.

"We can't wait that long," Moses insisted. "We've got to find
her now, to make sure she's all right." He pounded his fist into
his hand and walked away.

Simon felt the sting of Moses's disappointment. He should
have asked for the officer's help. He was as angry with himself
as Moses was. As soon as he could, he'd try to get the officer to
help find Rachel.

The block elder approached Simon. "Come with me," he said.

Simon followed him, wondering what was coming next.

183

The block elder led Simon to a small room in the front of the barracks. There were two metal-framed single beds separated by a lamp table. By the door were a desk, two chairs, and a metal file cabinet.

"This is where the work capo and I sleep. I sent for your lunch. It will come soon. In the meantime, I want to tell you the rules I've told the others." He motioned for Simon to sit. "The capo and I will wake the prisoners at four-thirty. You're to take care of your personal needs and make your bed and clean your area. You'll help clean the entire barracks with the others and then eat breakfast and be outside for roll call by five fifteen." The block elder was interrupted by a knock on the door.

"Come in."

Another prisoner entered with a tin cup of liquid and a piece of bread wrapped in paper.

The block elder jerked his head toward Simon. "Give him those and get out."

Simon took the cup and bread. He balanced the bread on his knees and took a sip of the liquid. He couldn't stop himself from making a face, nor could he tell what it was other than it was bitter and didn't appear to have any nourishment.

"Get used to it," the block elder said. "Eat while I finish."

Simon took another sip and ate the bread quickly. It was crusty and dry. He washed it down with the remaining liquid and tried not to make a face.

"Everyone will be assigned to labor and will be sent there after roll call," the block elder continued. "SS Muller has ordered you to work in the kitchen. The commander wants you to be interviewed by the capo of the orchestra. If he accepts you, you'll move there and not report to the kitchen until after roll call. Do you understand?"

Simon tried to take it all in. He would work in the kitch-
en. He could do that. And he'd have a chance to play his violin
again. One or both jobs might help him find Rachel if he was
careful and made no mistakes. "Yes, sir," he said. He'd ask Moses
and Aaron to fill him in on what he didn't remember.

"You're a lucky young man," the block elder said. "Officer
Muller has taken an interest in you. He wants me to look after
you. This may have gained you a longer life than you would have
had without his interest. Don't try to take advantage of me because of that. I'm still your boss while you're in this barracks. You
don't want the other prisoners to resent you because you get certain privileges. You treat me with the proper respect in front of
the others, and we'll get along fine." The block elder's voice had
an edge to it. Simon sensed his resentment. How was he going
to please him and SS Muller at the same time and not have his
barracks mates resent him?

The block elder sent Simon back to the prisoners' area, where
he met up with Moses and Aaron. They had saved him a place
next to them on the upper level of a three-tiered section of beds.
They'd be squeezed together in a space made for three people but
would have to sleep on their sides to fit. Their mattress, thin and
stuffed with straw, lay on a wooden board. Their brick barracks
held up to 180 prisoners. Simon could see the holes and spaces
in the roof where the sky was visible. This barracks was one of
several similar buildings surrounding theirs.

Simon frowned and said, "Why did you choose the top level?
It'll pour in when it rains."

Aaron shook his head. "Would you rather get peed or vomit-
ed on? That's what would happen if we slept down below."

Simon sighed heavily. He was right. He looked around.
"Where's the bathroom?" he asked.

The brothers took him outside to the back of the barracks, where there were long boards with holes in them set above trenches for them to use.

"The block elder said sinks and toilets will be built in some barracks by next year," Moses said. He shrugged his shoulders. "In the meantime, this is what we have."

Simon forced a smile. "I lived with your stink for two years. I can survive a little while longer."

Simon and the two brothers had lost track of time. The guards had taken their watches from them when they'd arrived. Their capo came in and sounded a gong for roll call. They went outside and lined up along with the other men in the barracks.

Once again, the prisoners stood in rows of five while their block elder counted them. There was confusion among the prisoners, resulting in a second roll call. When during that roll call a prisoner failed to respond, the counting started over. This process took two hours before the block elder felt his count was accurate. The block elder told the barracks group the capo oversaw labor assignments and would announce their assignments during roll call the next morning. He dismissed them for dinner, which consisted of a cup of soup and a piece of black bread.

They had free time until nine o'clock. Simon and the brothers talked with other barracks prisoners about their experiences earlier in the day and what they thought might happen next. Fear hung over everyone. Many of the men had wives and children from whom they'd been separated. They worried whether they'd get to see them. Moses, Aaron, and Simon made a pledge their foremost goal would be to locate Rachel.

A gong announced the nighttime silence. The three young men climbed up to their sleep area. Simon felt Aaron's breath on the back of his neck and the wiggling of his bunkmates trying to get comfortable. He couldn't let his body relax. The stresses of the day left his shoulders tight. His feet were sore from wearing wooden shoes without socks. His mind filled with uncertainties. *Where is Rachel? Is she safe? Will we find her?* Those thoughts came first, but then his mind went to Joseph. *Did he make it through?* And more ominously, *what did the block elder mean I might have a longer life because of SS Muller's interest in me?* Simon tried not to follow that train of thought too far, but everything he had seen in Auschwitz up to now made it easy to guess what might happen to him and all the others here. His last thoughts were of his parents. *Do they know about the ghetto's deportation? They must be terribly worried about me.* Exhausted mentally and physically, he fell asleep.

THIRTY-SIX

The first gong rang at four thirty the next morning, as promised. The capo called Simon to his room.

"Officer Muller left this for you," he growled. He handed Simon a well-worn violin and bow. Simon looked them over. He was disappointed they weren't the violin and bow he'd brought in his flour bag. This meant he wouldn't get his photographs back.

The thought of being separated from Moses and Aaron frightened Simon. How would he manage here alone without them? After it settled in, Moses and Aaron had acted as though they were glad to hear Simon's news. He could tell, though, that they, too, were sorry about the possibility of his moving away from them. He was helping them tidy up their sleep area when he heard his name called. A barracks mate pointed to Simon.

A young man who looked to be in his mid-twenties, dressed in clean and fitted striped prisoner's clothing, came to him.

"Hurry," he said, sounding winded. "The maestro has sent me to bring you to the music barracks."

Simon's chest tightened. He gave a darting look toward Moses and Aaron, worried about being separated so soon from the only two people he felt safe with. Simon shrugged his shoulders. He went to the capo's room, retrieved his violin and bow, and followed the man.

Along the way, Simon learned the name of his escort was Michal Galecki. He was one of the orchestra's flute players. He assisted the conductor in indoctrinating new members into the camp orchestra and helping them learn the orchestral arrangements.

In the music barracks, Michal took him to a small room like the capo's and block elder's room in his barracks. Then he left.

A tall man with rimless glasses and dressed in a well-fitting, pressed prisoner's uniform rose to greet him. His head was shaven, with a hint of a fresh growth of blond hair. His left eyebrow was separated by what looked like a scar. The man didn't appear quite as gaunt and pale as the other prisoners. Before he said a word, the man lifted his wrist to look at a round gold-rimmed watch with a brown leather band.

This man must have special privileges, Simon thought.

With a wide smile, the man said, "You're the one the commander wanted me to see?"

Simon held up his instrument. "Yes, sir."

"What's your name, son?"

Simon was surprised by his friendly tone. "My name is Simon Baron."

"Where are you from, Simon?"

"From Krakow, sir."

"Where did you study the violin?"

"I studied at the Krakow School of Music under Professor Kaminski."

"I studied at the conservatory in Vienna a while back. I'm the conductor of our little orchestra. As such, I'm also the capo of our barracks. My name is Borys Zubek, but the musicians call me Maestro. The commander seems to prefer it." He offered his hand to Simon, and Simon shook it. The conductor had a firm grip.

How different this man spoke to him compared to the capo and block elder in his barracks, Simon thought. Could he dare let his guard down and relax?

The conductor looked at his watch again.

"We're getting ready to line up to play for the prisoners as they march off to their assignments," he said. "There's coffee and a tray of bread in the barracks. Grab some. Then, when I give the signal, take your violin and bow, and go to the end of the line. You may not be familiar with what we play. Just pretend you're playing. We don't want the Germans to think you're in the musicians' barracks under false pretenses and drag you away. I'll try to keep you alive for as long as possible. We'll talk later." Simon's body stiffened as the smile faded from the man's face.

I'll try to keep you alive. The words sent a shiver up Simon's spine. This was the second time in two days his superiors had intimated the length of his life might be related to his musical abilities. He could easily imagine what might happen to him in this place if he couldn't make the Germans believe in his skill on the violin.

Soon Maestro gave instructions to get in formation. Simon stood behind the other musicians as he'd been told. Their leader stood in front holding up his baton. Simon kept his eyes on the man who, right now, was his best and only hope for survival, next to Muller.

Maestro called out the title of the march they were to play. The musicians paraded toward the stage, passing capos barking out orders to their labor crews to line up for their departures to work assignments outside of camp.

Once on the bandstand, the orchestra played ceaselessly while capos counted their prisoners. Simon did his best to make it look like he was playing along with the orchestra by pretending to move his bow across the strings and press the fingerboard. He felt he could have joined in and played his violin during certain pieces, but he thought it best to follow Maestro's instruction. An officer, dressed in a more commanding uniform than the others, periodically walked over to the stage and spoke with Maestro. He held a club behind his back and tapped it against his free hand to the music. Simon caught the conductor's eyes as he looked at him and nodded vigorously each time the man approached. He wasn't sure why, but he took this as a sign to make it look as if he were participating in the playing.

Two hours later, capos and labor foremen escorted their prisoners to their assignments. The musicians, back in their barracks, changed into their work clothes and went to their labor assignments. Maestro asked Simon to stay behind to meet with him in his room.

"Well, Simon, what do you think? How was it for you?"

"Fine, sir," he answered, but he was feeling nervous, sickened. The entire morning experience was tiring and frightening to watch. He didn't feel comfortable participating in a charade, watching beaten-down, weakened men being sent off to hard labor assignments while the orchestra played upbeat marches and other up-tempo music. Even from his place in the back row of the orchestra, he could see the disdainful looks given to members of the orchestra by other prisoners as they passed by them on their way out the gate and the woeful eyes of those he suspected might not return.

"You don't have to pretend with me, son. You can be frank."

Simon cautiously accepted the man's invitation. "It was uncomfortable, Maestro."

"Yes, it can be tiring standing there for two hours with nothing to do. Once we get you playing, time will go by faster. It won't seem as bad."

Simon took a chance. "That's not what I meant, sir."

"Oh?" Maestro tipped his head to the side.

"I saw the looks on the men's faces as they were leaving camp. I felt like I was betraying them. I was used to playing for appreciative audiences, people who wanted to hear music. Today I felt like I was participating in something evil, like marching men off to brutal work." Simon looked down at his entwined fingers.

Maestro leaned in. His face turned serious. "I'll let you in on a little secret, Simon. I'm not convinced most prisoners find courage in our music. To many it's downright annoying, and they despise the orchestra for it. But I'm told by others the sounds of the orchestra as they're returning to camp have inspired them to stay alive, that our music is like a marker they have survived another day, and they should not give up."

Simon looked up. "I'd like to think that's true, but I remember how I felt deceived when I heard music playing when I arrived outside the gate and then what happened inside." He rubbed his hand across his shaved head. "I don't like feeling my music will be used to deceive people."

"You're not unlike me and the other musicians in our little orchestra, Simon. We've all studied to have our music appreciated, but we're here now, and we're all doing our best to survive. Being in the music barracks gives us a better chance than most."

"How's that, Maestro?"

"You saw that man who kept coming up to me at the bandstand? He's the commander here. It was his idea to start this orchestra. He wants the orchestra to learn marches by Karl Obrecht. Obrecht made use of the violin. When he learned from Muller you were here, he had you sent to me. Because of him, if you work hard, don't antagonize anyone, and stay healthy, you might survive this place. You'll eat better, sleep on a firmer mattress, and wear cleaner and warmer clothes than the other prisoners."

Simon took this in. He felt guilty he'd get better treatment than Moses and Aaron, but being here might give him a better chance of finding Rachel.

Maestro motioned for Simon to stand. "Play something for me. Let's hear what you've got to offer."

"I just received this violin. I haven't had a chance to see if it's tuned."

Maestro nodded. "That's OK. Try it."

Simon stood and played a selection he had composed in the ghetto on the day he and Joseph heard the United States had entered the war. He wrote it to convey the excitement generated by the news among the ghetto's residents, who'd been longing for rescue. It ended with emotions expressed in a poem called "One Day When We Are Free," written by a ghetto resident to his children and read in the square the night of the news. Simon included the range of emotions he expected to feel upon the prospect of meeting his American father.

The beginning of the piece was joyous, with a tempo representing people dancing in the streets of the ghetto and singing their praises of American soldiers. The tone turned mellow, somewhat nostalgic, representing pieces of the lives of the ghetto residents that had been lost to them: their enjoyment of being with relatives, now missing, the taste of good food, the freedom to walk in their old neighborhoods, and the laughter that had once flowed from their hearts. Simon's inner turbulence about meeting his birth father appeared through the erratic sounds arising from the scratching of the bow across the strings. The piece ended with a lower pitch, implying a darker, sad, and more serious tone representing whether all that the residents had been hoping for could come true soon enough to save them.

"That's pretty good, Simon. Full of emotion, quite a range. You're right. The instrument can use tuning. You can work on that here tonight."

"Here? Tonight?" Simon gasped.

"Yes. I'd like you to move into this barracks tonight. I'll tell your capo at the other barracks. You can leave your violin here now and head over to the kitchen for your detail. I'll write a note to the kitchen capo to expect you after roll call each day and ask him to release you two hours early so you can come back with the other musicians to get ready for the prisoners' return. I'll see that Michal assigns you a bed."

Maestro stretched his arms behind his neck and leaned back in his chair. "Think of ways a violin can fit into a march. I'll go over marches by Karl Obrecht with you. Are you familiar with him?"

Simon shook his head.

Maestro adjusted his glasses and said, "I've got a few of his recordings. We'll listen to them later. We can show you off and give a bit more class to our marches."

The prospect of the conductor separating him from Moses and Aaron, and the promise of participation in the orchestra with like-minded people, scared and excited Simon.

Thirty-Seven

Simon felt dazed as he left the music barracks to report for kitchen duty. He reminded himself how careful he must be, how he must make no mistakes, no matter how much fear came over him. The thought of finding Rachel became his primary focus among all the other thoughts roaming around in his mind.

At the kitchen Simon introduced himself to the capo in charge. He was a tall, thin man with pencil-thin eyebrows and equally thin downturned lips sitting on a triangular-shaped face. He had the bluest eyes Simon had ever seen. They were the color of a cloudless sky on a perfect day. His shirt bore an inverted green triangle designating him as a convicted criminal, the same as Simon's barracks capo. He introduced himself as Klaus. Simon learned the police had arrested him in Poland before the arrival of the German Army. He had murdered his boss when the boss had caught him stealing. Following a guilty verdict, the court sent him to prison. He had worked in the prison kitchen before the Germans had invaded Krakow. The Germans sent him to Auschwitz.

Klaus told Simon they were in the process of making supper for the prisoners. He told Simon to grab a tin cup of soup and two slices of bread and eat before starting to work. Simon forced down two cups of watery soup and the bread. His bread was warm, as if recently out of the oven. The liquid was bitter, like the day before. He saw two of the bakers take a slice of bread for themselves and eat while they worked. They had a small pad of butter on their worktable. He wondered how the rest of the prisoners, who received only a cup of bitter liquid and a piece of bread for breakfast, managed to get through their work details.

A young prisoner named Ezra, one of the bakers, introduced himself. "You're lucky they assigned you to work here. We get to eat some of what we make, more than the others." Then he whispered to Simon, "Sew pockets in the inside of your clothing, and you can take some back to your barracks for bartering."

He thought of Moses and Aaron struggling somewhere, tired and hungry. He'd find a way to take Ezra's advice, not to barter the food away but to give it to them.

Klaus put Simon to work preparing soup in large pots over gas stoves. Simon, though six feet tall, stood on a stool to reach deep in to stir the meager slices of potatoes, turnips, and grains that sank to the bottom. Prisoners wearing the camp's red and yellow Star of David worked alongside Simon. Others sliced vegetables very thinly. Simon noticed one sneaking small pieces to eat as he sliced.

On the other side of the kitchen, men were rolling dough to make bread. There were eight ovens, larger than the ones in Simon's parents' bakery. There was a line of stoves along the back wall, where men were cooking sausage. Simon learned the prisoners would occasionally get a small piece of sausage for dinner along with their piece of bread and soup. Sometimes they might get a slice of cheese or jelly. He found himself thinking of the pastries he'd learned to make with cheese and jelly. Could he put that skill to use here, make something Klaus would appreciate?

The cooks and bakers alternated taking breaks for their lunch. The kitchen was hot and steamy. Klaus left the two doors to the kitchen open to bring in the cool outdoor air.

"It gets hotter here in the summer," Ezra said when he saw Simon wiping his brow on his shirtsleeves, "but it's better than sweating out in the fields or digging ditches."

Another, who had earlier introduced himself as Andrew, said, "Or working at the crematoria."

Simon tilted his head. "Crematoria?"

His mouth falling open, Andrew said, "You don't know about the crematoria? How long have you been here?"

"Since yesterday."

"I don't want to be the first to tell you," Andrew said. "Let someone else explain it."

"No, please," Simon said, grabbing Andrew's arm. "I want to know." What other horrors might be in store for him, Rachel, and her brothers, he wondered.

"All right but move away from the food. We don't need you throwing up in here."

Simon moved away from the stoves to the open kitchen door. Andrew told him how the camp administration sends half the arriving prisoners to their death in gas chambers.

"They burn their bodies in the crematories," Andrew said. "That doesn't include the prisoners who die daily of starvation, exhaustion, disease, murder by guards, and by suicide. That unbearable stench you smell in the air is bodies burning."

Is it the smoke of burning bodies I've been breathing since I got here? Simon thought. His stomach turned inside out. He clamped a hand over his mouth and ran out into the open yard. He started retching, bringing up the little he had eaten.

Andrew came up beside Simon and handed him a wet towel.

Simon wiped his face. "My girlfriend was in the same deportation as me. The guards separated us when we came through the gate. I'm hoping to find her. You've scared me."

Simon bent over, barely able to catch his breath. He could hear his heartbeat thrashing. He felt dizzy. His legs weakened. His body collapsed on him, and he fell to the ground clutching his arms around his belly. *No. no, God. Not Rachel, please, not Rachel.*

Andrew stayed outside with him. He tried to comfort Simon. "If she's as young and as valuable to the Nazis as you, she's most likely safe. Try not to worry. What's her name?"

Simon was breathing so hard he could barely get out her name. "Rachel, Rachel Rosenschtein," he sputtered.

"We'll ask around when we get to see the women. They can help us find her for you," Andrew said.

Klaus came out and told Andrew to get back in the kitchen or he'd have him replaced.

"I need workers, not slackers. Either you can manage the job or not. The only reason you are here is because SS Muller told me to take you," he said to Simon. "If you prefer, I can send you to the coal mines. You can play your violin for the workers there."

It took all of Simon's strength to pull himself together. If he had any hope of finding Rachel, if she were still alive, he had to be sure to retain his privileged place here. His voice shook as he apologized and promised Klaus he would work hard. Numbly, he followed Andrew back into the kitchen, fear and sickness still in his throat.

Thirty-Eight

Later, Klaus sent Simon back to the music barracks to prepare for the return of the prisoners. His work in the kitchen had stained and wrinkled Simon's clothes, and his breath smelled like vomit. The musicians in the barracks backed away from him. They were more sympathetic when he told them why he smelled.

Michal called Simon to his bed and held out a tube of toothpaste. He told Simon to take a small dab of it on his finger. "Brush your teeth and your tongue. I'll ask Maestro to get you toothpaste and a toothbrush," he said. "The commander likes the orchestra to look and smell nice when he visits. Maestro looks to me to make sure we all meet the commander's expectations."

Michal put his hands on his hips and looked Simon over. "We can't have you looking wrinkled like that on the bandstand. Just hide as best you can in the back tonight. I'll ask Maestro if I can take you to the clothing storeroom tomorrow to get you a set of clean clothes. You'll have one for your kitchen work and a clean one for the band."

Simon saw the other musicians changing their spotted and tattered clothes for clean, neatly pressed uniforms. It seemed as if everyone had a special set of clothes for their orchestra performances.

The musicians lined up, marched to the stand, and waited for the gate to swing open for the returning prisoners. By the time all detachments had returned and the capos had taken roll call, it was seven o'clock. The musicians got into formation and returned to their barracks to change back into their work clothes and eat dinner. Simon saw the older men had difficulty changing. Their fingers fumbled with their buttons, and they had to prop themselves against their bedposts so they could put on their pants. Simon observed two musicians asking their barrack mates to help them change their tops. The little nourishment they'd eaten during the day wasn't enough to sustain them for such long hours. Simon knew he was lucky to have eaten a better midday meal.

Soon Klaus appeared with someone Simon hadn't met. They rolled in a metal cart with a container of soup and a tray of black bread and another of sausage. They left, saying they'd return in half an hour. There was enough for each member of the orchestra to have two cups of soup, two pieces of bread, and a full piece of sausage. Simon saw fellow musicians who worked outside the camp's gate hide a portion of their dinner in their clothing. He assumed they were hiding this away for their lunches the next day. By the time Klaus and his helper came to take the cart back, the musicians had consumed everything on the cart. Simon saw what Maestro said was true. The orchestra seemed to receive more food than other prisoners, at least from his experience in the other barracks, but even at that, was it enough to sustain the older ones and those who had more arduous work assignments where they might not receive an afternoon meal?

Before curfew, Simon got permission from Maestro to see Moses and Aaron.

Moses lowered his head to Simon. "The camp may send us to work at a nearby factory. There are separate barracks for the men who work there. They haven't made it certain, but there's that possibility."

Simon knew that meant he might completely lose contact with Moses and Aaron. He stared down at his hands. His chest ached, but he looked up again and forced himself to speak cheerfully. "I've got some good news," he said. "The men in the kitchen have contacts in the women's barracks. They're going to help me find Rachel." He tried to make it sound like a certainty. "My capo is sending me to the clothing department to get a set of clean clothes for the orchestra. I'll ask someone there if anyone knows of Rachel. With her experience sewing at the Gruber factory, the camp may have assigned her to something related. I promise I'll ask my SS officer to help me find her too."

Moses looked into Simon's eyes. "I was cruel to you when you came to live with us, but you've become like a brother." He turned to Aaron. "Right?" he said.

Aaron nodded and placed his hand on Simon's shoulder.

"Take care of yourself," Moses said. "Find Rachel and tell her we're all right and to be brave. We'll find each other, if not here, when this is over. Tell her our mother and father are watching over us. We must survive for them."

The three embraced. "Shalom aleichem, our brother," Moses said. "Until we meet again, be safe."

Simon's shoulders drooped. "Aleichem shalom, my brothers. Peace unto you," he said.

Simon walked back to the music barracks with his head hung low. His steps dragged. He didn't know how much more loss he could stand, but Moses and Aaron had called him brother, and he had a responsibility to find their sister. He promised himself again he would find Rachel and give her their message.

In the music barracks, Michal led Simon to a bed designed for three prisoners for him to have to himself. "As more prisoners are assigned to the barracks, you'll have to share space."

Simon sat alone for a while, not wanting to talk with anyone. He wanted to savor the moment he had with Moses and Aaron. Their words gave him an additional reason to survive. Tomorrow he'd go to the clothing room and try to find Rachel.

Thirty-Nine

The next morning, after the last detachment left for work and the band members were preparing to head to their work assignments, Michal took Simon to get a set of clean clothes.

On the way to the clothing room, Simon told Michal about Rachel and how much he wanted to find her. He said he thought her capo in the women's section might have assigned her to the sewing room. Simon was speaking with the hope the SS had spared Rachel from the crematoria.

"We'll need to stop at the sewing room to get your Star of David sewn on your new clothes," Michal said. "You'll get a chance to find out if she's there."

The clothing room was a large storage area that held uniforms for men and women prisoners.

"The clothes are made in workshops at other camps and sent wherever they're needed to dress new prisoners," Michal said to Simon.

Simon tried on several combinations of pants, jackets, and caps before finding a set that fit nicely. Then, holding on to his new orchestra clothes, Simon followed Michal to the sewing room. Simon's heart pounded with a mixture of hope and fear. *What if I see Rachel? Will I recognize her? Will she recognize me without my hair? Will her supervisor allow us to talk to each other?* He didn't know which was more frightening, her being there but not knowing him or her not being there at all.

They stopped in front of a solid gray door, and Michal knocked. Simon closed his eyes and inhaled deeply. A female voice told them to enter.

When they stepped in, Simon saw a group of women leaning over sewing machines. The buzzing of the machines filled the air. All he could see of the women were the backs of their heads covered in kerchiefs. He couldn't tell if Rachel was there.

One of the women appeared to be the supervisor. She moved from machine to machine, eyeing the work at each. She seemed to recognize Michal and nodded. When she headed over toward them, one of the girls turned to watch her. Others turned also. Simon studied each of their faces and looked for their reactions. They turned back to their sewing machines and continued their work. Disappointment settled on him.

Another worker raised her hand and turned toward the door. Her eyebrows lifted, and her mouth opened.

Simon gasped. He nearly dropped his new clothes. He squeezed his eyes shut and opened them slowly to make sure he was seeing what he hoped he was seeing. Yes. It was Rachel.

"That's her," he whispered to Michal.

When the supervisor to came to him, Michal said, "This young man is in love with that girl. He's been searching for her. I think they'll each be more productive for us if we let them speak briefly."

Rachel's supervisor hesitated, then nodded and said, "Take them into the hallway, but you're responsible for them. I'll give them five minutes, no more. Leave the young man's clothes. I'll get his star sewn on."

The supervisor beckoned Rachel to them. Michal took Simon and Rachel out into the hallway and gave them space.

Simon and Rachel embraced.

Simon could hardly believe this was real. He put his arms around Rachel to feel her warmth and closeness. She embraced him back. He was thankful and almost brought to tears, but he managed to say, "I've been so worried about you. I promised your brothers I'd find you. Now I can tell them I have and you're safe."

"I've been worried too. I feel so much better knowing you're all right."

They didn't have much time. Reluctantly, Simon let her go and stepped back so they could see each other.

"Your hair," Rachel said. "Your beautiful hair."

Simon felt his shaved head. "They're trying to humiliate us, but we mustn't let them, Rachel. Your brothers told me to tell you to be brave and to be strong, that your parents are watching over you, that you must survive for them. My parents have said the same to me. Your brothers, you, and I will be together when the war is over." As he had found Rachel, this now seemed possible.

Rachel lowered her eyes. Simon saw her rub away a tear. He wanted to hold her and comfort her. She reached for his hand. His body filled with the pleasure of closeness as it had so many times before when she touched him. He couldn't speak. She broke the silence.

She tried to sound cheerful, he thought, when she spoke. "What have they assigned you to do?"

He did his best to match her high-spiritedness. "They've put me in the orchestra, and I work in the kitchen. That's our flute player." Simon nodded toward Michal. "He's helping me get adjusted to being in the orchestra. He's a good man. So is the orchestra's conductor. The kitchen capo I'm not so sure about, but I get to eat a little better working there. There's an SS officer who's taken an interest in me. He wants me to help him correspond with his girlfriend who's a violin student at the Leipzig Conservatory. But I'm talking too much. What about you?"

Simon wanted to hear about Rachel's duties, how she was holding up, whether she was getting enough to eat, but Rachel's supervisor came back into the hallway with Simon's clothes.

"Go back inside now," she said to Rachel.

Simon ached as Rachel let go of his hand. Their eyes remained on each other until she was inside the room and the door closed.

Simon took his clothes from the supervisor and followed Michal out. He couldn't wait to see Moses and Aaron after evening roll call to tell them he had found Rachel and she was safe.

Henry gave Simon a soft pat on the back. "Are you feeling better now?"

Simon nodded. "Thank you. Thank you for being kind to me."

"You're welcome. Do your best, and we'll help each other. Don't forget, you've got to become familiar with the music we play. I understand the commander has a special interest in a composer who makes use of the violin. Maestro wants to get together with you tonight to go over that as well as our normal repertoire. He wants to have you noticed as a contributing member of the band, or he fears you'll wind up in the kitchen full-time or worse."

"Don't worry," Simon said. "You can assure him I have an excellent memory. I'll learn quickly."

FORTY

When they returned to the kitchen door, Simon handed Michal his new clothes to put on his bed to wear for evening roll call. He apologized to Klaus for being away so long. "I had no control over it. I'll work extra hard right now to make up for it. Where do you want me?"

"Today we'll assess your bread making to see if you're as good as you say you are," Klaus said, his face twisted with skepticism. "Go over to the ovens. Ezra will get you started."

Simon felt he could do anything at that moment. He had found Rachel. She was well and had been given a safe job, one that wouldn't strain her body. Her supervisor had been cooperative with his capo in allowing them to have time together, as short as it was. His body felt light. For the first time in three days, he was free of the fear and anxiety that had taken over him not knowing where Rachel was. He walked over to the ovens. Ezra showed him where to find the ingredients to prepare the dough.

"You found Rachel, didn't you?" Ezra said.

"Yes. How did you know?"

"You're humming while you knead the dough, and you're being gentle with it. Most of us pound down hard on it as if it were the camp commander's head."

Simon's eyes widened. "She was in the sewing room, where I hoped she would be. She's safe and won't have to work too hard. I feel relieved, happy, light as a feather."

"Enjoy it while it lasts," Ezra said.

Simon ignored Ezra's warning. "Get me jelly and butter. I'm going to make jelly pastries for us all to celebrate."

Klaus was impressed with Simon's loaves of bread. He was more impressed with the pastries. With the ingredients Klaus allowed him, Simon made two for Klaus and four for the staff to cut up and share among themselves. He got no sneers from Klaus when he left early for band.

Later, after roll call, he sought out Moses and Aaron. Simon was told by their capo they had been transferred to the Monowitz concentration camp, where they'd be working at the Bauer Chemical Company plant.

"What's that?"

"It's a chemical plant. Among other things they make the gas for the gas chambers. The Germans lease prisoners to the company. It's still part of Auschwitz, but in another area about six miles from here."

Simon cringed at the idea of Moses and Aaron being located to another camp, especially one with such a sinister purpose. For a little while, since finding Rachel, Simon had almost let himself forget about the horrors that surrounded them all. Now it tightened around him again. He asked his former capo, "Will I be able to see them?"

"Probably not very often, if at all."

Simon turned away. He walked back to his barracks with his eyes fixed on the ground. He wanted to cry out, bang his fists on something, but he could only pray to God to look after Moses and Aaron. *What am I going to tell Rachel?*

He spent an hour before lights out listening to music by Obrecht with Maestro that included the violin, but he had a hard time concentrating.

Forty-One

Simon had no time to dwell on his latest loss of Moses and Aaron. He had to keep up with his work, and he had the hope of seeing Rachel as often as he could. Plus, Maestro needed him to help expand the camp orchestra and learn new repertoire requested by the commander. "I want to save other men from the worst of the camp work. I need your help to do this," he'd said to Simon.

The next evening Simon met with Maestro again to practice an Obrecht march that made use of the violin. Simon played along with a recording of the march on a player the commander had given Maestro.

As he practiced, someone rapped on the door. Simon's chair was blocking the entrance. With his back to the door, he moved over to allow whomever it was to enter.

A voice came from behind him. "Excuse me, sir, but my capo sent me to see you. He thinks I could be useful to the orchestra."

Simon couldn't believe his ears. He knew that voice. He spun around in his chair and jumped to his feet. He forgot about the new march and the orchestra. "No!" he exclaimed. "It can't be true."

But it was. It was Joseph. Simon had thought he might never see his friend again. With his violin in one hand and his bow in the other, he went to Joseph and threw his arms around him.

"When did you get here?" Simon asked. "Who's with you?" His joy wouldn't let him stop speaking long enough to listen to Joseph's answers. "Are you all right? I've been looking for you, hoping I'd find you."

When Simon let go of him, Joseph caught his breath and grinned. "I was hoping I'd find you too. Your transport was a day ahead of ours." His eyes sparkled and gleamed with delight. "I didn't know whether we'd be taken to the same place or not."

Simon turned to Maestro. "This is my best friend, Joseph. He plays the piccolo. He'd be great for the orchestra."

Maestro cradled his chin. "A piccolo player," he mused. "We could use a piccolo player. Obrecht frequently used the piccolo in his marches."

Joseph's eyebrows raised. "I learn quickly," he answered.

"He does," Simon said. "I can vouch for him."

"That's good enough for me," Maestro said to Joseph. He stopped to write something on a piece of paper. "Take this to your capo. It's a note telling him to transfer you here tonight. If he has any questions, tell him to come see me. Tomorrow after roll call, I'll have Michal, my assistant, take you to the Kanada warehouse to see if they've found any piccolos among the newcomers' belongings. While you're there he might as well take you to the clothing room and get you spare clothes for the orchestra." The conductor turned to Simon. "I can see you're too excited for me to get any more work out of you tonight. Go off with your friend. Enjoy your reunion but be prepared to work harder tomorrow."

Simon thanked Maestro and walked Joseph to his barracks. On the way, they chatted as exuberantly as boys in school. Simon thought of something. "While you're at the Kanada, see if you spot my flour bag. There's a framed picture of my family inside. My violin's in there too. Maybe you or Michal can sneak them out for me." Then he added the best news of all. "Rachel is working in the sewing room. When Michal takes you there to get your star sewn on your new clothes, he might be able to arrange for you to talk to her."

Joseph's eyes widened. "Rachel? You've seen her? What about Moses and Aaron?"

"Yes, I've seen Rachel," Simon said. "Michal asked her capo to let us talk while my stars were sewn on." His delight faded. "I'm afraid Moses and Aaron have been moved to another camp. If you see Rachel, please don't tell her. She'll be upset. I'd rather tell her myself."

The next evening, after roll call, Simon found Joseph in the orchestra's barracks holding a piccolo.

"Look under your mattress," Joseph said.

Simon found his family picture folded into a square. When he unfolded it, the smaller picture of his biological mother fell out.

Simon stared at the pictures. Tears formed in the corner of his eyes. "How did you manage to find them?"

Joseph spread his hands. "Like you said, your flour bag stood out. The workers hadn't processed it yet." He patted Simon's shoulder. "Go see Maestro. He has another surprise for you."

"My violin?"

"Yes."

Simon gripped Joseph's shoulders. "Thank you. Thank you. I promise to repay you for this. What about Rachel? Did you see her?"

Joseph lowered his head and shook it.

Simon patted Joseph's shoulder. "That's OK. I'm sure she's safe where she is." Simon hoped Rachel's supervisor allowing him to see her earlier hadn't gotten her in trouble. He placed his family pictures back under his mattress and went to Maestro's room. His violin and bow were by the door waiting for him.

"What's so special about that violin?" Maestro said.

Simon picked up the instrument and ran his hand along its smooth back. "An elderly woman in the ghetto gave it to me. It belonged to her husband, who died there. It gave her pleasure to give it to another violinist, and it helped me to have it. I promised her I'd take safe care of it."

"Good," the conductor said. "I'll take the one I gave you and give it to someone new. Tomorrow, while you're all at your work details, I'm going to the commander's office to get paper for the men to copy a new song the commander has requested. I'd like you to give it a look and see how we might play it with a bigger ensemble. The commander is adding more men to the orchestra and giving us more rehearsal time by reducing our labor assignments."

Earlier, while Joseph had been getting his additional set of clothing, Simon had prepared a space next to his for Joseph to sleep. He slept a little easier that night having found his best friend. He had learned, however, in the few days he'd been in Auschwitz, how quickly things could change.

Maestro arranged for Joseph to work at the Kanada warehouse. It wasn't unlike the work Joseph had done in the ghetto's distribution center, but Joseph told Simon it felt different. He hated having to process the treasures new inmates had brought with them to the camp knowing the enemy would use them to provide weapons and materials for the German army. Joseph told Simon he was worried about his father. "I feel guilty leaving him alone knowing he's depressed over being separated from my mother," Joseph said.

Simon had never seen Joseph cry, but at night, in bed, he felt Joseph's body shaking. In the mornings he couldn't help noticing Joseph's eyes were red and tired looking. Simon understood the pain of being separated from family, and he looked after Joseph. He needed his friend to keep up his own spirits.

Forty-Two

Simon knew he had to tell Rachel her brothers had been transferred to another camp. She'd be worried to death about them. Simon persuaded Klaus and Maestro to let him miss the first hour of kitchen duty to take a new orchestra musician to get his orchestra clothes. He promised to make up his time by helping to take dinner carts to the barracks and returning them. He'd skip his own dinner to meet with Maestro. Michal was a good sport and went along with it.

"I'll write you a note in case you're stopped," Maestro said. "I'll ask the sewing room supervisor to let you see your Rachel. Don't take long. You don't want to get her in trouble. Be back at the time you promised Klaus. I'll have Joseph look for an accordion for our new member."

The next morning, Simon walked the new orchestra member, an accordionist, to the clothing room. On the way they spoke to each other in German. Simon learned the young man's name was Daniel. He came from Hungary and had studied at the Prague Conservatory of Music.

Simon waited impatiently until the clothing room workers fitted Daniel with a set of clean clothes. Then he walked Daniel to the sewing room. Simon knocked on the door. His heart started beating faster. He prayed Rachel was there and he'd have a chance to speak with her.

The sewing room supervisor opened the door and sighed heavily. "Another star?" she said. She shook her head and took the clothes Simon was holding.

"Yes, and I have a note from our conductor," Simon said.

The supervisor read the note. "Wait here," she said.

Simon and Daniel waited in the hall. Simon was too nervous to talk with his new barracks mate. He paced back and forth.

Minutes passed before the door opened.

Rachel appeared, standing beside her supervisor.

"I'll give you a few minutes," the supervisor said to Simon. "That's all. Leave the door open. You come in with me," she said to Daniel.

Simon hoped for a minute or two of happiness with Rachel, but her immediate concern was for her brothers. "How are they?"

Simon hesitated. He hated knowing how much what he was going to say would hurt her. "They've been moved to another camp to work in a factory." He quickly added, "The camp is near-by, though."

She wrung her hands. "Will you get to see them?"

"I don't know. Their capo here said it might be possible." Simon put his arms around her. "Try not to worry. They're together. I spoke with them before they left. They said to tell you to be brave and to remember your parents are watching over you and them. They'll find you when the war is over."

Rachel grabbed his forearm. "Oh, Simon. I'm scared. They're all I have left."

He pulled her in toward him. "No. You have me. Remember that. I'll try to see you often. Quick, before your supervisor comes back, tell me your barracks number. I'll find a way to see you there."

Before Rachel could tell him, her supervisor came out with Daniel. "Go back now," she said to Simon.

Rachel went inside, but before the door closed behind her, she held up four fingers behind her back.

When Simon returned to his barracks that night, Daniel was surrounded by a group of the musicians playing with them. As much as Simon wanted to join in, he fulfilled his promise to Maestro. He'd managed to eat enough leftovers from the kitchen to stay alert while working with Maestro.

Forty-Three

It wasn't until early in April that SS Muller came to the orchestra's platform after a Monday morning roll call and spoke with Maestro. Simon had passed his eighteenth birthday on March 19 without fanfare.

"He wants you to meet him at the barracks and bring your violin with you. He's cleared it with the commander and with the kitchen," Maestro said to Simon. It had been weeks since he'd seen SS Muller. Simon was beginning to think the man had lost interest in him, but he hadn't given it much thought since he felt protected in the music barracks under Maestro's care.

The day before, Simon had taken Ezra's advice and asked another prisoner to sew a hidden pocket into the inside of his pants near the hip so it wouldn't be noticed under his jacket. He also had the lining to his cap partly unstitched so he could hide food there. Now he felt disappointed he wouldn't get to work his shift in the kitchen to lift food. Joseph's father was suffering from the lack of nourishment. Simon had wanted to sneak food for Joseph to take to him. Instead, he had to go with Muller.

Simon had difficulty keeping up with the officer's long strides. He didn't want to stumble and risk damaging his violin.

Once in Muller's office, Simon said, "You seem to be in a good mood." He immediately regretted his comment, knowing it was much too familiar.

Muller didn't seem to mind. "I am. I have received a letter from my sweetheart. She has written to me she is studying a Bach concerto."

"Which one?" Simon said, still standing, holding his violin. He hadn't been invited to sit.

Muller rubbed his chin. "How many are there?"

Simon thought quickly. His knowledge of Bach was limited. "As I recall there are three, two for one violin only and one for two violins."

Muller smiled. His eyes crinkled. "I see I made a wise choice in selecting you." He pulled out a letter from its envelope and unfolded it. He scrolled his fingers across the letter, his head bearing down on the print, until he raised his eyes and said, "Bach's Concerto in A Minor. Do you know it?"

Simon had heard this Bach concerto played only once. Even with his exceptional memory, he didn't think he was familiar enough with it to give Muller what he wanted to impress his girlfriend. He panicked. While he tried to figure out what he needed to do, there was a knock on the door.

"Damn it, who is it?" Muller shouted. The fierceness of it caused Simon to jump.

The door opened. It was another SS officer. "The Commander wants to see us in his office in fifteen minutes."

"What about?" Muller barked.

"When the Commander calls, I don't ask. I just go," the other officer said and closed the door.

Muller's jaw tightened. He picked up a pencil and threw it down on his desk. He muttered an expletive under his breath, rolled his chair back, and stood up.

"Get yourself to the kitchen," he said to Simon, his tone deepening. "We will meet again tomorrow. Be prepared to play this Bach concerto to me and help me write a letter to my girl that will make me look informed."

Simon felt his stomach churn. This man, who he'd thought might be a source of protection and safety, had a hard and vulgar side. Did he have as much to fear from him as he now thought? He needed to talk with Maestro as soon as possible. He needed his help to learn enough about the Bach concerto to play parts of it to Muller and help him write an intelligent letter. But first he had to go to his kitchen assignment, or he'd be in trouble there.

Time moved slowly for Simon in the kitchen. Images of what could be flashed through his mind. What if he couldn't help Muller write a sufficiently impressive letter to his girlfriend?

Later, back at the music barracks, Simon told Maestro about his meeting with Muller.

"I've played that concerto a few times," Maestro said, "but it's been a while." He thought a moment. "Don't worry. I know who can help you. After the prisoners return, I'll take you to her. Try to remain calm." What if he couldn't remain calm?

Simon had difficulty concentrating while the orchestra played during the prisoners' return. The quick turn of Muller's mood when the other officer interrupted him, and his threat that Simon be prepared to help him write an intelligent response to his girlfriend, made him feel he was losing control of the little bit of security he had managed to gain over his imprisonment. Would Maestro really be able to help him out of this situation?

FORTY-FOUR

After roll call, Maestro told Simon to keep hold of his violin and bow. With his own violin case in hand, he took Simon to meet Maria Belinski, a prisoner in the Birkenau Women's Camp Orchestra. They met in her room in her barracks.

Simon had heard of this woman. She'd appeared at the school of music during his second year. At the time, she was a highly respected professor at the Warsaw School of Music and a violinist with the Warsaw Symphony Orchestra. She was also a friend of Professor Kaminski. He wondered if she knew about the professor's whereabouts, but now was not the time to ask. Their time together would be short.

Maestro explained the need for Simon to quickly learn enough about Bach's Concerto in A Minor to help Muller write an intelligent letter to his sweetheart. His safety depended on it.

"That's a pretty big undertaking for one evening," Miss. Belinski said.

Simon's chest tightened at the prospect of her being unwilling to help.

She looked at Simon. "How well do you play the violin?" she said.

"I'm a very good player, and I learn quickly." Maestro nodded in agreement.

"Then let's get started." She went to a file cabinet, pulled out sheet music, and put it on a music stand. "There's a pad and a pencil on my desk," she said to Maestro. "You'd better take notes of some of what I explain about the concerto while I teach this young man to play some of its sections." He obliged willingly.

Within two hours, Miss. Belinski felt Simon had mastered enough of the concerto to play for Muller. The concerto contained multiple melodies weaving in and out of each simultaneously. It was not an easy piece to play, especially for a young man like Simon whose music education had been prematurely interrupted. Maestro assured Simon he had taken notes that would give the information he would need to include in a letter.

The two men thanked Miss. Belinski for her help and headed back to the men's music barracks before curfew. On the way, Simon hummed the pieces he had learned. He spent the night studying Maestro's notes under his blanket with a dim flashlight loaned to him by the conductor.

The next morning Simon was tired during roll call. When he saw Muller stop by the orchestra's stage and speak to Maestro, he suddenly felt his body wake up. While playing, Simon repeated in his mind what he'd learned the night before. Muller was waiting for him outside the barracks after roll call. Simon's felt as though his stomach was filled with butterflies. He changed quickly and grabbed his violin.

Back in Muller's office, Simon stood waiting for Muller to start.

"The Bach violin concerto," Muller said in his clipped speech. "Play it for me."

Simon sounded a few notes on his violin, adjusted the tuning pegs, and began playing parts of the first and third movements.

Muller clapped enthusiastically when Simon finished. Simon was relieved his mistakes had passed unnoticed. "Now," Muller said, "tell me whatever you can about this piece, so I sound knowledgeable when I write my letter."

Simon told Muller what he had learned from studying Maestro's notes. He explained that scholars believed the concerto was composed in the mid seventeen hundreds while Bach was employed by a prince to compose instrumental music. He called Muller's attention to the multiple melodies weaving in and out of each other and replayed an example for him. Muller paid close attention and scribbled on a piece of paper from the pad on his desk. As Simon explained more, Muller would occasionally ask Simon to slow down and repeat what he'd said. Simon played the ending again to demonstrate a rapid string-crossing technique Bach had used in this concerto.

When he finished, Muller rose. "You have done well today. I am most pleased. Come. I shall walk you back to the kitchen and see you get your lunch and a bag of bread to take back to your barracks.

Simon was overjoyed to have extra pieces of bread to share with Joseph and Joseph's father. That night, before falling asleep, he thought of other things he might be able to teach Muller that would keep him in the SS's good graces.

FORTY-FIVE

With the arrival of spring, the orchestra grew. The commander requested more of the group. Many of the musicians had died of diseases from poor nutrition and sanitation, as had so many of the other prisoners at Auschwitz. With the constant turnover of the orchestra, Maestro relied more on Michal, Simon, and other younger, fit members of the orchestra to bring new members up to date on musical arrangements. The commander gave the orchestra members two days a week free from their work assignments so they could rehearse. Their work supervisors, including Kraus, weren't pleased.

"Tell your conductor fewer cooks in the kitchen means less food," Klaus said to Simon on his workday. "As for you, Mr. Fancy Violinist, less time here means less sneaking food for yourself and your friends."

"This isn't Maestro's fault or mine," Simon said to Klaus. "It's the commander's. He's the one who's demanding more of us."

"Humph," Klaus responded. "Get to work."

Simon knew Klaus was right. Despite his being able to sneak a few extra pieces of bread and some pieces of vegetables in the linings of his clothes, he'd lost weight from working less. He hoped Maestro had a way of making sure he and the other orchestra members didn't starve.

Forty-Six

Later in April, Muller summoned Simon to his office. He was told to bring his violin. Muller's office door was open when Simon arrived. Simon watched Muller pacing about his office humming. When Muller noticed Simon, he grinned widely and waved him in.

He looks downright giddy, thought Simon. He stood waiting for Muller to tell him the reason for their meeting.

"My lady friend's birthday is in August," Muller said. His voice was bubbly. "I want you to teach me to play 'Happy Birthday' so I can record it and send it to her with a picture of me holding a violin."

Simon's mind raced. Muller's excitement suggested he wanted Simon to make him a violin virtuoso right away. He'd seen signs of Muller's impatience when he'd been interrupted and his frustration when he'd helped him with the Bach letter. He had his doubts about Muller's ability to learn this, but he felt he had to comply with his request.

"It's an easy song to play, but we'll have to start with some basics. You'll need to have some patience.

"Yes, yes. I understand. Let's start now."

Simon began this session by teaching Muller the various parts of his violin. Muller was impatient and wanted to learn how to begin learning the song immediately. He grabbed for Simon's violin. Simon felt he had no choice but to hand it over. He attempted to teach Muller to hold the instrument properly and pluck a few strings to the tune of the song. Muller was clumsy with the instrument. He had difficulty gripping it without it slipping from under his chin. Twice he dropped his bow, showing irritation. He jerked his head toward the floor, instructing Simon to pick it up. Simon tried to overlook Muller's spewing of profanities and blaming looks toward him when he had difficulty holding the bow correctly to sound the notes Simon was teaching him. Muller clenched his jaw; the gritting of his teeth showed a sign of this man that frightened him.

Simon swallowed hard, trying to hold back his anger over the mistreatment of his treasured violin. Mrs. Goren would be disheartened if she knew. He tried to be encouraging to keep in Muller's favor. He worked with Muller on his stance, which improved his control. This enabled Simon to move on to teaching Muller the string notes for the first two words of the song.

Simon's body ached from the tension of this session. He was relieved when Muller ended the meeting but apprehensive when Muller said he wanted to meet with Simon weekly.

Back at the musicians' barracks, Maestro asked Simon how his meeting with Muller had gone. Simon scratched the back of his neck and said, "The man is a child. I don't understand how he became an officer." Simon kept his voice down, knowing how dangerous it would be if anyone overheard him. "If he's an example of what our allies are fighting, I don't understand why they haven't won the war by now."

That night Simon couldn't sleep. He was frightened Muller was expecting too much of himself and thus of him. What would happen to him if he didn't succeed in helping the officer with his goal?

The next evening Joseph told Simon Muller had been at the Kanada looking for a violin.

Simon looked up in surprise and stopped buttoning his jacket. "Did he find one?"

"Yes. My supervisor took care of him. Your SS grabbed it from his hand and walked off without a word of thanks. I heard my supervisor mutter what an arrogant so-and-so your Muller is." Joseph patted Simon on the back. "I hope he treats you with more respect."

Simon shrugged and finished his buttoning, trying not to worry, but this more excitable, irrational side of Muller, combined with a complete lack of musical ability, wore on Simon even more. At least, Simon thought, Muller now had his own violin to abuse.

Three days later, on one of his scheduled days to work in the kitchen, Muller summoned Simon to his office again.

Klaus was annoyed. "I'm going to have to report this to the commander. I can't keep having men cover for you every time your Muller gets a whim."

Simon didn't like it any more than Klaus. Not only was he losing his own access to food, but he also didn't like being in the position of trying to teach Muller something he probably couldn't learn.

The door to Muller's office was open when Simon arrived. Muller was posing in front of his mirror with a violin on his shoulder and holding the bow in playing position.

Muller waved Simon in and told him to close the door. "I look handsome, don't I?" Muller said, assuming different stances. "Which way do I look best?"

Simon was angry. Not only was Muller stupid and vain, but he was also oblivious to, or didn't seem to care about, the fact he'd taken Simon away from his kitchen work. Simon wondered if he should tell Muller about Klaus's threatening to report him to the camp commander, but he thought better of it. *It would make him angrier, and he'd take it out on me. Besides, Klaus might not do what he said.*

Muller placed his violin and bow on his desk and sat down.

"I have a friend over in the main camp whose father is an engineer at AEG. He has one of their tape recorders, a Magnetophon. I will borrow it so you can record 'Happy Birthday' for me to practice with. I shall have it here the next time we meet." Muller leaned back in his chair. "When you have taught me well, I shall record it and have a picture taken with my violin to send it to my girl in time for her birthday."

Simon was wary of Muller's use of the phrase "when you have taught me well" rather than "when I learn it." *Suppose I fail, not because of my own lack of skill, but because of his inability to succeed? What will happen then?*

"May I see your violin?" Simon said. "I want to check its tuning for you."

Muller gladly handed it over and watched Simon pick at the strings and adjust the tuning pegs. Simon handed it back to Muller. "I think it's all right now. Would you like to try to continue learning to play?"

Muller nodded.

Simon began to play the notes needed for "Happy Birthday" on his violin. Noticing Muller seemed anxious to join in, Simon gave an inviting nod. Muller's playing wasn't perfect, but it was improving. They practiced two more rounds of the song. Muller quickly corrected his mistakes without the extreme expressions of frustration he had shown before.

Muller got up and reached for his coat. "Come, I shall walk you back to the kitchen."

On the way, Muller sang along with Simon the names of the notes to the tune of "Happy Birthday." Muller waved his arm with exaggeration to the notes, and he paid close attention to Simon's gently correcting him when he made mistakes.

While Muller was talking with Klaus, Simon managed to sneak extra sausage into the lining of his cap. Klaus asked Simon to stay behind when the others left. He handed Simon a bag of bread and shook his head with disgust. Simon looked at Klaus sheepishly when he took hold of the bag. Muller had placed them both in awkward positions.

The sooner I can teach Muller what he wants, the sooner he'll be satisfied and leave me alone.

FORTY-SEVEN

By the end of May, Simon felt he was making progress in teaching Muller to play "Happy Birthday." He had recorded it himself on Muller's borrowed recorder and repeatedly gone over it with him. He was beginning to think Muller might be able to pull it off.

One Sunday afternoon in early June, Simon was sitting in the back of the barracks with other members of the orchestra. He saw Muller walk into the barracks with another officer. Muller spotted Simon and waved him over. Simon excused himself from his barracks mates and approached Muller.

"This is Officer Wolff," Muller said to Simon. "Our good friend, Officer Becker, will be celebrating his thirty-fifth birthday next month. We want to give him a surprise party and want the men's orchestra to play at the party."

Muller waved his hand toward Simon. "This is my music slave," he said to Wolff.

Simon felt his cheeks turning red. He felt humiliated by Muller's reference to him as his slave.

Wolff stood with his hands behind his back, looking Simon up and down but not acknowledging him.

Muller held his shoulders back and his chin high. "Where is the conductor?"

He's trying to impress his companion, Simon thought. He paused, then said, "I'm not sure he's here. Let me go check." He didn't want to give the men the satisfaction of an immediate response to their request. Because of their rudeness, he'd make them wait. Simon knew he was letting his emotions get the better of him, but he couldn't help himself.

He walked slowly to Maestro's room and told him he had visitors. He reported how Muller had referred to him.

"Come with me," Maestro said.

Maestro greeted the two officers with a sunny smile. "My assistant says you'd like to see me."

Simon appreciated being referred to as his assistant.

"Yes. Can we meet in your office?" Muller said.

"I'm so sorry. I'm afraid I don't have enough chairs. I think we'd be more comfortable over there?" Maestro pointed to the musicians' tiered beds.

Simon licked his lips in admiration of the way Maestro showed his contempt for these men by appearing to be ingratiating and, at the same time, disrespectful.

Maestro led the way.

Muller and Wolff glanced at one another. For a split second, it looked as if they didn't know how to respond. They followed the conductor, who sat and pointed for them to sit opposite him. "Join us please, Simon," Maestro said.

Simon sat next to Maestro, practically knee to knee with Wolff. He watched the discomfort of both officers.

Muller managed to get past his unease to tell the conductor why he and Officer Wolff were there. Maestro said he'd be pleased to participate in their surprise and asked them if they had any musical preferences. The two officers gave their suggestions, and Maestro said he'd prepare the orchestra for the party.

After the two officers left, Maestro said to Simon, "It will be extra work to get ready for this party, but it will be worth it, having seen the looks on their faces when I asked them to sit on the barracks beds. It was as if I asked them to kiss our behinds." But Simon knew Maestro was also doing this for his benefit, to keep him in good graces with the precarious Muller.

Forty-Eight

Two weeks later, the sound of horns from the guard stations awakened the prisoners in the Birkenau men's area. The roll call area lit up with floodlights. From his bed, Simon heard a rattle of shots and the screams of men.

In the dark, someone said, "It's another escape attempt."

Joseph jumped down from his bed and ran to the barracks' door. Simon knew Joseph was terrified for his father. For weeks he had worried his father was so depressed and sick he might run into the electric fence to kill himself.

Simon jumped out of his bed, following Joseph. He feared Joseph would run out into the yard and guards would think he was trying to escape and shoot him.

Simon had just enough time to grab the tail of Joseph's jacket, pull him back, and wrestle him to the floor.

Joseph struggled to get free.

"Someone, help me," Simon shouted. Filip, the trombonist, came to help hold Joseph down. At first Joseph tried to fight them both off, sobbing with anger and desperation. Then he seemed to give up all at once. He lay there, his body limp with exhaustion.

The entire barracks had crowded around the three of them. Simon and Filip sat with Joseph.

Breathing hard, Joseph whispered to Simon, "Go see if you can tell who it is."

Simon went to the door while Filip stayed with Joseph.

"The floodlights are lit, but I can't see who the bodies belong to. Their faces are down. Guards are surrounding them. It's impossible to tell."

Simon sat with Joseph as Filip stood and hovered over them. The other musicians began to disperse. Simon held on to Joseph's forearm until he heard Joseph's breathing quiet down. Then he signaled to Filip to go back to his bed.

Simon attempted to offer hope to Joseph. "It's not him," he said. He wanted to believe it himself, even though it might be.

Joseph rolled over to his side and sat up. His voice broke. "I think it is, and it's all my fault. I killed him."

"Of course you didn't. Don't even think it," Simon said.

"I did. Last night I went to see him and told him the truth, that my mother was sent to the gas chambers upon her arrival here."

Simon's voice rose in pitch. "How do you know that?"

Joseph told Simon the Germans transported Leah, a girl who lived in the apartment above his in the ghetto, with him. She'd been assigned to the Kanada the same time he was. He'd asked her if she'd seen his mother. "She looked down sheepishly and said she hadn't," Joseph told Simon. "I didn't want to believe it at the time, but I felt she was lying. I asked her to search around to see if my mother was in one of the women's barracks." Joseph rubbed his arms. "She kept avoiding my asking, saying she stayed close to her own barracks in the evenings. She didn't travel to the others." With audible stress, Joseph said, "Finally, with my constant pushing, she admitted my mother had been selected to go into the line that led to the gas chambers."

Simon tried to comfort his friend. "I'm so sorry, Joseph. This must have been horrible for you to learn."

Joseph's eyes were red with tears of remorse. "I visited my father last night and told him. I thought he'd feel a sense of resolution knowing the truth and would grieve and go on, but I was wrong. That's why he ran out into the fence, to commit suicide. I'm sure of it." Joseph hid his face and started sobbing. His body trembled. "I shouldn't have told him. I should have let him hold on to his hope. It's my fault." He pounded his fists against the floor. "It's my fault."

Simon squeezed Joseph's shoulder. "You can't be sure it's your father out there. Let's wait until tomorrow and hope for the best. No matter what, I'm here for you. You're not alone, my friend. I need you to be here for me. Please don't do anything rash."

Simon didn't sleep well that night, listening to his friend's breathing. He stayed up watching to make sure Joseph didn't harm himself.

The next morning, before roll call, Maestro went to talk with Joseph's father's capo. He returned to the barracks with the sad news. Joseph's father was one of the men executed the night before.

Joseph took the news badly. Simon stayed closely by him. He wished he could alleviate his friend's pain, but he knew there were no words to comfort Joseph. He felt an ache in his own heart for his friend and was determined to do anything he could to help his friend get past this.

That morning, during roll call, Maestro led the orchestra in playing the Polish melody for the kaddish in memory of Joseph's father. The Germans were too busy readying their men for labor deployments to notice the Jewish melody, but Simon saw prisoners slightly bow their heads as the orchestra played.

Forty-Nine

At eight o'clock on the evening of Becker's party, on the last Friday in July, Maestro led the orchestra to a building for the SS officers' relaxation. There was a room with a kitchen reserved for their receptions.

Two SS officers stood watching the prisoners come in and out of a door from the kitchen. One prisoner carrying a tray let a sandwich fall on the floor. He stooped to pick it up and placed it back on the tray. An SS officer with a scar on his cheek approached the prisoner and slapped his face hard. The prisoner dropped the entire tray. Sandwiches fell across the area. Simon saw tears bead in the prisoner's eyes. Simon's hands began to sweat. Maestro shook his head and put a finger to his lips to calm the members of the orchestra.

The officer pulled out his pistol and asked the other officer to do the same. He forced the prisoner he had slapped to kneel. "You," he said, pointing to the other prisoner. "Put down your tray and come here." The other prisoner did as he was told.

Simon saw the fear on the face of the second prisoner as the kneeling prisoner begged for forgiveness and mercy. The officer with the scar handed the second prisoner his pistol and ordered him to stand behind the kneeling prisoner and shoot him in the head. "If you don't, Officer Schmidt, standing behind you, will shoot your brains out. Your choice," he said, without emotion.

Simon watched the second prisoner tremble as he held the gun to his fellow prisoner's head. He heard a click from Officer Schmidt's gun warning the second prisoner what would happen to him if he didn't comply. The standing prisoner winced and pulled the trigger, killing the clumsy prisoner. He then fainted. The two officers called others from the kitchen to remove both prisoners.

The two officers put away their pistols and slapped each other on the back, laughing and taking no notice of the gasps and dazed looks on the faces of the musicians. Maestro responded quickly by tapping his baton on his music stand and shouting out a march for the orchestra to play. The orchestra started off slowly but picked up with their conductor's exaggerated baton movements.

Soon other officers began arriving, greeting one another robustly and standing around drinking and eating sandwiches. The officers spoke about their experiences during the past week. It appeared to Simon as though some of them had started drinking before their arrival. While the orchestra played soft background music, Simon and his fellow musicians were forced to listen to the SS officers brag about the number of dead bodies brought back that week from their labor crews, the number of cremations they'd supervised, the greater number of infants they'd buried this week than the week before, and the number of men and women prisoners they'd hung or shot for trying to escape or for disobeying orders.

Simon's body tensed at their attempts to outdo each other in their boasting. He watched the pained expressions on the faces of his fellow musicians as they struggled to hide their revulsion. He fought his compulsion to flee by recalling the words of his father to be brave and to use his talents to get by. This evening soon would be over, and he'd be back in his bed, safe for the night.

At ten o'clock, an officer on guard at the door switched the lights off and gave the signal SS Becker was on his way. Officer Becker arrived on the shoulders of Muller and Wolff to the shouts of "surprise" while the orchestra played "Happy Birthday."

When Muller and Wolff let Becker down, Muller swaggered over to Simon. Simon's eyes widened when Muller reached for his violin and tore it and the bow away from him. Muller walked to the front of the orchestra and started playing along crudely and singing along loudly. A crowd formed around him. Two of the officers hoisted Becker onto their shoulders, and the gathering sang another verse. When the singing ended, Muller turned to face the orchestra and tossed the violin and bow over his shoulders into the crowd. The officers reached up to catch them. Simon watched in horror as the violin and bow flipped from hand to hand and landed on the floor. He heard the crunch of wood and laughter. When the men dispersed, he saw the shattered pieces of the violin and bow. Simon looked at Muller with disgust, then over to Maestro. With the breaking of that precious violin and its bow, Simon felt an aching in his heart. He had disappointed Mrs. Goren by not fulfilling his pledge to keep these items safe as a lasting remembrance of her husband.

Soon after, the commander arrived to offer his congratulations to Becker. As the commander circulated among his officers, other officers escorted a group of women into the room. Simon watched them pair off with the officers to dance. Maestro led the orchestra into slow, romantic music. Simon had heard from Ezra about the camp brothel and how the officers sought sexual favors from these prisoners. Simon was happy to learn Jewish women weren't selected for the brothel. German men were prohibited from sexual relations with Jews, but according to Ezra, that didn't prevent camp officers from abusing Jewish women prisoners sexually or otherwise.

After the paired couples disappeared from the social hall, SS Wolff escorted an elegantly dressed blond-haired woman into the room. The commander approached her, and the two disappeared together. Simon wondered if the commander's wife knew about his relationship with this woman and what his two children would think if they saw him with her.

The party continued until eleven o'clock, at which point the officers had had their fill of food and alcohol and were barely able to stand. The orchestra prepared to leave, and prisoners from the kitchen began to clean up. Once the officers were gone, one of the kitchen staff offered leftover sandwiches and cakes to the musicians. Out of sheer hunger, they accepted this food, but the bitterness of the evening stayed with them.

FIFTY

Muller called Simon to his office every Sunday morning to continue teaching him to play "Happy Birthday" and help him respond to his girlfriend's letters. Maestro had given him another violin to replace the one Muller had broken. Simon found it difficult to work with Muller after the incident at Becker's party, but he knew his own self-interests depended upon it.

He found it more irritating that Muller wanted to see him on Sunday mornings, when he and other prisoners looked forward to catching up on their sleep and having time to themselves. However, meeting with Muller on Sundays eased Klaus's complaints about Muller pulling him away from his scheduled time in the kitchen, and Simon's annoyance was softened by his knowing he would get a chance of seeing Rachel after the orchestra's Sunday afternoon concerts for the SS officers.

By mid-July, Muller had learned to play "Happy Birthday" well enough to record it himself on the Magnetophon and send it to his girlfriend a week before her July 28 birthday, along with a photograph of himself holding his violin.

A week later, SS Muller appeared at the music barracks ahead of roll call. Simon and Joseph were cleaning their area before their morning coffee.

Muller called out, "Where is that Jew bastard, Simon Baron?" Simon's heart jumped at the seething anger in his voice.

Muller walked between the rows of tiered beds rubbing his thick stick along the wooden bedposts. He stopped in front of Simon. His eyes were glazed over with rage.

"Come with me," he snarled.

236

Helpless, Simon looked at Joseph. Joseph's chin was trembling. Simon was confused by Muller's behavior, but he tried not to show him how frightened he was.

Maestro came out of his room. "What's the trouble here?" he said.

"Stay out of this," Muller threatened. "This is none of your business."

"It is my concern. He reports to me, and I report to the commander."

Muller put his hand on his gun holster and told Maestro to step aside. The conductor obeyed. Simon knew Maestro had no other choice, but fear caused his head to swirl and his stomach to tighten. He followed Muller to his office, knowing he was in serious trouble. What could have aroused such fury, and what could he do to save himself? Muller had the power of life and death over him

Once they were in Muller's office, Muller closed and locked the door behind them. He took a letter off his desk and shook it in Simon's face.

"She has broken up with me. She has found another man. This is your fault." Muller's nostrils flared on his red face. He took off his jacket and rolled up his shirtsleeves and picked up the heavy stick he had brought into the barracks.

Simon was trembling. He started to back away, looking for a safe place to move to. "No, sir. I taught you…" Simon began.

Muller didn't let him finish. "Shut up!" He slapped the club against his palm as he walked around the desk toward Simon. "You did not teach me well enough to win her completely. You will pay for this."

Simon started to shake. Muller had locked the door. He'd never reach it and unlock it in time. *If I scream, no one will help. It will only make him angrier.* For the barest instant, he wondered if he could stand up to Muller. He was taller and younger. But Muller had a club and a gun. *Can I get hold of one of those before he hurts me?*

Simon stepped back and held up his hands, but Muller came in with the club. The heavy wooden object swung through the air and thudded against Simon's left leg. When Simon fell forward, gasping in pain, the club connected with the back of his head. The room spun, and Simon saw stars. His teeth came together on his tongue. He tasted his own blood. Then the club smashed into his side. Pain ripped through him again, and he screamed in agony.

Through the haze of pain and agony, Simon heard a knock on the door. "What's going on in there?" a voice called out. The doorknob rattled. "Open this door immediately," the voice said.

Muller shouted, "Go away." He was breathing hard.

Simon managed to drag himself around Muller's desk, push the chair away, and squirm into the knee hole. He scrunched as far back as he could and called out for help.

The door burst open. "What's going on?" the voice said again.

This was Simon's only chance. "Please help me," he called from under the desk.

Hands reached for him. An SS officer he'd never seen before pulled him out and hauled him upright. Two other SS officers had hold of Muller. They were marching him out of the room, and he was ranting, "He has ruined my chances for marriage. I shall kill the damn Jew."

Simon felt blood trickling down his neck from the wound on his head. He couldn't stand up straight from the blow to his leg. Neither could he draw a full breath because of the pain in his side. He wondered if his ribs were broken.

Once on his feet, balanced by the officer who had pulled him from out under the desk, Simon saw the commander standing in the doorway. Maestro was by his side, looking grieved and anxious.

The commander ordered his men to take Muller to his office, and he called the infirmary to bring a stretcher to take Simon for an examination of his injuries.

Maestro stayed alone with Simon until two men came to take him to the infirmary. While waiting, Maestro gently placed his hands on Simon's shoulder and asked him if he was all right. Simon, unable to speak, squeezed his eyes tight and nodded.

Two men arrived and helped Simon onto a stretcher. Maestro said he'd come to visit him as soon as he could and told him to concentrate on getting well.

FIFTY-ONE

At the infirmary, Dr. Fridman examined Simon. Upon learning Simon's full name, the doctor recognized him as the boy who once stood up for his son, Nachum, against a schoolyard bully. Simon asked if the doctor's son was also in Auschwitz.

"Thank God I was able to get him and my wife out of Poland before the final deportation. I waited too long to get myself out, trying to protect our property. They're safe in France."

Dr. Fridman gave Simon a complete physical. He told him his leg wasn't hurt badly. He had no broken bones there, only contusions that would heal. The cut on the back of his head was deep and required stitching, and he did have two broken ribs.

"I'll keep you here for a while," Dr. Fridman said. "I'll report your leg is fractured, you have a concussion, and that you must rest for your ribs to heal. They won't dispose of you. You're too valuable to them. I've heard you play at Sunday concerts." The doctor whispered into Simon's ear, "I'll look out for you, like you looked out for my son."

Simon stammered his appreciation as best he could.

Dr. Fridman patted his shoulder. "Thank me by following my directions."

Before the day was over, Simon's leg was in a cast and the doctor had given him crutches, for show. He found them difficult to use with broken ribs. Dr. Fridman had cleaned and stitched the wound on his head and covered it in gauze wrapping.

Two days later, Simon was feeling better. He realized Rachel would have heard what had happened to him and would be worrying. He told Dr. Fridman about Rachel and his relationship with her.

"What barracks is she in?" Dr. Fridman asked.

"She's in barracks four and working in the sewing room. Is it possible to get a message to her?"

Dr. Fridman scratched his head. "I may be able to do better."

Two days later, Rachel was working in the infirmary helping take care of Simon and other patients.

Simon clasped Dr. Fridman's hand to thank him. "How did you manage this?" he said.

"She's the daughter of my rabbi. Rabbi Rosenschtein gave spiritual guidance and a sense of tradition to our congregation. I have an obligation to pass that on. You and Rachel are my only ties to my past. I couldn't let her feel she was alone. Plus, we're short of nurses. I figured I could train someone skilled in sewing to help with stitching wounds. I was able to convince our head doctor to bring her here from the sewing room." Dr. Fridman winked. "Just try not to act too friendly, if you know what I mean."

From his bed, Simon watched Dr. Fridman give Rachel short talks on anatomy and physiology as she followed him while he examined patients. She told Simon what she had learned about the symptoms of common diseases prisoners suffered and how Dr. Fridman taught her to take and record pulse and temperature readings.

Rachel took care of Simon daily. She took his pulse and temperature three times a day, helped him wash, fed him, checked the cut on his head, and replaced his bandage. Every week she brought him fresh clothes and changed his bedding.

Simon's feelings for Rachel grew the more she took care of him. When she expressed continued concern for her brothers, Simon felt frustrated he was unable to shed light on their situation, but he reminded her of their last words to her through him. When she told him of the horrors she had heard about at the women's infirmary, he listened and held her hand.

One evening, while changing Simon's sheets, Rachel said, "Do you know what they're doing to women who become pregnant?" She shuddered. "They're sending them to the gas chamber because the Germans have no use for them if they can't work. Dr. Fridman told me there are Jewish doctors in the women's infirmary who are secretly providing abortions so women may escape the gas chambers and live long enough to have children when we're freed."

"That's horrible," Simon responded.

"Oh, Simon, why are they doing this to us? What did we ever do to them to make them so cruel, so inhuman, to hate us so? It makes me feel I don't want to have children if this is the kind of world they'll live in."

Simon understood that as horrible it was to give abortions to pregnant prisoners, what the Jewish doctors were doing was an act of humanity, their attempt to keep women alive, but he thought it best to hold Rachel's hand and kiss it without responding. Inside he felt the same. *We exist, that's all. We just exist. We've become their scapegoats.*

Simon received a visit from Maestro once a week during the month he was in the infirmary. When Simon asked him what happened to Muller, Maestro said he just seemed to disappear. Rumor had it the army sent him off to fight on the battlefield, but Maestro doubted it. "He has no control to be a soldier. I suspect he's at another camp working in a sauna torturing new prisoners."

During the first week of September, Dr. Fridman said to Simon, "I can't keep you here any longer without raising suspicion. It's time I release you back to the music barracks. I'll give you a note saying you need to return to the infirmary once a week for follow-up care. This will give you the opportunity to see Rachel."

Fifty-Two

In September, Maestro welcomed Simon back to the music barracks. Simon was surprised to learn so many of the older orchestra members had died from an outbreak of typhus. Others had been weakened by vitamin deficiencies. The camp had reduced food rations among prisoners, which affected the orchestra members as well.

Simon resumed his responsibility of orienting newer barracks members to the musical arrangements of the orchestra's repertoire. Also, now that he was out of the infirmary, Klaus expected Simon back at his kitchen detail.

Joseph had lost even more weight. Simon hoped he wouldn't wind up in the infirmary.

"What's going on with you, Joseph?" Simon chided. "I thought one of the benefits of working in the Kanada was finding food in the suitcases left on the train platform."

"I've lost my appetite. Ever since my father died, I can't stop thinking about how he must have felt to take his life that way. I feel guilty having left him to move to the music barracks, then telling him the truth about my mother."

"I understand," Simon said more softly. "But he wouldn't want you to suffer. He'd want you to do your best to stay alive. We've got to fatten you up. Please eat what you can in the Kanada. I'll bring you what I can sneak from the kitchen."

During September and October, Simon went to the infirmary weekly for his follow-up visits. Dr. Fridman made sure Rachel was by his side as he examined Simon, and he allowed them time alone. Simon returned to his barracks after these visits feeling secure that Dr. Fridman was looking after Rachel, but he wished he could see her more often.

FIFTY-THREE

The harshness of the winter fell upon the camp. The commander continued to allow the orchestra the two days free of their labor assignments to meet his continued demands for new music. The musicians suffered less than those being sent out or returning from their detachments. They were provided with warmer clothing to wear when performing during roll call.

One Sunday afternoon, Simon visited Rachel outside her barracks. They took a walk in the cold to have privacy. He was dressed in his heavier orchestra clothes. When he saw her shiver, he took off his coat and gloves and gave them to her. His coat seemed to bury her.

"Sometimes when we're on the bandstand," he said, "and we musicians are bundled up, I see the eyes of the shivering prisoners being sent off to work to their outside assignments. They're filled with resentment toward the orchestra. Their lives are futile. I want to take off my coat and give it to one of them. But then I think, which one? How would I choose?" He shook his head. "It's so unfair. I feel like I'm aiding and abetting the Nazis."

She patted his arm. "It is unfair. No, it's worse. It's cruel and evil, but what are we to do? We have no power. We have no control."

He released her so they could face each other. His face stiffened. "One day we will," he said. "One day. You must not give up hope. We're going to get through this." His eyes brightened. "Remember that day you let me read your poems, I said to you one day we were going to live in a penthouse in New York, have lots of children and servants, that you'd be a famous poet and I a famous composer? You said the war had spoiled our dreams." He took hold of both her arms and held them tightly. "We cannot let that happen, Rachel. We must hold on to our dreams. Promise me you will."

She fell into his arms and pressed against him. Tears filled her eyes. "I'll try, Simon. I'll try very hard."

He tilted her face toward his and kissed her forehead. She stood on her toes. Their lips met in a deep kiss. "I love you, Rachel," he said.

"I love you too."

When they let go and held hands, Simon felt a spark of electricity jump from his fingers to hers. They looked at each other in amazement.

"That's a sign from God," Simon said. "He has blessed us. Now I'm sure we're going to make it through this war."

Fifty-Four

The winter of 1943 to 1944 passed slowly for Simon. During the colder months, the orchestra didn't play as frequently for the entertainment of the SS officers on Sundays, but he visited Rachel's barracks regularly. He brought her slices of bread and sausages he'd been able to sneak from the kitchen for her to share with some of her friends who didn't have as much access to extra food.

Although the musicians received larger portions of food than other prisoners, they were affected by the rationing. As members of the orchestra succumbed to the diseases and malnutrition that ran rampant through the camp, the influx of new prisoners made up for the labor needs. The commander saw to it the orchestra remained complete.

Simon became aware of prisoners from a camp in Terezin, Czechoslovakia, arriving at Auschwitz-Birkenau in several transports. Large numbers of them, he learned, were exterminated upon arrival. The survivors lived in a separated area of Auschwitz-Birkenau called Terezin. They were unseen by other prisoners and received special privileges, including not having their hair shaved and being allowed to wear their own clothes. Nevertheless, they were treated as prisoners.

One evening Maestro gathered the musicians and told them representatives from the International Red Cross had received special permission to visit and inspect the Terezin camp. The orchestra had been invited to perform for them.

On June 23, 1944, Maestro led the orchestra to the Terezin camp. Simon took note of the neatly swept streets and the beautifully mowed and planted gardens. Adults and children wore clean civilian clothes. They walked past normal living quarters. The setting looked carefully staged and unlike any part of Auschwitz he'd seen. The orchestra played on a sheltered bandstand wearing special clothes provided for the occasion. Chairs were set up for the Red Cross representatives, German dignitaries, and Terezin SS officers. The Terezin prisoners did not participate.

The men in the orchestra knew they were taking part in something fraudulent. Simon vowed when he was free, he'd let it be known what really went on that day. He told Rachel about his feelings about this experience.

The following week, while he was walking hand in hand with Rachel, she said, "I told Dr. Fridman about what you said about playing for the Red Cross."

Simon stopped, let go of her hand, and faced Rachel. "What did he say?"

"He said he thought the only reason the Germans would have let them come was to convince them there was no German plan to murder Jews."

Simon frowned. "If that is true, the German's strategy likely worked."

FIFTY-FIVE

On the morning of November 2, 1944, Maestro came into the barracks looking agitated. His face was reddened. He told the musicians to get in formation for the morning detachments. Simon stood next to Joseph and wondered if his friend was experiencing the same discomfort he was feeling from the look on Maestro's face. Maestro stood rubbing the back of his neck until they were in place. He cleared his throat and said, "Tomorrow morning will be our last roll call. The orchestra is being transported to Sachsenhausen tomorrow evening."

Simon's mouth slackened. *Is he kidding?* He looked at Maestro to see if this was a joke he was playing. Maestro's eyes looked serious, and there was a grim twist to his mouth. Simon felt lightheaded. He turned and caught Joseph looking at him. Joseph's head was shaking, and his mouth was open. Simon looked around at the other musicians. Their faces showed surprise and confusion. Some let out short gasps of breath.

What does this mean for me and Rachel? Simon thought. *I can't be separated from her. I love her. My future is with her. She'll fall apart when she hears this. I'm all she has.* He had to figure out a way to prevent this. His violin fell to his side. His shoulders tightened from the fear of danger as he waited for Maestro to explain.

"The Russians are making their way toward Poland," Maestro said. "Auschwitz is being readied for evacuation. They're starting with the orchestra and some of the other men's barracks. The Germans are nervous. I've seen it for the past few days. Now I understand why."

Simon grimaced. "Where is Sachsenhausen? he said.

"It's near Berlin. We'll be sent by train and get there some-time the day after tomorrow. You're not to take your instruments, just the clothes on your backs." There were gasps.

Their conductor added quickly, "I want you to look at this as a good thing. If the Germans are afraid, it must mean the Allies are getting closer. It may not be long until we're freed. I want you to play with that in mind this morning. We'll start off with the Polish patriotic march the 'Marz Generalski.' The guards and SS officers are so distracted they won't notice. We'll end with anoth-er Polish anthem, the 'March of the First Brigade.' That will be a slap in Hitler's face. Too bad he won't be here to hear it."

Simon wrinkled his brow. "Won't that be asking for trouble?"

"We'll be out of here tomorrow evening with a group of oth-er prisoners. What can they do to us?" Maestro said. "Right now, they're worried about their own hides."

Simon watched the capos and SS officers take roll call while the orchestra played the two defiant pieces. They didn't seem to notice, but Simon saw the grins and winks on the gaunt faces of the prisoners when they walked their worn bodies past the orchestra and out the gate.

While playing, Simon thought about how lucky he'd been at Auschwitz: the commander's favoritism toward the orchestra and the special privileges he'd received as a result; Maestro's kindness toward and protection of him; his less-demanding labor deployment in the kitchen; his being in the same barracks as his best friend; and most of all, his being able to keep contact with Rachel. These had helped him survive the worst horrors of Aus-chwitz. Except for the beating from Muller, he had escaped much of the psychic and physical trauma he'd seen run rampant in the camp. Now, a move to another camp would force him to face a new set of challenges. Would he be up to them? Would Joseph?

FIFTY-SIX

After roll call, Simon went to his bed and removed the folded pictures he kept hidden there. He received Maestro's permission to go to the infirmary to tell Rachel about the transport. On the way he practiced what he'd say to avoid frightening her, to give her hope. She'd be as upset by the separation as he was.

At the infirmary Dr. Fridman told Simon and Rachel to go to the medical supply room for privacy. Simon spoke as gently and hopefully as he could about where he was going, saying that he knew he would find her again. Rachel's eyes went wide with horror. She caught hold of the wall, breathing fast.

"I feel dizzy," she said. "I need to sit down."

There was no chair in the closet. Simon held her, and they slid to the floor.

"I'm afraid," Rachel said. "I don't want to lose you. You're all I have left."

"I don't want to lose you either. You're the only thing that's made my life bearable since the war began. I love you, Rachel." He moved closer to her and put his arm around her. Her body fell into his. She hid her face against his shoulder and started to cry.

"I love you too," she sobbed. "But it's hard to love here. It's taken away from you too fast. I've lost my parents. I've lost my brothers and so many of my friends. Now I'm losing you. I'm afraid to love anybody."

Simon swallowed his own tears. "Please don't talk that way, please. We'll have a future together. I'm determined. There's no proof your brothers are gone. You need to think of them as alive. You've got to hold on to hope."

Simon took her chin and gently raised her head. "We survived five years since the war began. It won't last much longer. Maestro said we're being sent away because the Allies are getting closer. That means there's hope the war will end soon."

Rachel gave a faint smile.

They didn't have much more time. Nurses would be wanting to come into the room for supplies, and he had to get back to his barracks.

"Look, we need to make a plan," he said, "but first, promise me you'll follow it and be there for me when this is over."

Rachel looked at him. Her eyes were damp. "I promise," she said.

Simon looked at the traces of tears on her face, at her thin, flushed cheeks, and he became profoundly moved by her vulnerability. "Good. No matter where you are, repeat these words to yourself over and over. 'I'm strong. Be brave. The war will be over soon, and Simon and my brothers and I will be together. My parents are watching over me.' Got it?" His own voice quivered as he said this.

Rachel nodded.

"Say it with me."

Rachel repeated the words.

"Say it again."

Rachel wiped her eyes and repeated it. Simon could now see the real hope and determination in her voice and on her face.

"Now, here's the plan. We'll meet at my parents' bakery when we're free. If you get there first, my parents will take care of you. I'll help you find your brothers. OK?" Simon believed in this future. He could envision it.

Rachel nodded.

"We're going to make it, Rachel. We are. Just follow the plan. Now, I have something to give you to take care of for me."

He reached into his cap and pulled out the folded photograph of his family and of his biological mother. "I'll be stripped when we arrive at our new camp. They'll take these from me. They have a better chance with you. Keep them if you can. They're something to remember me by and to give you hope we'll be together again." He handed the photographs to her.

She held the precious objects in her hand. She looked frightened. "But what if they're taken from me?"

"Then so be it but think positive. Look at the picture of me often. See how cute I was as a little boy?"

Rachel smiled.

"See, it's made you happy already."

"It's not the picture that made me happy. It's you."

Simon pulled Rachel to her feet and gave her a last hug.

"Be strong. I love you," he said.

He had to leave before he broke down. Just as he turned away, he saw her kiss the unfolded picture.

FIFTY-SEVEN

On November 4, 1944, Simon and his fellow prisoners from Auschwitz disembarked at Oranienburg, Germany, one train at a time. The train ride to Sachsenhausen had been long and crowded, with no food. They had traveled in the dark cold of night. Their shared body heat hadn't been enough to keep them warm. The guards at Sachsenhausen had lists of the names of prisoners on each train and their tattoo numbers. As the prisoners disembarked, guards with truncheons and dogs organized them into separate rows. By the time the guards had lined up the 350 men, many had collapsed from weakness and the cold. Simon watched the guards drag them away. He never saw them again.

Another line of guards with rifles walked alongside the prisoners as they trudged the short distance to the Sachsenhausen gate. It was a freezing November day with snow on the ground. The prisoners wore only their blue striped uniforms with their thin coats and caps. They hadn't been allowed to take their warmer orchestra clothes. Snow found its way into their wooden clogs. Their sockless feet made walking difficult. They reached the entrance, scared, hungry, and weary. Simon felt numb. Auschwitz and Rachel were a lifetime ago. He could barely remember the warmth of his last embrace with her.

The guards stopped the prisoners when they came to a stone wall.

"Look," a guard said through a megaphone. "That wall is ten feet tall and surrounded by barbed wire. The fence is electric. See those towers. There are nine of them. Guards stand ready to shoot you if you try to escape. It will be impossible."

Simon turned to see Joseph's reaction. Joseph's eyes closed. His body swayed. "Stay calm, my friend," Simon whispered. "I'm as scared as you. I need you to be strong for me."

Once they were inside the gate, a guard took each group to the sauna of Sachsenhausen. There Simon felt the same degradation he had felt at Auschwitz as his captors made him strip, shaved his head and body, forced him to shower, deloused him, and provided him with ragged, ill-fitting clothes.

When a group of prisoners finished in the sauna, the guards would take them to their assigned barracks. Simon's barracks had beds like in Auschwitz. There was a main area for washing and personal hygiene. The capo there allowed Simon's group an hour to select their beds, eat, and use the toilets until the other groups were ready for roll call. Guards with dogs and pistols stood at the barracks door. Two guards rolled in a pair of carts with tin cups, steel containers of soup, and slices of bread.

Simon and Joseph sat next to each other on the edge of one of the lower beds while they ate.

"You're very quiet," Joseph said. "It can't be because you're savoring this swill."

Simon's head sank. His forearms dangled from his thighs. He ignored the soup that spilled from his cup onto the floor. "I'm thinking about Rachel. The deportation came so quickly, we didn't have much time together."

"She's in good care," Joseph said quietly. "Dr. Fridman will look out for her."

Simon pounded his fist against his thigh. His voice rose. "You don't understand. I had plans for my life. My parents had expectations of me. They gave me an education, a chance to fulfill my dreams. I thought that was all I wanted, but I've fallen in love with Rachel." His voice broke. "I want more. I want a life. Where is God? What did we do wrong for him to punish us like this? Why is he allowing this?"

Joseph put an arm around Simon's shoulder.

Simon's voice softened. "I'm sorry, Joseph," Simon said. "I have no right to complain after what you've been through."

"No. Don't apologize. I've had the same feelings. It seems like God has forsaken us. It's hard not to feel that way."

Their capo called his new inmates from their barracks for roll call. The floodlights from the guard towers illuminated the semicircular area in front of the buildings, causing a haze and discomfort among the prisoners. Each barracks capo called the names of the newly transferred captives according to lists Auschwitz had provided. An SS officer stood with each capo. Simon wasn't used to participating in roll call. It was hard on the body compared to playing in the orchestra, or at least a different kind of discomfort.

Later, after roll call, Simon's barracks capo came and told the inmates to line up for their labor assignments. Simon prayed he and Joseph would receive the same detachment. His prayers were answered. Their capo assigned them to the munitions factory. Two guards escorted them to a separate barracks nearer the plant. After that, Simon never saw Maestro again.

Simon's job at the munitions factory was to sweep away excess brass falling from a cupping press used to make bullets. He worked alongside prisoners who had been at Sachsenhausen longer than he and who knew the process. Joseph worked in the packaging area, where he boxed shells for forwarding and distribution.

One morning a prisoner whose job it was to sweep, like Simon, missed a sharp piece of brass. An SS officer walking by stepped on it. It pierced his shoe. The officer jumped and held on to the penetrated foot.

"Which one of you idiots missed this?" the officer shouted.

A prisoner six feet from Simon slowly raised his arm. His face looked pained. The officer limped over to the offending prisoner. Spit flew from the officer's mouth onto the prisoner's face as he yelled, "There'll be no lunch for you. You'll pay for this by spending the rest of the day squatting with your arms outstretched in front."

Later that evening, Simon described the punishment to a barracks mate. "That's the 'Sachsenhausen salute,'" his fellow captive said.

"You be careful not to offend an officer, so you don't get sent to the marching strip," another prisoner said.

"What's that?" Joseph said.

"You weren't at the main camp long enough to see the strip around the perimeter of the roll call area. Prisoners sent there are forced to test military footwear. All day they walk across cement, stones, gravel, and sand wearing different shoes. Sometimes they're given shoes smaller than their normal sizes and carry sacks on their backs."

Joseph grimaced and shook his head.

With these warnings Simon and Joseph did their best to stay out of trouble.

November slipped into December, and 1945 arrived. Simon and Joseph were losing weight, as were their fellow prisoners.

One brutally cold night in February, Joseph said, "I'm not sure I can go on much longer. I'm hungry all the time, and my body's sore from packing and lifting all day. I feel sick and tired."

Simon looked at his friend. "You can and you will go on. We got through those hard days picking up debris from the destruction sites in Krakow. Those German officers were heartless. Remember the ways they made fun of the old men, how cruel they were? We managed to get by. Our work is easier now. We're working indoors, at least. It can't be much longer before we're rescued."

Simon was talking as much for his own benefit as he was for Joseph's. He realized he'd been doing this a lot lately. He had something to live for. Joseph had no one left. Simon watched Joseph's will fail. He had to hold him up. His will was failing, too, but he kept it alive by repeating his father's words and hoping Rachel was repeating what he'd told her. Whenever he felt discouraged, he pictured Rachel working in the infirmary, protected by Dr. Fridman. In the evenings, he imagined her kissing his likeness on the photograph he had given her to protect. This was keeping him alive. He prayed it was doing the same for her.

FIFTY-EIGHT

On March 19, 1945, Simon turned twenty. Another birthday came and went without his noticing. One day was like another at the camp.

In the early morning of April 21, 1945, the blasting of horns from the guard towers awakened Simon. His capo roused the prisoners from their beds.

"Get up quickly, and prepare for roll call," the capo said.

The men lined up in front of their barracks. SS officers sat in jeeps by the gate, rifles in hand. Guards stood in their towers pointing rifles at the prisoners.

"We're evacuating the camp," a voice over the loudspeaker said. "Follow your capo. They've been instructed to shoot anyone not following directions."

The men looked at each other.

"Where do you think they're taking us?" Joseph said to Simon.

Simon shrugged, but he hoped it was a good sign the Allies were near, and the Germans were nervous. If this were true, he had to hold on a little longer. He wondered what had happened at Auschwitz. Had the Russians liberated the camp as Maestro had suggested they would? Was Rachel now free? Had she followed their plan? Was she waiting for him at his parents' home?

After a final roll call, the gate opened. Guards led the thirty-three thousand inmates, including women and children, in groups of four hundred, out on a forced march.

"This must be serious," Simon whispered to Joseph. "There are enough jeeps in front to hold every SS officer in the camp." He opened his hopes to Joseph. "The Allies must be nearby. They're acting like Maestro had said they had at Auschwitz when they sent us here." The smallest tendril of hope woke in him. *My father will be among the rescuers.* He knew it was a foolish thought, but he couldn't help it.

"Quiet," his capo said, passing Simon.

A prisoner behind Simon asked, "Can you at least tell us where you're taking us?"

"Come with me," a guard said. He pulled the man out of line.

Simon heard the crack of a pistol shot. He turned his head and watched the man's body being dragged away.

"Any more questions?" the guard shouted to the others.

Simon dug his fingernails into his palms. He looked straight ahead and swallowed hard to stop from crying out. *I'm brave. Stay strong. The war will be over soon, and I'll be with Rachel and my family again.* He believed this. He had to in order to survive.

They began their march away from the camp in their skimpy clothing without their morning coffee and bread.

The morning passed, and the noon sun peeked through the clouds intermittently. The day was bitter cold. A light snow from the night before covered the ground. Hunger gnawed at Simon's stomach, and weariness dragged at his eyelids as they passed through the countryside.

Prisoners fell around him. Guards pulled them off to the side. Many were shot. The guards left those too weak to move where they dropped. Other guards and capos surrounded the prisoners in line shouting for them to keep walking.

Joseph whispered to Simon, "I'm not sure I can go on."

"You can. You must," Simon said. He barely had enough strength to keep himself moving, but he wrapped his arm around Joseph's waist. Joseph put his arm around Simon's neck and shoulders. "Try not to falter. I need you, my friend," Simon said, encouraging him.

Soon the guards ordered the prisoners to stop and sit. Simon saw SS officers up ahead get out of their jeeps and stretch. They sat alongside the road, ate with their hands, and drank out of canteens. They provided no food or drink to the prisoners. Simon gathered snow in his hands and swallowed it. It chilled his mouth and insides. He gathered more for Joseph and blew on it. "Slurp at it and swallow it slowly," he warned Joseph. They swallowed a little more before the guards took them and other prisoners into the woods in groups to perform their bodily functions. Not long after, the guards told the prisoners to prepare to continue the march.

Simon asked a barracks mate to help support Joseph as they walked. Many prisoners were unable to move and were pulled from the line by their arms and legs into the woods. Simon heard gunshots. He felt his heart beating faster with each pistol blast. He gulped down breaths to stop from crying out. He forced himself to keep moving.

Toward nightfall, the guards again told the prisoners to sit. The SS officers lit fires alongside the road to keep themselves warm. Simon heard sounds of laughter coming from around the campfires. He could see the officers sitting around eating and drinking.

The guards made fires of their own and took turns watching the prisoners. Simon sat quietly with Joseph. He was too tired and too weak to talk. The only real thing in his mind was the image of Rachel.

Some prisoners, exhausted as they were, tried to make a break into the woods to escape. Guards shot them before they reached the edge of the tree line.

Simon looked up at the sky and swore he would do whatever it took to survive. He knew to do so he'd have to separate his mind from his aching, hungry, and exhausted body. He had to keep his mind in the future, no matter how hard this would be. He'd have to do this for Joseph, as well.

The next morning, before sunrise, guards forced the prisoners to continue the march. The day went as it had the day before. More prisoners died from exhaustion and starvation.

Over the next two days, the guards marched their prisoners through small villages and towns where they slept in overcrowded barns or outside in the cold. Some townspeople took pity on the prisoners and gave them food and water. Others turned their heads in indifference. Each day Simon noticed there were fewer SS officers and guards on the march. Four days after the beginning of their march, the guards took the remaining prisoners to a barbed-wire-fenced camp and left them with no provisions.

Simon felt close to death. He tried to distract himself from the cold and his hunger by tending to Joseph, whom he feared was dying. He offered Joseph assurances they'd be rescued soon, but he was losing hope himself. He thought about Katrina, Lena, and his grandmother. Would he be joining them soon? In moments of delirium, he found himself speaking to Rachel and begging for her forgiveness for his not being strong enough to follow the words he had given her to survive. He thought about his mother, how frail she looked when he last saw and embraced her and how she'd react to the news of his death. He fretted about how he'd disappoint his father if his words had not given his son the strength to survive. He curled up next to Joseph to keep them both warm and listened to the shallowness of his friend's breathing. His own breaths began to synchronize with those of his best friend. At least they wouldn't die alone, he thought, before falling asleep.

Simon awoke to the feel of a gentle shaking. He looked up through bleary eyes to see a man in uniform offering him water. He looked over at Joseph. A man in the same uniform was offering him water also. Unstable and unable to walk without assistance, he and Joseph were carried on stretchers by other uniformed men to a truck. They were moved to an emergency provisional hospital nearby.

Simon learned the men in uniform were American soldiers who had liberated the surviving prisoners near the town of Schwerin, Germany. He and Joseph and other survivors were cared for by American Red Cross workers and US Army doctors.

FIFTY-NINE

Simon and Joseph were skin and bones from starvation. Their bodies needed time to heal. Their swollen and blistered feet needed care. Their stomachs needed to adjust to eating normally. Medical staff fed and treated them. Simon improved more quickly than Joseph. Within two weeks he was able to tolerate soft foods and was using crutches to walk a few minutes every hour for exercise. Joseph's body wasn't tolerating food as easily, and he wasn't gaining weight. Simon did his best to boost Joseph's spirits, but Joseph picked at the special diet the nurses provided him, and he rejected Simon's requests to walk with him. Simon became worried by his friend's lack of progress.

"We've made it this far, Joseph. We're free. Soon we'll be going home. You'll come live with me and my parents. We'll be your family, Joseph. You've become like a brother. Please get well. I need you." Simon reached over to hold Joseph's hand. Joseph reached for and held Simon's hand.

The two friends unclasped their hands when a nurse came to attend to the sores on their feet. She was new and wore an American Red Cross uniform.

"You're American?" Simon said in the little English he had learned while in the hospital.

"Yes," she smiled.

"Do you know a violinist named Adrian Mazurek?" This was a question he had learned to ask all the Americans at the hospital.

She looked thoughtful for a minute while she checked his bandages. "I'm afraid I don't. Why?"

"He's my father."

When the nurse left them, Simon looked over at Joseph. His friend's arm dangled over the edge of the bed. His head was turned toward Simon as if he were about to speak, but his eyes were blank and lifeless.

Simon screamed for the nurse.

Part Three

Sixty

On September 1, 1945, Simon jumped from the back of the US Army truck and waved goodbye. He stood outside the bakery. The sign over the store's entrance and the words in the window no longer read "Baron's Bakery." They were repainted to read "Bakery on the Square." Simon remembered his dream when he knocked on the bakery door and a stranger peeked out the upstairs window and told him the Barons no longer lived there. The stranger in the dream had tossed him an envelope with a message from his parents telling him where to find them. Simon wondered how true that dream would turn out to be.

He used the darkness of the early morning hour as an excuse to not knock on the door nor ring the bell. He was fearful of what he'd find when someone answered.

The city was asleep. The streetlamps and the fading moon provided the only light. Simon walked over to the square. Nothing had changed, except a four-story apartment building stood where the synagogue used to be. The destruction Simon had passed as the truck had brought him through other cities in Germany and Poland was absent here. It was as if the war had never happened. When he closed his eyes, however, he relived the nightmare he'd witnessed in broad daylight on the square six years ago and what had come afterward. Those events were ingrained in his mind.

Simon sat on a bench where he could observe any movements in the bakery. He felt restless. A small black cat walked to him, curled against his legs, and meowed. Simon picked it up.

The cat jumped off his lap, wandered to a trash container, and poked its nose around the bottom.

Simon got up and walked idly toward the cat, thinking he might see if he could find it something to eat. He stopped and turned when he heard a voice calling from the apartment building.

"Minka, where are you? How did you get out? Come home, Minka."

The cat ran to a woman standing at the front entrance to the apartment house.

Simon was grateful for the temporary distraction. He returned to the bench and looked at the bakery. After a while, a light came on in the second-floor room that looked out over the square. Simon gripped the edge of the bench. He couldn't take his eyes off the window. He waited to see a silhouette cross it, someone he knew.

Simon started to sweat. *What if my parents aren't there? What if Rachel isn't there?* Part of him wanted to run away, but then he thought, *What if I leave, and they are here?* He wished time would speed up so he could have his answers. If only he could shut up the questions that swirled in his head. He took a deep breath, stretched his shoulders to release his tension, and got to his feet. He slowly walked to the front door of the bakery, pushed the doorbell, and waited.

His heart pounded in anticipation. He couldn't have said how long he waited before someone appeared on the other side of the glass door. A shape, vague at first, came toward him, and then he saw a face he knew.

Rachel.

Simon felt his jaw go slack with disbelief. She was here. He had hardly dared to believe it. He saw her hand fly to her mouth. They stared at each other through the glass, suspended in astonishment. Rachel fumbled with the lock. Simon struggled free of his backpack. Then the door was open, and she was in his arms.

He thought he'd never let go of her again. At first they could only kiss and hold each other in wordless joy. Then he heard her whisper, "Simon, I can't believe it's you."

He found his voice. "I was afraid you wouldn't be here." His lips pressed against her smooth hair. "I don't know what I would have done if you weren't."

She stepped back. "Let me look at you."

They stood apart, holding hands, gazing at each other. She looked stronger, healthier than when he had last seen her. Her hair had grown in curlier, and her skin was smoother. She was almost back to her weight in the ghetto. But there was something in her bearing and her eyes that showed the suffering she'd gone through and the losses she'd experienced.

"I prayed and prayed you'd come to find me," she said. "Come upstairs." She tugged at his hand. "There are people I think you'll want to see."

He became filled with certainty. *My parents are here.* He ran up the steps behind her.

Berta stood in the kitchen. When she saw Simon, she clasped her hands. Her broad smile faded into tears as she hurried to hug him. "Simon, thank God you're alive." She pulled away and looked at him. "You're so thin. Those bastards, how they treated you. Sit. Let me prepare breakfast. What would you like? Whatever you want, I'll make it."

Simon glanced around. The kitchen looked much the same except for the curtains. They were light blue instead of the red ones his parents had. *Where are my parents? Are they still asleep? Why aren't they preparing to open the bakery? What is Berta doing here in her bathrobe?*

A tall bulky man appeared in the kitchen wearing pajamas and scratching his chin. "What's all the fuss?" His eyes lit up. He pointed. "You must be Simon," he said. "Am I right, Berta? Is this Simon?"

Berta nodded, and she introduced the man to Simon as her husband, Louis. He placed his hand on Simon's shoulders and said, "It's great to have you back, boy. We've waited a long time for this day." He thrust his chin toward Rachel. "This young lady has had her head out the kitchen window every day looking for you. Whenever the bakery door opened, she looked up to see if it was you. This is a momentous day. We must celebrate."

Simon couldn't hold himself back. He looked at Berta. "Where are my parents?"

"Let me fix you something to eat, and I'll tell you where they are. They'll be joyous to know you're here."

Those words encouraged Simon, but he was too curious to eat. He begged Berta to tell him about his parents first and cook later.

Berta gave in and sat down at the table. "Your parents are in Germany with your aunts and uncles."

Simon felt sick. He had seen so much destruction and rubble in Germany along the way here. "Germany is destroyed," he said, trying to keep his voice steady. "Where are they in Germany?"

"They're in Berlin. I have their address and phone number," Berta said.

Simon held back a desire to scream at her. "Have you spoken to them recently?" he asked.

He saw her go pale. She picked at her fingers. "No," she admitted. "The phone lines are disconnected."

Simon couldn't stay in his chair. He got up and started pacing around the table, trying to compose himself. "Tell me whatever you know about them," he said. His own voice sounded harsh in his ears. Rachel stayed where she was, twisting her hair nervously, her eyes on him.

Berta asked Simon to sit down again. "Louis, make us some tea," she said.

Simon reluctantly pulled a chair out, scraping its legs against the floor. He sat down heavily.

Berta sat next to Simon. "When you left, your mother worried about you all the time. She fell apart." Berta sighed. "Your father asked me to come back to help, but he soon decided, for your mother's sake, it was best to go live with your aunts and uncles in Berlin. When he and your mother left, the Germans took over the bakery and gave it to a German family. That family kept me, Lucas, and Peter on."

Simon was becoming impatient. He wanted to know where his parents were.

"When the war was over, the family decided to leave and agreed to sell the bakery to the three of us. We've turned it back into a Polish bakery now that the Germans have gone. Your father stayed in touch with us until near the end of the war. He called or wrote to us every week, but then his calls and letters stopped."

Simon felt shivers down his spine at the word "stopped." Visions of the buildings destroyed by the Allied bombing of Germany raced through his mind. He questioned if his parents could have survived that. If so, where would they be now? Simon remembered how delicate his mother had looked the day his parents took him to the rabbi's house. The losses of Katrina and Lena had aged her and made her frail. He could imagine how his leaving and the prospect of losing him, too, must have been more than she could bear. If she was still alive, he wanted to see her, to let her know he had survived and was OK. He wanted to hold her and promise her he'd never leave her again. But he had no idea where to start looking for her. His mind became foggy.

Then Berta said, "Your father left a message for you. He said you'd know where to find it."

Simon raised his eyebrows. "A message? What kind of message?"

"He didn't say. He just said you'd know where to look," Berta said.

Simon thought a moment. Then he jumped from his chair and ran from the kitchen. Rachel, Berta, and Louis followed him to his old room.

Simon flung the closet door open, took out the clothes, and threw them on the bed. He pushed the hidden lever that exposed the secret room. Everything was exactly as he had left it. His violins were safe in their cases. The box containing Rachel's letters, his music compositions, and composition paper sat in the middle of the floor.

Simon pulled out the box and opened it. On top was a white envelope with his name printed on it. He opened it with shaking hands and found a handwritten letter.

Dear son, our precious boy,

If you find this, it means you've been brave and strong and have done what you needed to survive to come back to us. You've been through the worst and know you can survive anything.

Your mother and I moved to Berlin to be with my brothers and their families. We will be waiting for you. Berta, Lukas, and Peter will be at the bakery to greet you and take care of you to make sure you are able to journey safely to us. They have our address and phone number.

Your mother and I pray the rabbi and his family are safe. Please tell them they are welcome to come with you. We owe much to them. They will always be a part of us, in our hearts and minds.

I sold the old Fiat and left the money in this envelope for you to travel here. Berta and the boys promised to drive you to us.

We pray you will soon be in the comfort of our arms.

Your loving parents

Simon handed the letter to Rachel. He was filled with sadness and longing. He wanted to travel to them as soon as possible. The fact that Berta had told him that her contact with his parents had stopped filled him with fear.

Berta and Louis left Simon and Rachel alone in the bedroom.

"What do you want to do now?" Rachel asked.

"I want to go to Berlin and find my parents." Simon wanted to leave immediately, but when he looked at Rachel, he saw tears in her eyes. Simon realized he had no idea what had happened to her since their parting in Auschwitz, what new griefs might have found her then.

He felt ashamed. He took her hand. "I'm sorry, Rachel. I haven't asked a thing about you. How long have you been here waiting for me? Have you heard anything about your brothers?"

Rachel told him she and Dr. Fridman and many others were left behind when the Germans abandoned Auschwitz before the Allies arrived. She looked down. "Those of us who survived were sick and starving. If it hadn't been for Dr. Fridman, I would have died there. He helped keep up my spirits." The Soviets arrived in time to help those of us who were alive. Dr. Fridman helped me look for my brothers, but no one could give me any information about them."

Simon looked at the pained expression on her face. "You've been through hell, but now you're safe and we're together. Let's hope Moses and Aaron are safe too. Did you leave a note at your house saying they could find you here?"

Rachel nodded. "The people living there now promised to give it to them."

"Good," Simon said. "What happened when the Allies came?"

"They were shocked. They couldn't believe what they saw. Thousands of the prisoners were dead from hunger and illness. It was as if the rest of the world had no idea what was going on in the camps." Simon reached for her hand. He understood what she was saying. "They rescued us in January," Rachel said. "I had six months to get well. Every day I wondered where you were." Simon kissed her hand and said he'd been wondering the same about her.

Rachel moved her kissed hand to her cheek and closed her eyes. After a moment she continued, her voice lowered. "Soviet medics took care of us, and the Red Cross came soon after the Soviets arrived. They clothed and fed us until we were strong enough to leave." She looked into Simon's eyes. "Every day I repeated your words to be strong and my promise to return to you. Dr. Fridman helped me get to the bakery. I've been here waiting for you since June."

Still holding Simon's hand, she said, "How is Joseph! Did he come back with you?"

"Joseph died. In the bed next to me while a nurse was taking care of us. One minute we were talking and holding hands. Then his hand dropped, and he was gone." Simon fought back tears as he told her this.

Simon told her about the death march. "Joseph was too weak to survive it. One day I'll tell you more, but not today." The memory of Joseph was too fresh. Joseph was the best friend Simon had ever had. He couldn't yet release Joseph's memory from his heart. He needed to pull himself away from those painful memories. "Let's go back to the kitchen," he said. "I'm feeling hungry. How about you?"

"A little," Rachael laughed. "I can't tell you how good it feels to know I can eat whenever I want." Simon enjoyed hearing that laugh of hers again.

Simon started to replace the top on the box when he saw the picture of his father. He pulled it out.

"Who's that?" Rachel asked.

"It's my biological father." He stared at the picture for a few seconds and thought, *I've made it through the war, Father. There's still a chance we might meet sometime, but if we do, it will be on my terms, not yours.*

"Wait here." Rachel left the room. She came back after a moment with the photographs Simon had entrusted to her. "I saved them, like you asked." She gave him the cut-off picture of his mother.

Simon matched the picture up against that of his father. "Is that the picture of my family?" Simon asked about the folded picture she was holding.

Rachel nodded and handed it to him. He kissed it. "Come," he said, "let's go to the kitchen to see if they have any tape."

At the kitchen table, Simon taped together the backs of the pictures of his birth parents. He'd never gotten to know and love his biological mother, but this picture would bind him to her forever. Although he had strong feelings about his biological father's abandonment, he couldn't yet let himself throw away the half of the picture he'd cut off years ago.

He stared at the larger photograph of his family and thought about how happy they had once been. He would never forget the love he had shared with them, especially with his sisters and grandmother. Some day he would have a photograph of him and

Rachel and their children to treasure. God willing, it would include Moses and Aaron.

Now he had to focus on reuniting with his parents. He placed the smaller picture of his biological parents and the folded, creased picture of his family into the envelope with his father's letter. He got up from his chair.

"I'll be right back," he said to Berta, who was waiting to dish up breakfast. He skipped down the steps to the bakery and returned with his backpack. He placed the envelope in it.

At breakfast Simon learned Berta and Louis were sharing the house with Lucas, Peter, and their wives. This kept their living expenses low. They lived comfortably together in the large space, and it was convenient for them to live upstairs from their work.

Simon looked around. "Where are Lucas and Peter?"

"They went off with their wives for the weekend," Berta said. "Today is the anniversary of the German invasion. We decided to close the store. They'll be back tomorrow afternoon. They'll be thrilled to find you here."

Simon wanted to get to his parents quickly. He asked Berta to drive him and Rachel to Berlin in the automobile they all shared when the boys and their wives got back.

"I'll pay your expenses with the money my father left for me," he said.

"You still look thin and pale," Berta said, encouraging him to stay two weeks more. "You need to put on more weight and gain more strength."

Simon was determined to go to Berlin right away. Rachel understood how he felt. She told Berta gently, "You'd want to do the same, get back to your parents as fast as possible."

Simon said to Berta, "If you're unable to take us, Rachel and I will take the train." Berta gave in when Louis said he'd go with her.

"Perhaps you're right," Berta said. "The Jews who have returned haven't been treated kindly. There is much prejudice toward them. We've kept a careful watch over Rachel."

Sixty-One

On September fifth, they neared the street where Simon's father wrote he, Simon's mother, and the family were living. Despite the destruction they'd seen along the way, Simon refused to believe his parents were harmed. Passing each block, with no house nor building intact, with the rubble of bricks and glass everywhere, he clung to the idea his parents' residence had somehow been spared.

The car slowed. Simon's mouth went dry. The house was gone. It was nothing more than wreckage, like all the others. *But they must have survived*, he told himself. *They've escaped. They're safe somewhere.* He felt Rachel take his hand.

"They should have written to give you their new address," Simon said to Berta. There was a bit of hurt and anger in his voice. "They knew we'd come here eventually."

"Simon—" Berta started, but Simon cut her off.

"No," he said. He understood she wanted to stop looking, and he even understood why, but he wouldn't listen. "Keep driving, he insisted. We'll find someone who knows where they are."

He closed his mind. *They're safe somewhere. We'll find them.* The truth couldn't penetrate the walls he held up.

Simon saw a group of men shoveling debris away from a church on the next corner. "Stop!" he cried out to Berta. He pulled his hand free of Rachel's, jumped from the car before it came to a full halt, and ran up to the men.

Breathlessly he said to them, "I'm looking for my family, the Barons, who lived down the street. Does anyone know them, where they are?"

"We're just a work crew," one of the men said. "The priest is in there." He jerked his thumb at the building. "What's left of it."

Simon ran into the church. Surely his parents had come to services here, he thought. The priest would be able to tell him where they were.

A man was at the altar sifting through rubble. He looked to be around his father's age but thinner and taller. He was wearing plain clothes. Simon made his way over through the heaps of scattered stone and broken wood.

"My name is Simon Baron," he huffed. "My family lived down the street, the Barons. This is where they would have prayed. Do you know them?"

The man looked up, startled. He stared at Simon. "No, I'm afraid I don't. I'm Father Schneider. I was the priest here before the Nazis arrested me in 1940 and sent me to Dachau. I've only recently come back to see my church. It's quite disheartening to find it in shambles." He wiped his hand on his pants leg and offered it to Simon.

Simon looked around without returning the priest's reach. One wall of the church was half-blown away. The light of the sky shone through holes in the roof. Pews were splintered and shattered. Stained glass windows were either seriously riddled with cracks or blown out. Shards of glass were scattered in the mess on the floor.

Simon removed his wool cap. He couldn't swallow. *But they got out. They're safe somewhere.* The truth pressed against him.

Gently the priest asked, "Are you alone?"

Simon managed to say, "I have friends in the car outside."

"Let's sit," the priest said. He led Simon to a pew only partly damaged, and he brushed away the debris. When they sat, he turned to face Simon. "I'm sorry, but your parents, your whole family, likely didn't survive the bombings. The whole city, as you must have seen, has been destroyed. Thousands of lives were lost. I'm so sorry, my son." The priest looked down at his entwined hands. "The irony is," he said, "I was the one in a concentration camp expecting to die, but I survived. They were in their homes, expecting to live, but…" He bit his lip and splayed his hands.

Simon felt nauseous. His chest ached as if it would cave in. He didn't want to believe any of this, but he could see it all too clearly.

"I'm sorry," the priest said again.

With that, Simon couldn't sit there any longer. He jumped to his feet and squeezed past the priest. Near the exit, he stopped and clutched his hair. He looked around, not knowing where to turn. He looked for something to throw. He saw a wooden crucifix near the altar. He ran down the ruined aisle, grabbed the cross, and hurled it with all his strength. It hit the stone foundation of the church and broke. Simon fell to the ground. Sobs ripped at his throat. The tears were warm on his face.

The priest knelt beside him. Simon felt a gentle hand on his shoulder.

"I'm so sorry, son. I'm so sorry," the priest said.

Through the grief, he heard another voice. "Simon, I'm here."

It was Rachel. Simon was aware of the priest getting up and leaving the two of them alone. Rachel put her arms around Simon and held him until he caught his breath.

When he was able to stand up, he saw Berta and Louis had come inside with the priest. The five of them gathered by the altar. The priest listened to Simon's story about his search for his parents. He asked if Simon and Rachel wanted to return to Krakow with Berta and Louis or go to a displaced persons camp with the goal of moving away from Europe and its bad memories. Simon wasn't sure what he wanted. It was too soon for him to think beyond his grief. Rachel decided there was nothing for her in Krakow. A displaced persons camp might lead her to her brothers. She made the decision for them both. Rachel told Berta she'd let her know where they were in case her brothers came looking for her.

They said their sad goodbyes. Berta hugged Simon and Rachel. "We've had too many goodbyes," she said. "Promise me you'll always stay in touch." Rachel promised they would. Simon removed his and Rachel's belongings from the car. He and Rachel stood beside the road and waved as Berta and Louis drove away.

They were prepared for a new life.

Sixty-Two

Father Schneider took Simon and Rachel through a hidden door and down five narrow steps leading to an area in the basement of the church that had been spared destruction.

"I hid two Jewish families here before I was caught and arrested," he told them. "You're welcome to stay here until you're ready to move on."

Simon looked around the small room. There was a single bed against the wall. A small wooden table stood beside the bed with a candlestick on top and a porcelain bowl under it. Another table held a small heating device and a metal pot. A shelf above held a ceramic cup, a bowl, a plate, and eating utensils. Books were scattered on a chair at the end of the bed. A doorway led to a single step down, beyond which were two other rooms no larger than the first. Simon saw two single beds in each room, nothing else. None of the rooms had a toilet or sink.

Simon wondered what it must have been like to live hidden here. In the ghetto he had had room to roam and fresh air to breathe to feel somewhat human. He shuddered at the vision of the families hiding here and the fear they must have felt when Nazi soldiers had discovered them.

"There's a displaced persons camp in the American zone southwest of Munich," the priest told them. "It's a Jewish installation camp called Foehrenwald established by the US Army. It was originally built to house employees of a chemical company, including forced laborers, there and at Auschwitz. That might be a place for you to settle until you get your bearings," the priest said.

Simon looked at Rachel. "A chemical company," she said, her eyes lighting up. "Weren't my brothers sent to such a place at Auschwitz?"

Rachel turned to Father Schneider. "Would the Germans have moved them from Auschwitz to Munich?"

Simon saw hope in her eyes.

"I don't know," Father Schneider said. "The company had several factories. I guess it's possible prisoners from other camps were sent there."

Rachel put her hand on her heart. Her face shone. "We must go there," she said to Simon.

"I've been told it's a good place," Father Schneider said. "I've spent some time at the Wildflecken camp, and I've heard about it from the United Nations people who are operating both camps."

Simon knew he couldn't refuse Rachel. She had come with him to find his parents when he knew she wanted to stay in Krakow in the hope her brothers would come home. "How do we get there, Father?" he said.

"Why don't you stay here with me for one or two nights," the priest offered. "I'll help you find transportation."

Simon and Rachel agreed.

SIXTY-THREE

Simon and Rachel arrived at Foehrenwald on September 10, 1945. About four thousand residents were already living there in well-constructed buildings with central heat and running water. The buildings were originally built for far fewer workers of the chemical factory, now closed. The residences were grouped together on streets named after American states. Residents kept their buildings neat and clean. Simon and Rachel were placed in separate buildings for single people. Families were assigned to double bunks for two persons to share. Blankets fell from the ceilings between the bunk beds to allow privacy.

The streets of Foehrenwald were tree-lined and litter-free. There was green space all around the camp. People looked healthy, wore nice clothes, had fresh haircuts, and ate regularly, thanks to the American Jewish Joint Distribution Committee. Men and women had jobs and could learn new skills at schools set up by the Jewish Organization for Rehabilitation through Training. Children went to school and competed in athletics. In many respects, it felt like an ordinary town from before the war.

Simon worked as a cook and baker in one of the camp's kitchens. He served on Foehrenwald's fire brigade, and he joined a small orchestra formed by the residents. He now used his own violin. He put his childhood violin to beneficial use teaching the six-year-old son of a coworker to play.

He spent as much time as he could composing. He was determined to write a concerto to express and release the anger and rage he replayed in his dreams, beginning with that first day on the square when the Germans entered Krakow and ending with the death march from Sachsenhausen and his loss of Joseph.

After his nightly visits with Rachel, Simon sat on the side of his bed writing down the music that poured from his heart. The notes came readily as he remembered the horrors he and his family suffered after the invasion: the deaths of his sisters, his forced labor in the city, his required separation from his family and the indignity of life in the ghetto, the nightmare of Auschwitz and what had followed.

Rachel worked as a teacher at the camp's Orthodox Hebrew school. After school hours she took care of children whose mothers were still at work. Rachel had posted a notice on the camp's bulletin board to try and locate her brothers. Sometimes Simon would go there to see if anyone had responded with good news.

At Foehrenwald Simon and Rachel found wondrous joy in the freedom of being able to meet after work and walk holding hands as they discussed their days. They smiled at friendly faces they had no reason to fear, people who smiled back, people they knew, who would be there, alive, and fearless on the days that followed.

Simon knew his friends in the camp saw him and Rachel as a couple, and they were. They were in love, and they both knew it. Sometimes his coworkers in the kitchen would nudge him playfully. "When are you going to propose to that girl of yours?"

Simon wasn't sure he was ready to take that step. He decided to talk with Rabbi Strouse, a young Polish Jewish Orthodox chaplain in the camp. Simon liked Rabbi Strouse. He seemed genuinely friendly and down-to-earth. They had spoken once when Simon and his band played at a wedding at which the rabbi officiated. Afterward, the rabbi pulled Simon aside and said his uncle was a trained violinist in Palestine. He told Simon he saw something special in him, the way he held his violin, the look on his face when he played.

One afternoon in mid-October, while on a break, Simon mustered his courage and went to Rabbi Strouse's office. The rabbi rose to greet him.

"Ah, the violinist," he said. "Welcome. Please come in. Have a seat."

Simon sat in the chair in front of the rabbi's desk. The desk was strewn with papers. Simon guessed the rabbi had been in the middle of work.

"Would it be better if I came back another time?"

Rabbi Strouse smiled. "No. I can always catch up with this. Tell me what's on your mind, Simon. That's your name, isn't it?"

Simon was pleased the rabbi remembered his name. That easy welcome helped him relax.

"I've got a lot on my mind, things I can't seem to figure out on my own. I need someone to help me think them through." Simon felt relieved to finally speak out.

"You're not alone, Simon. Everyone here has lived through terrible experiences. It will take time to adjust to your new freedom, to trust yourself and others, and to figure out where you want to go from here."

Simon nodded and clenched the woolen hat he held. He was unsure what to say next.

"I'm glad you came to see me, Simon. I'd like to be able to help you sort out your feelings and what you would like to do with your life."

"I'd like that too," Simon said. "How do we do that?"

"We'll set up times to meet to talk about what's on your mind, what decisions you need to make, so when the time comes, you can leave here feeling you've pulled your life together and you know what to do next."

Simon was disappointed by not being able to launch into the things he wanted to talk about right away, but this sounded like exactly what he needed. "How soon can we start?"

The rabbi reached for a book on his desk and shuffled through its pages. "Let's plan to talk for about an hour, say twice a week? What time is best for you?"

They set up a schedule, and Simon thanked the rabbi. He walked back to the kitchen feeling light-footed, freed by the thought he would get his life in order.

SIXTY-FOUR

Simon thought about the most important things he wanted to talk about with Rabbi Strouse. He was living in a camp without any awareness of how long he'd be here and what his future would be. Where did he want to live when immigration laws allowed? Where could he fulfill his dream to become a skilled violin performer and composer? A decision in one direction could determine his fate in another. How could he use his time at Foehrenwald to decide? Without knowing the answers to these questions, how could he make a commitment to Rachel? Simon presented his worries to Rabbi Strouse during his next visit, on October 20.

"Many people here are struggling with the same things," the rabbi said. "The fact that the war disrupted your career goals, and you lost your family, complicates things for you. Try not to be too hard on yourself. It's better you've decided to bring your feelings out in the open. That is your path to figuring out your future."

Simon felt at ease from the rabbi's sympathetic, reassuring tone. "I'm in love with a girl named Rachel who lives in this camp," he began. "We've both lost our families, but she's still hoping to find her brothers. She's the daughter of a rabbi. We're both from Poland, and we have known each other for a long time. I want to marry her, and I believe she wants to marry me too."

"What's holding you back?"

"I have no future."

"Of course, you do," Rabbi Strouse said. "Everyone has a future. You need to determine what yours will be. Tell me, have you decided where you want to settle when you leave here?"

"I see only two choices," Simon answered. "Either Palestine or the United States."

"Do you have a preference?"

"I think I'd prefer the United States."

"Why is that?"

"There may be more opportunities there for me to develop my violin skills. I've wanted to be a violin soloist since I can remember. I was a student at the Krakow School of Music until the Germans invaded and closed it down." He paused, lowered his head to avoid the rabbi's eyes, and added, "I have a father in the United States who's a famous violinist."

Rabbi Strouse tilted his head to the side and moved his chair closer to his desk. "I thought you said you had no family."

"I hadn't learned about my real father until the Germans came and I discovered I was born to a Jewish mother who died in childbirth. I've had no contact with my biological father and have many conflicting feelings toward him, from outright hatred to a desire to be loved by him."

"I see we have a lot to talk about. There's much there to uncover, but first let's talk about you and Rachel. Have you and she discussed your goals for the future, where she wants to live after here, what she sees for herself? Chances are you both are going to be here anywhere from two to three years." The rabbi looked Simon in the eyes. "Both of you need to think about where your heads will be when that time comes. Will part of that preparation be making a life together here? In other words, will you move on from here together or separately?"

The rabbi's directness hit at the core of Simon's inner conflict. He'd been feeling he had nothing to offer Rachel but his love. How would he support her if they married and moved to another country? How would he develop his career as a violinist? He had no idea what she really wanted. The war had strangled them both. They were struggling to survive, having suffered the losses of their families, having had little time to adjust to freedom. The freedom they needed lay in this camp filled with other people going through the same struggle of trying to find themselves and make lives for themselves.

The next evening was on the chilly side. Clouds floated through the moonlit sky. Simon and Rachel wore warm coats and gloves on their walk. The enticing odors of the supper meal floated from the dining hall into the air outside.

Simon said to Rachel, "Where do you want to go after Foehrenwald?"

"That depends," she said. "Where do you want to go?"

"I've been giving it some thought. I want to go to the United States." He looked for her reaction.

She let go of his hand and turned to look into his eyes. "Then that's where I want to go."

His eyes widened. "Really?" he stammered.

"Of course. I want to be with you, wherever you are."

Simon couldn't help asking the same questions that had gone through his mind so many times. "How would we live? What would we do there?"

She smiled up at him. "I'll get a job, and you'll study violin. When you've finished your training, you'll perform and get rich, and I'll stay home and take care of our children."

The picture she drew dazzled Simon so much he could hardly think. She stood before him with the brightness and enthusiasm of a vibrant young woman, freed from the chains of her imprisonment. Out of the swirl of confusion and new hope, he managed to ask, "Our children? How many?"

"Let's start with one and see where it goes from there."

"It will be that easy?" Right now, looking into her beautiful eyes, he remembered the day in the ghetto when she shared her poems with him and his outburst to her about the wonderful life they'd have living in a skyscraper in New York with lots of children and servants. Back then she squeezed his hand and said, "The war has interrupted our dreams. Let's wait and see what happens." With the war now over, could they truly pursue their dreams? He was the one feeling apprehensive now, knowing how difficult it would be. She was the one expressing total optimism.

"Maybe not but look what we've lived through. We can make it," she said. She took his hand again. "We've got to make a life for ourselves. It's like you said. We owe it to our parents, and there are Jewish agencies in the United States that will help us."

She was brave, strong, and wise. She was more than he could ever deserve, but she had told him she was his. His heart could have burst with joy. The words fell right out of his mouth. "I love you, Rachel. Will you marry me?"

"Yes," she said. "Yes, yes, yes."

She threw her arms around his neck. He lifted her off the ground, and they kissed. Passersby whistled and clapped. Simon looked up and grinned, then went back into their embrace.

Sixty-Five

Simon beamed as he sat down for his next session with Rabbi Strouse. "I'm engaged, Rabbi. You're a miracle worker."

The rabbi's eyes and mouth opened wide. "Tell me what happened."

"I talked with Rachel, like you suggested. She said she wants to go wherever I go. She had no hesitations. She agreed with you. We must start our lives here to be ready for when we can leave."

"How do you feel about this?"

"I'm a little scared." It was hard to explain how he felt. Part of him still couldn't believe Rachel wanted to share her life with him, and part of him was afraid he couldn't live up to her expectations. "Being engaged is different than dating or seeing each other. There's a real commitment."

"That's true. Are you ready for that?"

"I hope so." Simon hesitated. "I know I might be hard for her to live with."

"How so?" the rabbi asked.

Simon looked down. His voice lowered as he began talking about himself. "I like to be alone a lot, especially when I'm composing or practicing. I can be standoffish. I've never had many friends." He rubbed his nose. "At school I was competitive, and people didn't like me for that."

Simon's eyes stung as he thought about Joseph and what he was about to say. "I've only had one good friend in my life, Joseph, and he's gone. He accepted me for what I am. We had fun together. And now..." Sadness welled up in him. "I'm not who I thought I was. I felt responsible for my sisters' deaths and now for my parents'. Sometimes I cry myself to sleep." He was about to cry now. He forced it down. "How could I burden Rachel with that?"

The rabbi said gently, "Marriage, a good one, means two people love each other enough to accept each other's burdens. Didn't you tell me you lived with Rachel's family in the ghetto? You'd been through many bad experiences by then. You got through them. Sometimes such circumstances bring people together, purely because of the circumstances, but when the situation changes, feelings change. Do you think this is the case with you and Rachel?"

"No." Simon felt certain. "I think we truly love each other."

"It's not unusual here, Simon, for people to cry themselves to sleep. We've been through the worst of experiences, and we've survived more than any human being should have to. To not cry, to not mourn, would be unnatural. I'm sure you've heard others cry at night, haven't you?"

"Yes," Simon whispered.

"Do you ever feel like comforting one of them, say the person sleeping above or next to you?"

Simon nodded.

"Why don't you?"

"I don't want to embarrass them"—he paused—"or myself. It isn't manly." The tears were rising in his throat again. It took all his determination to hold them back.

"It's human," Rabbi Strouse said.

Simon couldn't help it anymore. The sobs forced their way out, tearing at him. He couldn't stop. He heard the rabbi's chair scrape against the floor. Then he felt a gentle hand on his shoulder. "It's all right," the rabbi said. "It's all right."

It felt like a long time before Simon spent his tears. When he raised his head, Rabbi Strouse handed him a tissue.

"This is what you can do for Rachel," he said, "and she for you. Let her in, and let her let you in. That's part of marriage."

SIXTY-SIX

On January 3, 1946, Simon and Rachel stood under the chuppah before the chief rabbi of the camp. Rachel wore a borrowed wedding dress from a woman who had borrowed it from another woman. Simon wore a suit given to him by the Jewish Joint Distribution Committee. During the wedding ceremony, when the rabbi spoke of Simon's and Rachel's departed parents, the couple looked at each other and squeezed their hands together tightly. There was the glint of a tear in each of their eyes.

When it came time for the vows, Simon placed the ring on Rachel's index finger and said, "Ha-rei aht mekudeshet Li, be-tehba'at zoh, k'dat Mosheh v'Yisrael. With this ring, you are consecrated to me, as my wife, according to the tradition of Moses and Israel." He stomped his right foot on the wrapped glass. Their friends shouted, "Mazel Tov." Simon kissed his bride. Rabbi Strouse was the first to pat Simon on the back and offer his congratulations to the newly-weds.

Simon's co-workers from the kitchen made them a two-tiered wedding cake. Others brought food, and everyone danced joyously while Simon's musician friends played. Simon couldn't stop smiling, and he couldn't look away from Rachel, whose eyes seemed to sparkle and gleam at him. During the traditional wedding dance, the hora, he danced so joyfully he stumbled and landed on his bottom. Once others helped him to his feet, Rachel led her hobbling husband to a chair and insisted he sit for a while.

They spent their first night together in a small home nearby. Other camp newlyweds had used it. Simon had saved for three months to rent the room for the night. This was the first time they'd made love. It felt natural for Simon to share this act of intimacy. He held and kissed his bride, looked into her eyes, and caressed her face. Their lovemaking was slow. He held her tightly and called out her name and whispered in her ear he loved her. When it was over, they fell into each other's arms. He held up her hand and kissed her finger. "I'm sorry I couldn't afford a real ring." The ring he had given her was a simple metal band made from melted bronze by a craftsman in the camp.

"I love this ring more than if it were gold," Rachel said. She kissed him and snuggled deeper into his arms.

Simon told her how happy he was their lives had come together. He promised Rachel that despite the hardships they each had suffered, they would make a life together. When he saw tears in her eyes, he held her tighter. "I know," he said. "I know." He knew she was thinking about her parents and her brothers. He was thinking about his family too.

"We've got to make a life for them, our parents, to show it wasn't for nothing. It's over now, and they'd be happy for us and want us to carry on." These were words he repeated often to himself to get through the rough days, the rough remembrances.

SIXTY-SEVEN

Simon and Rachel had been married a month and were living in a building on Ohio Street. The population of the camp had risen to fifty-six hundred occupants. Simon and Rachel slept together in the bottom of a two-tiered bunk bed. They shared the building with twenty-four other families. They held the same jobs and were living as happily as a newlywed couple could in such crowded conditions.

One day, while on his break from the kitchen, Simon went to the bulletin board that listed the names of missing persons who camp residents were attempting to locate. There wasn't a response to Rachel's note about her brothers, but there was a list of names the new camp director had posted asking the people named to come to his office. Simon saw his own name there.

Curious as to why the director wanted to see him, Simon walked to the administration office and announced he was responding to note on the bulletin board. An assistant directed him into an office and told him to take a seat. Soon the director entered. He said he was pleased to meet Simon and asked about his experiences at Foehrenwald. After the small talk, he came to the point.

"Do you have any relatives in the United States?"

Simon thought the director might be interviewing him for his request for immigration to the United States.

"None that I've ever had contact with," he said.

"Does the name Adrian Mazurek mean anything to you?"

Simon's jaw dropped. Whatever he might have expected, surely it hadn't been this. He managed to say, "My biological father's name is Adrian Mazurek, but I've never net him." He felt embarrassed admitting this.

"Do you know anything about your biological father?"

Simon kept his voice calm. "I understand he's a violinist in the United States."

"Well, it certainly seems to fit. There is a man named Adrian Mazurek in the United States, a well-known violinist, who is looking for a man your age named Simon Baron. He says he's your father and wants to be reunited with you. I have all the information you need to contact him." The director handed Adrian a sealed envelope. "He wants to know if I can tell him you've been located and if you'd allow me to tell him how to reach you."

Simon was speechless. He had dreamed of this day for years. Now he didn't know how to meet it. On the one hand, Simon wanted to punish the man who dared call himself his father by denying him his request. On the other hand, he longed to meet Adrian Mazurek face to face and tell him what he thought of him. He wanted to show him the son he'd abandoned had grown into a strong, proud man, a survivor, despite everything that had happened to him. Simon knew it was best not to do anything before he talked with Rabbi Strouse.

"Can I get back to you about that, sir? I need to think about it."

"Sure," the director said. "I see I've shocked you. I'm sorry. Take as much time as you need."

"Thank you." Simon managed to get to his feet.

"This may be a wonderful opportunity for you, Simon," the director said. "Find someone to talk it over with before making your decision. I understand you may be conflicted."

"I will, sir."

Simon was late getting back to work from lunch. He put in extra time to make up for it, trying all the while to take his mind off his visit with the director, but he kept replaying the

conversation in his head. *Adrian Mazurek. Well-known violinist. Wants to be reunited with you.*

When his shift was over, Simon walked to Rabbi Strouse's
office but found it closed. He met Rachel back at their building.

"You look upset," she said. "What's the matter?"

He told her about his visit with the camp's director.

"Let's find a private place to talk," she said.

Hand in hand, they walked quietly to the library. It was din-
nertime, so the library wasn't busy. They found a table away from
others.

"What are you thinking?" Rachel asked.

As if the question had broken a dam inside him, Simon
found he could speak. In fact, he was so full of anger he was
ready to burst. "If he thinks he can just walk into my life after
all this time..." Simon slammed his hand flat on the table. Two
people who had just arrived stopped to stare. Simon flushed and
gave them an apologetic look.

Rachel's eyes narrowed. "I thought you wanted to find him
and move to America to be with him."

He rubbed the hand he'd banged on the table. "I don't know
what I want. Why didn't he take me to America with him twenty
years ago?" Simon couldn't keep himself from raising his voice.
"What right does he have to think he can march into my life
now?" His face felt hot. He stared down at the table. He knew he
was acting badly, but he couldn't help himself.

Rachel reached for his hand. "If he had taken you to America," she said, without reproach, "we would have never met. We
wouldn't be married."

She was right, as always. Simon looked up and wrapped his
fingers around hers. "I'm sorry, Rachel. I'm not thinking straight.
Let's get out of here. I need to walk."

They walked around the camp, passing the fire station, the school, and the chief rabbi's synagogue. Simon concentrated on the feeling of the hard ground under his feet, the rhythm of his steps that almost, but not quite, managed to drive the questions and confusion out of his head.

"You're walking too fast, Simon. I can't keep up." Rachel pulled the collar of her coat around her neck and said, "It's getting dark, and I'm cold. Can we stop for dinner now?"

"Sure. I'm sorry." He turned, took her arm. "I'm being a bear."

They went to the dining hall and ate quietly for a while until Simon broke the silence. "This all started when I stopped by the bulletin board to see if anyone had responded to your search for Moses and Aaron. That's when I saw the note for me to see the camp director. I'm ashamed, Rachel. All those people looking for their relatives, and they may never find them..." Simon stopped. He hadn't meant to suggest that Rachel might never find her brothers.

Rachel looked at him steadily "You feel guilty," she said." You're one of the lucky ones because someone is looking for you, but you aren't even sure you should feel lucky. Be grateful for the opportunity to be able to decide whether you want anyone to find you. When is your next meeting with Rabbi Strouse?"

"Thursday."

Rachel placed a gentle hand over his. "Why don't you make a list of the things you want to talk about? You have a lot on your mind."

After dinner they went to their residence. Simon played lullabies on his violin and sang at the bedsides of young children who had difficulty falling asleep. This had a soothing effect on him and took his mind off his meeting with the camp director until he and Rachel went to bed.

"You're grinding your teeth," Rachel said.

He rolled away from her. "Sorry." But despite what Rachel had told him, despite her very presence in his life as a better angel, he couldn't stop thinking about the ways he could hurt Adrian Mazurek. The easiest way, Simon thought, would be to ignore his letter, but that wouldn't give Simon the satisfaction of knowing the pain, if any, he had caused "that man" by ignoring him. He needed to know if his father suffered. With those thoughts in mind, he fell asleep.

Sixty-Eight

Simon sat in Rabbi Strouse's office waiting for the rabbi to finish a note he was writing. He sat with his hands folded tightly, tapping his foot, until the rabbi put his pen down and said, "What would you like to talk about today?"

Simon told him about his meeting with the camp director.

"Tell me what you're thinking."

Simon pushed the words out through clenched teeth. "I'm feeling hatred for the man. I want to punish him."

The rabbi understood Simon's anger toward his father. "How would you do that?"

"By ignoring his request, refusing to contact him."

"'Hatred'" is a strong word, Simon. Are you sure it isn't anger you're feeling?"

"You sound like Rabbi Rosenschtein."

Rabbi Strouse raised his eyebrows. "What do you mean?"

"He said the same thing to me six years ago."

"Apparently it didn't take. Maybe we'd better talk about it again."

Simon twisted in his chair. "What's the difference between hatred and anger? Why does it matter?" he said flippantly. Then Simon relented. "All right, you start," he sighed.

"You're being sarcastic, but I'll play along," Rabbi Strouse said. "People hate other people for who they are. We get angry at people we otherwise like for something they did or didn't do. If Rachel were to come home late from work when you had an important date, you might be angry, but you wouldn't hate her.

You don't know enough about your father to hate him, but you can be angry for what you feel he did to you."

Simon couldn't contain himself. He pushed himself out of his chair. "He abandoned me!" he shouted. "He left me here to suffer. He's responsible for the deaths of my sisters and my parents. Why shouldn't I hate him?" He turned his back on the rabbi and forced himself to take deep breaths, trying to calm down.

From behind him he heard the light tapping noise of a pencil against the desk. Then he heard the rabbi's voice.

"We need to look at these thoughts one at a time," the rabbi said. "You don't want your feelings to be a negative force in your life, to destroy you. Right now, your hatred, your anger, whatever you want to call it, can cause you to lose your perspective, prevent you from having a happy life with Rachel, from becoming the great violinist you want to be."

Simon didn't want to turn around, but he made himself face the rabbi. "What do you mean?"

"Let's talk about your feelings about being abandoned. Describe them for me."

Simon didn't know why he should bother but said, "When my mother died, he left me and went to the United States, never to be heard from again. If he had taken me with him, I wouldn't have suffered as a Jew here in Europe. I wouldn't have been sent to the ghetto and to Auschwitz."

The rabbi offered Simon an understanding nod, and with a thoughtful expression, he asked, "Didn't you tell me he was nineteen years old and had a breakdown of sorts after your mother died?"

Simon paced the floor in front of the desk. "That's what my parents told me."

The rabbi put down his pencil. "Let's see, you're only a year older than he was then. How would you feel if, God forbid, Rachel died in childbirth, and you were left alone to care for your newborn child while in the middle of your schooling to become a concert violinist?"

If Rachel died? The question shocked Simon. He turned his back again to not look at Rabbi Strouse's face. For a moment he couldn't answer. Then in almost a whisper, he spit out, "No matter what, I'd never leave my child."

"But would you be heartbroken? Confused? Unable to think or make decisions?"

"I don't know." Simon squeezed his eyes shut at the rabbi even suggesting the possibility of Rachel's death. "I haven't faced that. I hope I never have to," he stammered.

"Before we see each other again, I'd like you to think about it, not just from one viewpoint, but from other possibilities."

Simon sat down. He was beginning to get a headache. "What do you mean?"

The rabbi leaned forward and placed his forearms on the desk. "Was it your father's sole decision to leave, or did someone suggest it to him? Was he told it would be best, for your sake and his, because he was ill- equipped to care for a child alone? Did he arrange for you to live with a loving family before he left, people he knew would care for you?" The rabbi leaned back. His voice softened. "Did he make a bargain, for your sake, that he wouldn't interfere with the arrangement, so you'd never worry that one day he'd come to take you away from people you'd grown to love? Did he suffer from this decision, regret it? Did something happen to prevent him from contacting you sooner, like the war, for example?"

During the next and future sessions, the rabbi and Simon dealt with Simon's feelings about his father abandoning him, his anger and guilt over the deaths of his sisters and parents, and how to decide if he could make peace with his father by taking the first step toward contacting him. The two spoke about Jewish views on anger and how Simon could control his anger to improve his relationships with people, including himself.

"Remember," the rabbi said, "someone is always watching you. If not another person, God. People may judge you by your expressions of anger. If you think about the consequences before you act on your anger, you may behave differently, but if you slip, always do your best to apologize. The hardest thing you will need to understand is, whatever happened to make you angry is God's doing. This means the person you're angry with is just the messenger. You need to ask yourself what God is trying to tell you at that moment."

Simon began to consider the possibility his father's leaving him to be raised by the Barons was a choice he had made for Simon's own sake. If his father had taken him to America, where he knew no one, who would have raised him, how would his father have afforded to continue his education and care for a child?

Rabbi Strouse, like Rabbi Rosenschtein, helped Simon to see that neither his own nor his birth father's actions were responsible for Katrina's and Lena's deaths. These were the results of the philosophy and actions of the Nazis, under Hitler. Katrina would have lived a happy and useful life, despite her impairment, had there been no war, and Lena would have been spared the tragedy and consequences of seeing her sister killed.

Simon began to understand his father could not have foreseen the events that had affected him and the Baron family so profoundly. If Adrian could have known what was coming, he might have come to Poland to rescue them all and bring them to the United States. Simon also began to understand rescuing him and his family might not have been that simple. The United States was on the other side of the Atlantic, not an easy journey, and its tight restrictions on immigration made it harder yet.

Early in the second week of March 1946, Simon made up his mind. "I think I'm ready to contact my father in America," he told Rabbi Strouse. "I've struggled with the idea of whether I'd be betraying the Barons by meeting my father, but I think they'd want me to be happy. He was their nephew, and I learned from them he and my mother brought joy into their lives."

"I'm happy you've come to peace with this and the things we've discussed over the past few months, Simon."

"Besides, Rachel and I want to raise our baby in the United States. He or she will need grandparents to have a complete family."

The rabbi slapped his hands against his cheeks. "Does that mean what I think it means?" he said.

Simon couldn't help grinning. "Yes, Rachel is three months pregnant. The baby is due in October."

"Mazel tov, Simon. Give my best to Rachel. I will, too, when I see her. Now let's discuss the letter you're going to write."

They talked about Simon writing in terms of his own feelings, not accusing his father of things. "Let him know what's been on your mind," Rabbi Strouse said. "Give him a chance to explain himself without being defensive. Get to know each other. Don't judge him. You may find you like him. Then again, you may find you don't. Nothing says you must. Correspond until you feel comfortable deciding by the time it comes for you to leave here."

That evening Simon sat at a desk alone in the library and started to write.

Dear Mr. Mazurek,
I understand you're trying to get in touch with me.

This began the correspondence between Simon and his birth father.

Sixty-Nine

Simon visited the camp post office daily during his lunch break to see if he'd received a response to his first letter to his father. On Tuesday, April 9, 1946, the postmaster placed a large, wrapped box and an envelope on top of the counter and said, "Looks like you may have hit the jackpot here. It's from the United States. It's big, but it's not heavy. Let me put string around it to make it easier for you to carry."

Simon opened and read the letter while waiting for the box to be wrapped with cord and folded on the top to serve as a handle.

Dear Simon,

I've waited years to hear from you and am relieved to learn you are safe. I've worried about you all through this long war, wondering if your Jewish heritage had been discovered by those heartless Nazis and, if so, its effect upon you. I've punished myself many times over for having abandoned you and for promising my aunt and uncle I wouldn't interfere in their raising you. That's why you haven't heard from me until now. I pray you can find it in your heart to forgive me for any suffering that decision caused you.

To make it up to you, I want to sponsor your, Rachel's, and my grandchild's immigration to the United States, if this is where you want to come. My entire family knows about you and wants you to join us. Please consider it seriously. I'm hoping through our correspondence you get to know me better and realize my sincerity.

You and I have so much to talk about. I'm sure it was a shock to learn about me and you have many mixed feelings about our developing a relationship. No matter what, I want you to know I've never forgotten you. I hope you can forgive me for my sorrowful behavior after your mother's death.

A box should soon arrive for you. On top of its contents is a photograph of your family in California, so you and Rachel will become familiar with us. When you go through the box, you will see you have always been in my thoughts.

Love,

Adrian

That night Simon and Rachel spread the contents of the box on a common table in their building and went through them. He learned in vivid detail the effect their long separation had had on his birth father. They found twenty-one birthday cards from Adrian and scores of handwritten notes of all sizes. One expressed the same sentiment written in his letter. Other notes spoke about aspects of his life over the years, including his experiences in New York with the Eleventh State Symphony Orchestra. He asked if Simon had found the violin he'd left for him and if he'd inherited his musical talent. There were notes about his attempts to connect in spirit with Simon by working with the government to sort out American Nazi sympathizers, him and Suzanne, his wife, moving to Hollywood, California, and his work as the music director of a film studio that had as its goal to make films to encourage the American public to enter the war.

"It's evident," Rachel said, "he's regretted leaving you behind and has never forgotten you."

Simon nodded. What she said was true. But he still had feelings he had to shake off.

Simon went to see Rabbi Strouse.

"You were right, Rabbi," he said.

"How so?"

"I received a letter and a box from my birth father filled with cards for each of my twenty-one birthdays and hundreds of notes written by him showing me how much I've been in his thoughts over the years. He wants me and Rachel to come live with him and his family in California until we get settled on our own. He says he'll do everything he can to help make it happen."

"That's wonderful, Simon. Does Rachel share your enthusiasm?"

"Oh yes. She's been hoping I'd reconcile with him and, like you, has urged me to forgive him."

Rabbi Strouse tilted his head to the side. "Do you have any doubts?" he asked.

Simon bunched his lips and nodded. "I'm a little nervous. We're still strangers."

"How will you resolve your doubts?"

Simon smiled. "I'll correspond with him, and hopefully I'll get to know him better. And" he added, "I'll come to you with my thoughts when I'm conflicted."

"Wonderful. Just what I hoped you'd say."

SEVENTY

In June of 1947, Simon's father wrote, "Immigration laws in the US have been slow to allow immigrants into the country. Members of Congress are concerned about the admission of Communists and other subversives. The immigration quotas reflect discrimination against Jews, as well. I'm exerting whatever influence I have to speed up your visa approval and passports. We're trying to be patient here. Please don't lose hope. We will be together, I promise."

It wasn't until July 1948 that the Immigration Bureau announced 205,000 displaced persons would be allowed to enter the United States under careful screening. Finally, in September, Simon and Rachel were told their visas had been approved. Simon's father sent them funds to cover their travel expenses.

In October 1948, the day before they were to begin their journey, while they were packing, Rachel confessed, "I'm scared, Simon. I feel comfortable here. I don't know anyone where we're going. They're your family, not mine." She was rubbing her forearms. She spoke in a quiet voice.

Simon stopped what he was doing. He wasn't used to seeing Rachel this vulnerable since they'd come to Foehrenwald. He went to her and wrapped his arms around her.

"I'm scared too. Despite our correspondence, they're still strangers to me, but we've got to make a new beginning. Who better with than our American mishpachah." Rachel grinned at his use of the word. "Foehrenwald won't be here forever. Think of this move as our first step. Subsequent steps will be easier and better." He lifted her chin and looked into her eyes. "By next year, California and the United States will feel like home, I promise."

Their son, Moses, started to make sounds of waking from his nap. "You go to him while I finish packing." Rachel's eyes glistened. "I'll be all right." Simon kissed her cheek and went to tend to his son.

Later they went to their last dinner at the camp. They'd be getting an early start the next morning and wanted to get Moses and themselves to bed. On the way to the dining hall, Simon held Moses in his left arm and swung Rachel's left hand as they sang the nursery rhyme "Jack and Jill," to Moses's laughter.

SEVENTY-ONE

The next morning, Simon, Rachel, and Moses boarded a bus with eight other Foehrenwald families. A soldier from the camp drove them to the Wolfratshausen train station in Munich. There they boarded with other arrivals for an eleven-hour ride to Bremerhaven, Germany, a port city on the country's North Sea coast. They ate lunch and dinner on the way.

Upon their arrival, American soldiers greeted them and drove them to a small hotel to spend the night. The next morning, buses transported them to the port where American ships were waiting to take them to the United States.

Simon looked astonished. There was a large banner welcoming the group as the first immigrants to the US under the DP ACT of 1948. Camera crews were filming them.

Military personnel greeted them, guided them onto a ship named after General W. M. Black, and helped them with their luggage. Ship staff led Simon and his family to their first-class cabin. His father had advised sailing first-class, explaining first and second-class passengers received speedier quarantine inspections upon arrival in New York and would bypass Ellis Island. This would speed up their reunion in California.

The passage took one week. Simon had a bout of seasickness for the first three days, leaving Rachel to care for the often-crabby Moses. He didn't take to the confinement of the ship and the extra precautions his parents took to keep him safe.

Family members of Suzanne, Adrian's wife, greeted them when they arrived in New York. Having kept abreast of the ship's progress, they provided them with plane tickets to California for the next day.

SEVENTY-TWO

As the plane began its descent, Simon leaned back in his seat and looked over at Rachel and his son. He remembered the words of the father who raised him, the words that enabled him to survive and reach this day. You are strong. Be brave. Use your talents. Do what you must to survive. These words had brought him here now to meet his other father, his birth father, a man with whom he'd spent most of his life, in his heart and mind, struggling to make peace. Simon vowed never to forget the promise he'd made to the father who raised him: No matter how old he was, no matter where he lived, no matter what happened, he would always be the son of David Baron.

He leaned his head back on his headrest and thought about all he and Rachel had lost: their youth, their homes, their families, their friends. Now was his chance to form a new family and begin a new life in a place called Los Angeles, the City of Angels. He was both nervous and excited as he watched the speck of people on the ground grow closer.

Rachel reached for his hand. "You're sweating," she said.

"I've waited for this for so long. I've both cursed him for deserting me and prayed for this day when we'd meet. I'm not sure how to react when I meet him."

She patted his thigh. "Just let it happen, be natural. Follow his lead. He's made it clear he wants you. He wouldn't have searched for you and brought us here if he didn't want us. Wait until he sees Moses. His heart will melt."

Who's reassuring whom now? Simon thought, remembering how he had had to soothe Rachel's fears the day before they had left Foehrenwald.

He closed his eyes, and the events of the past nine years passed before him: his capture on the square, his learning he was adopted and Jewish, his expulsion from music school, the deaths of his sisters and the guilt he felt and his fear for his family, his life in the ghetto with the rabbi and his family, and all the other events that led to this day. It was so much to happen in a short lifetime, so much heartbreak. He and Rachel had survived, however, and together they would form a life that would honor all those they had left behind.

When the plane landed and rolled slowly to a stop, he saw a family waving small American flags. They were the people in the picture his birth father had sent to him. He knew them all by name.

"There they are," he said to Rachel. He reached for Moses and held him up to the window. "That's your American family, your mishpachah," he said to his son. "Can you say 'mishpachah'"? Moses bounced up and down on Simon's knee giggling. Simon took hold of his son's arm and moved it to wave to those waiting for them.

EPILOGUE

Simon completed the first performance of his concerto. Adrian stood behind the curtain and watched his son take his bows from center stage of the Hollywood Odeum Center. When the applause ended, his father joined Simon. He embraced his son and whispered, "Well done, son, well done." He walked to the microphone.

"Ladies and gentlemen. You've read about the long separation between me and my son. Finding him alive after the war and bringing him and his family to live in this great country of ours was a longtime dream. All parents want to share something special with their children, something beautiful that binds them together. Simon and I have our music. You may not know that the two of us have violins made by my father and Simon's grandfather, Dominik Mazurek. Tonight, we'd like to pay tribute to him by playing a piece together, Bach's Concerto for Two Violins in D Minor."

A gentleman walked on stage and handed Adrian his violin. Simon gave his signal to the conductor, and they began to play. Their eyes stayed closed as they played. Each of them was one with the music, each feeling his individual part. Only at the end, when they came out of their dreamlike states and the audience rose in appreciation of their performance and the story behind it, did they clasp hands to take their bows and look at each other with love and gratitude.

The End

Author's Note

I wrote this novel with the utmost sensitivity and respect for those who suffered and survived or perished because of the Holocaust. A person as far away from it as I can only imagine and endeavor to convey what they experienced. The realities and emotions that I strived to put into this story will never compare with the testimonies of the survivors.

It is my hope this book and *CONCERTO: BOOK 2, ADRIAN* will serve two purposes: [1] to educate those whose lives are too young to remember WW 2 and the Holocaust and to encourage them to learn more, and [2] to sensitize anyone of any age, race, ethnicity, religion, political ideology, sexual orientation and/or gender identity to the happenings in today's world, and to what these happenings could lead to if we don't pay attention and learn from past events. Working together creatively as human beings, rather than destructively, is the more fruitful path.

Fred Raymond Goldman is a native of Baltimore, Maryland. He lives in the suburb of Lutherville with his wife, Abigail. They have four children and ten grandchildren.

This is his first of two companion novels. The second is titled *CONCERTO: BOOK 2, ADRIAN.*

ACKNOWLEDGEMENTS

I am grateful to those who helped me along the way to accomplish my long-time goal of writing a novel. This novel and the next to follow, a companion piece to Simon's journey through WW II and the Holocaust, were over three years in the making and began at the Lutherville branch of the Baltimore County Public Library, where Kris Faatz, a talented author and pianist, voluntarily taught a writing class. Members of that group, all extraordinarily gifted people, including Cece, Christina, Gerald, Loni, Melissa, Rachel, Rebecca, and Toula, contributed to critiquing what eventually became these companion books. I was blessed to meet and know you all.

I give credit to the library staff for their patience in helping me learn their computer system before I broke down and purchased my own laptop. They came to my aid every time I raised my hand for assistance, which was quite often. To paraphrase my favorite television Superman, Dean Cain, and to give credit to songwriter, Adam Young, librarians are "heroes without capes."

Several people read the first draft of my novel, originally titled *THE AUSCHWITZ CONCERTO*, to give me feedback. This was quite a feat since it was six hundred and fifty-six pages before I divided into two novels. Their enthusiasm about the story and my writing, gave me the push to have it published. Thank you, Marcia, Marlene and Joel, Carl, Mark and his mom, Arlene, and particularly my aunt Bessie, an avid reader, whose love for me gave her no cause to be prejudicial.

I have had the privilege of having two persons help with the editing of these volumes before turning them over to Palmetto.

Thank you, Kris Faatz and Herta Feely, both successful published authors. Kris, through her praise of my storyline, egged me on to forge ahead, and Nicolas, my editor at Palmetto, was so unrestrained in his praise of *Book 1, Simon*, he gave me the self confidence to believe I was not being self-indulgent in deciding to self-publish.

The staff at Palmetto has been incredibly supportive in leading me through this process. I'd like to thank Roy, V.P. of Author Services, Savannah, my Project Manager and guide through the publication process, Nicholas, my Palmetto editor, Jackie for the cover design and Carlene for the interior design. Thanks, also, to Kristin and all the others behind the scenes who have been generous in indulging me in my ignorance through part of the process.

Without the help of my family, I'd still be struggling with breakdowns of my computer and printer and never finishing these works. Thank you, Molly, Beth, Rebecca, and Mark, for always being there for me and sticking by me through this long process. Thanks to my wife, Gail, for putting up with me during this arduous project. A shout out to my grandchildren who believe in me. These books will be part of my legacy to them.

Read on for an excerpt from the companion novel to
CONCERTO: BOOK 1, SIMON
by Fred Raymond Goldman

Part One

ONE

On Monday Evening, September 4, 1939, Adrian Mazurek, concertmaster of the Eleventh State Philharmonic Orchestra in New York City, stood in front of his bathroom mirror and finished tying the bow tie of his tuxedo. He lingered awhile staring at himself and thought about how far he'd come since arriving in the United States fourteen years ago. Back then, he was a shattered young man who sought refuge in his studies at the Walter Sanfried School of Music to overcome his tragic past. He'd focused on his studies to become a proficient violinist and avoided close relationships, lest people think poorly of him once discovering the reason for his retreat from Poland. Since then, he'd become a confident and respected artist who associated with the most prominent musicians of his time. Despite that, he'd kept his prior life a secret. Now, he was in love with Suzanne and wanted to make a life with her. He was prepared to tell her about his earlier years in Poland before proposing marriage after the fundraiser tonight. He was sure of her love and felt confident that she'd accept his proposal readily.

The limousine arrived half an hour later. Adrian was waiting outside his building. He slid into the back seat. Suzanne was sitting in the middle. Her father, Marcus Reitman, the Director of Annual Giving of the symphony, sat on the opposite window side. Mr. Reitman greeted him with a friendly nod. Suzanne moved over to give Adrian more room to balance his violin case on his lap. They were on their way to the home of the Count and Contessa Uberti, who were hosting the fundraiser for the symphony. Adrian was their guest of honor.

Suzanne had attracted Adrian's attention immediately at a welcoming party for Alistair McGowan in November 1937. The occasion was Mc Gowan's selection as music director and conductor of the symphony. Suzanne was with her fiancé, Bill Henderson. A hunting accident resulted in his death three months later, shortly before their forthcoming wedding. Adrian waited a month past the scheduled nuptials to phone her. He considered this to be a respectable length of time to delay before asking her out to dinner. They dated intermittently until this past April when they became exclusive.

Adrian studied Suzanne. Her dark brown hair fell softly to her shoulders, accentuating her skin, clear and creamy. The bright red of her lipstick defined the fullness of her lips. He looked into those deep brown eyes of hers and thought of Chana. She, too, had been beautiful like Suzanne, with the same smooth skin and full lips. He wondered if Chana, had she survived, would have felt comfortable being driven in a limousine to the home of a Count and Contessa, where he'd perform to a hand-picked array of New York's elite. Would she have been able to bask in this moment with him, like Suzanne?

He'd come to realize Chana and Suzanne were different people. Youth, inexperience, and family didn't restrict Suzanne as it had Chana. She was mature, a person in her own right, well established in her career and secure in herself. She, unlike Chana, could manage whatever came her way, including the demands of his profession. What's more, he and Suzanne shared many of the same interests and values which, to him, made them compatible. There was no reason not to propose to her. He wouldn't hurt her like he had Chana and leave behind a mess as he had in Poland.

Suzanne interrupted his reverie. "What are you thinking?"

He turned his attention back to her. "Nothing. What's that perfume you're wearing? You smell delicious."

She gave him a playful punch on the arm. "It's Joy. You should know my favorite perfume by now."

"Be careful. My arms are my fortune. I've got to play well for the Contessa and her dinner guests if we're going to raise enough money to meet the orchestra's contractual demands."

Mr. Reitman's patted his daughter's knee. "Amen," he said smiling. "Perhaps you'd better keep your hands off Adrian tonight, my dear."

Adrian leaned over and gave Suzanne a light kiss on the cheek. He knew she'd be fussy about getting her lipstick smeared. She immediately pulled out her gold compact to check her lipstick and hair.

Adrian felt good about tonight. Playing the violin was his love. It was something he did with his life, a gift with which he'd been blessed and to share with others. He was pleased the Contessa had invited him to help the orchestra raise money. The Depression had placed a financial strain on the institution. Due to previous contractual obligations with the musicians, lower ticket sales, and annual deficits, the Endowment Fund had taken a hit. Currently there was a significant deficit from the 1938-1939 season and, of course, that new round of negotiations with the musicians was about to begin.

The Contessa and Mr. Reitman had gone to great pains to plan a special evening. They'd invited a select group of guests, hoping their donations and bequests would place the symphony on a sounder footing. Adrian's presence would not only provide entertainment but put a familiar face to the symphony. People would find it a privilege to share an evening with him. Reviews of his concerts by *The New York Times* and other large east coast city papers labeled his performances compelling, mesmerizing, and enthralling, that he had the ability to bring about difficult sounds and moods from his violin when the music demanded it. Adrian had learned the invitation to tonight's gathering had drawn an immediate response, leaving others the Contessa hadn't invited to feel disappointed.

Adrian was feeling a bit uncertain about the first selection he'd chosen to perform this evening, a short piece he'd composed. He'd recently become intrigued by the trend in avant-garde music, which went beyond the expectations one might anticipate hearing from a classical performer like himself. His piece was unconventional with little melody or form and with erratic, scratching sounds. Now, he wasn't sure this selection was right for this conservative gathering. Once at the Contessa's, he'd look the guests over and determine whether they'd appreciate a composition composed in this style. He had other pieces memorized to substitute if he felt them more appropriate for this soiree.

Adrian readjusted himself in his seat. He tried not to allow his hesitation about playing his own composition tonight take away from his excitement about what was going to happen after the party when he was alone with Suzanne. He couldn't wait to see the look on her face when he proposed.

To take his mind off his uneasiness, Adrian teased Suzanne and her father by announcing,

"If things go well tonight, I have a little surprise up my sleeve."

"Oh, oh," Suzanne said, poking her father. "You'd better stay close to him tonight. He's in one of his playful moods. Why don't you tell us, Adrian, so we're prepared for whatever comes and not sit all night holding our breath?"

"Now, now, Suzanne," Mr. Reitman said "We all know how focused Adrian is. He's probably been practicing for this evening for weeks. I'm sure he's out to make an excellent impression by being on his best behavior."

Adrian raised his eyebrows. "You'll just have to wait and see," he said.

Traffic had slowed down. "There's a log jam ahead," the limousine driver said. "I'll try to find a way around it, but it looks blocked. We may be late."

"Do your best," Adrian said, tapping his foot. Being late might not give him the time he needed to familiarize himself with the guests to decide whether to substitute his own piece for another and to allow him a few additional minutes of practice if he were to decide to change. He kept glancing at his watch. Every minute lost would take away from his preparing for his recital and delay what he had planned with Suzanne afterward.